BLISS

A LENNY BLISS MYSTERY

BOB SLOAN

SCRIBNER

SCRIBNER
1230 Avenue of the Americas
New York, NY 10020

Set in Caledonia

DESIGNED BY ERICH HOBBING

Manufactured in the United States of America

1   3   5   7   9   10   8   6   4   2

Library of Congress Cataloging-in-Publication Data
Sloan, Bob.
Bliss : a Lenny Bliss mystery / Bob Sloan.
p. cm.
I. Title.
PS3569.L5B57   1996
813'.54—dc20   96-21512
CIP

ISBN 0-684-82250-4

For my wife
Randi
and my kid brother
Larry.

ACKNOWLEDGMENTS

Gracious thanks to Chaz Lawther, Josh Reibel, Susan Lesher, Craig, Barbara, and the ebullient Jane Rosenman for their support.

Revenge, like borscht, is a dish best served hot or cold.
                    —Old Russian proverb
                    (Or if it's not, it should be.)

BLISS

Like most of the great sex in Lenny Bliss's life lately, this time, too, it wasn't going to happen.

He was lying on a large bed somewhere in Cairo. An Egyptian princess dancing before him. The Sirocco, or was it Mariah, gently fluttered her veil and he could see her exquisite beauty, teeth white against ocher skin; lips wet, parted slightly in an inviting smile. "Come, come with me down the Nile." Her brothers, the princes, the *fellaheen* fellas, were searching the streets in ballooning red silk pants, giant curved cardboard swords stuck in their bright green sashes, huge mustaches falling off their lips as the sweat loosened the spirit gum. They'd seen him with their sister and now they wanted to cut off his nuts and feed them to their pet ibis. But he and the princess had escaped, running through winding back alleys until they arrived at this secret place where he was lying naked on sheets of the finest cotton and she was kneeling down next to him. He could feel her breath on his belly. His follicles were aflutter. He was outstretched, reaching for her, like the arms of the teenage girls at Kennedy Airport waiting for the Beatles to walk out of the plane, straining over the barricades, panting in anticipation, when suddenly a cold fist connected to his temple. The princess floated away and he woke up.

It was dawn. His wife was Floyd Patterson in her sleep. Bliss was about to put his knee in the small of her back, as he usually did, and shove her across the bed, when he realized it wasn't his wife who clocked him, but his kid. Which one? The youngest. The six-year-old. Cori. She must have snuck into their bed during the night. He hated having an erection when his kids were in his bed. Cori purred and smacked her lips. She looked so beautiful in the morning light. Then she caught him in the cheek with a solid right hook. Bliss was pissed. Should have seen it coming.

His daughter catching more flush than any collar had in his eighteen years on the force. This was his kid, all right.

He turned away from Cori and dealt with getting rid of his woody. Not always an easy task. He conjured up Margaret Dumont as Mrs. Rittenhouse in *Duck Soup,* filling out the folds in her huge satin dress. "Oh Mr. FIRE-fly! Oh RU-fus!" No dice. This one was ornery. He worked harder. He thought about Bishop Tutu—looking saintly in his long robe and beanie and his assortment of idyllic expressions. Shit. He was still as hard as Japanese arithmetic. He tried Bishop Tutu in a tutu, which made him laugh but didn't change his profile. So he played his trump card, and hunkered down and focused hard on the image of Lyndon Johnson, yes, he could see him now, sitting on the Oval Office toilet taking a dump while he talked to his staff. His boxers down by his ankles, groaning, and as the president started wiping his butt it was gone. One hundred percent success. LBJ never failed him. Hey! Hey! LBJ! Make my boner go away! Bliss knew that if he ever had to play a sex scene in the movies, he'd never embarrass himself by getting hard as long as he kept Lyndon on his mind. It wasn't much, but it was one less thing he had to worry about.

The phone rang. Bad news. Bad news came by mail—worse news came by phone.

"Drop your cocks and put on your socks." It was his partner, Ward, who always sounded as if he'd just been poisoned.

"What's wrong?" his wife asked, propping herself on her elbow.

"I don't know," said Bliss. "It's Ward."

"Fuck him," said his wife, Rachel, falling back asleep.

Bliss returned to the phone.

"Status report, Spock."

"Body," said Ward. "Type dead. Female."

"Another Gary Puckett?"

"No young girl this time."

Bliss was relieved. They were working on a case involving a sixteen-year-old who'd been left in a Dumpster. He stroked his daughter's hair.

"This one's twenty-two, twenty-three, judging from her jugs," said Ward. "Maybe older, if she never had kids or if she didn't breast-feed."

"In mufti?"

"Negativo, Captain. If there was a breeze she'd be shivering."

"Bottoms up?"

"No. On her back. Aureoles skyward. Ready for ring toss."

"Give me the coordinates."

"Set a course for three-five-eight-nine mark Third Avenue."

"The Manhattan Nebula."

"Yes, Captain."

"That's Klingon territory."

"Affirmative, Captain."

"I'll be there warp factor six."

"Oh, and Captain, this one's messy."

"They're all messy, Spock. Captain out."

He hung up the phone. There was a gentle rustling of sheets, then a whisper.

"Where you going, Daddy?" Cori said.

"I have to go work," he whispered back.

She rubbed her eyes. "Do I need to get up now?"

"No," he said. "Wait for the alarm."

"You forgot to read to me last night," she said.

"I didn't forget. I just got home late."

"It's okay," she said, wiping the sleep from her eyes. "Mom finished the book. The bull got to live under his tree."

"Good."

"He didn't have to fight anyone. Even though he was the biggest and strongest bull, he didn't believe in fighting."

"Great."

"His name was Ferdinand. He could have stuck his horns in people and hurt them but he didn't."

"Right."

"He just stayed under his tree."

"Good bull."

"Smelling the flowers."

"Nice bull."

"Daddy?"

"Yes, Sweetie?"

"Are we safe?"

Cori was starting to sound like a cop's kid in a B movie.

"Mmm-hmm," he told her. "We're very safe."

Glenn Ford, the cop in *The Big Heat,* pats his kid on the head, tells him everything's all right. Then his wife, played by Jocelyn Brando, starts the car in the driveway and it gets blown to shit. Luckily Bliss lived in Manhattan, so they didn't need a car.

"Does Bob the doorman keep us safe?" Cori asked.

"Yes. Bob and Daddy and Mom keep you and your sister very safe."

She smiled and closed her eyes and took a deep breath. He bent down and kissed her on the cheek. He would have kissed Rachel, but she was on the other side of the bed. Asleep. Lately, it seemed whenever they were in bed, one or the other or both of them were sleeping.

3589 Third Avenue was a four-floor walk-up. Bliss flashed his detective badge. The woman officer on the steps told him it was apartment 3-RF. Bliss headed up the stairs. "RF." What the hell was that? "Rear-Front?" The slumlords in New York give their apartments exotic letter appendages to make them sound more appealing. Like they were suites, instead of oversized broom closets. Bliss suspected 3-RF would probably look more like 3-SH, for Shit Hole. He stopped at the first landing. The hallway reeked from the pungent smell of Lysol. Probably a Polish super. They loved Lysol. Trying to wipe away their past sins.

A young woman was leaving her apartment. She was wearing a tank top and those nylon running shorts that are loose and flap enticingly. She was taut and muscular and carried a bicycle on her shoulder. Bliss was glad it was only the second floor, so he wasn't yet out of breath. He took out his badge.

"Anything out of the ordinary happen last night?"

The woman looked at the badge without flinching. Then at Bliss.

"Where?"

"Here. In the building."

"Not that I know of."

"You didn't hear noises, anything that sounded like a struggle?"

"No. What's the matter?"

"Nothing much." Bliss took a step toward her and ran his fingers through his hair.

"That a mountain bike?" he asked.

It was on the "b" of bike that he realized that in his rush to get out of the house that morning he hadn't brushed his teeth. The girl scowled.

"Yeah. It's a mountain bike. It's got thick tires. Thick. You know about 'thick'?"

She brushed past him. A pedal jabbed his thigh.

"Hey, I'm a cop."

"You smell like it," she said. The front door slammed. Bliss imagined her getting on her bike, arranging herself on the seat, wiggling to make herself more comfortable, her shorts inching up her thigh. Who was it . . . the poet William Blake said something about seeing the world in a grain of sand. But Bliss, he couldn't see a *beach* full of sand if there was one bikini in sight, so preoccupied was he with bosom and pudenda. He was turning into a parody of himself. A parody of a travesty. All wrapped up in one salacious, flatulent package. He reached into his pocket for a package of mints and bit one off. It tasted chalky. It was probably a Tums. Same difference.

The best he could figure, RF stood for Right-Front. It was a studio. No rugs. No furniture except a cheap but tasteful foldout couch. The woman was on her back, stretched out on the bare floor, one arm draped across her eyes. She could have been lying on a chaise, protecting herself from too much sun. There were several short, red marks on her belly, slits that were made by a small and very sharp instrument—perhaps a scalpel.

"Check out her neck," Ward said. He was standing by her feet like she was a deer he'd just shot. He took a swig from a bottle of designer water.

"Hey Ward, I hope you're not getting parvenu on me."

The truth was the Evian looked right on Ward, like he could have been a model taking a break during the shoot. Tall and muscular, his eyes black, his mouth set in a bemused pout, his skin smooth and softly shaded, the subtle mixture of light browns and deep reds that didn't have a name but gave Ward his "permanent tan," which he said began the night the plantation owner crept into his great-grandmother's shack and had changed hues every generation since. His hair was soft, lying in natural curls (no Geri curls they) that Julius Caesar would have envied. He was quite a package, his partner. Lenny's wife liked having him around, knowing any damsels in distress the two knights encountered would swoon over Ward before they even got a whiff of her husband.

"It was the only thing cold in her fridge," Ward said, taking a deep swig of the water.

"It could be evidence."

"Could be. I think this is tap water. I think she refilled the bottle."

"You should know," Bliss said. "You're the detective."

Bliss looked at her neck and saw the bright red marks. You could almost discern the outlines of the individual fingers.

"Archie Bell and the Drells," Ward said, shaking his head.

"Yeah, 'The Tighten Up.' Any prints?" Bliss asked.

"Nope. Rubber gloves. This could be the work of a demented proctologist. Forensics will tell us whether the cuts on her stomach happened before or after strangulation. Someone slit her a few extra cunts."

"That's repulsive, partner."

But it wasn't Ward's vulgarity that got to Bliss. It was his habit of coming up in every case with some particularly graphic image that burned into Bliss's mind. Last month it was a bullet-ridden crack dealer with his brains spilling out on the sidewalk. Ward took one look and said "couscous" without missing a beat, and now whenever Bliss heard the word, which granted wasn't too often, he pictured the oozing frontal lobe leaking from the head of an eighteen-year-old kid. This time, whenever he made love to his wife, just before the big moment, he'd see this woman lying dead on her floor, her belly an indecipherable map of cuts crusted with dried blood.

"We got a name?"

"Nothing I can pronounce," said Ward.

"Try."

"El-len-ah Kor-roh-shevvv-esss-ky."

"You're reading's improving."

"Hooked on Phonics."

"What is she, Russian?"

"At least someone wants us to think so. She's got these books in Russian on her shelves. She's got letters written in Russian with Russian stamps. She's got postcards of Russia taped to the mirror in her pissoir. She's got everything but a hammer and sickle tattooed to her ass."

"How do you know? She's lying on her back."

"Maybe she wasn't when I got here. The point is, El-len-ah Kor-roh-shevvv-esss-ky or *someone else* is going a great deal out of their way to make it appear as if this woman was from Russia."

"Unless she actually is from Russia."

"I'm glad you're here, partner."

Bliss looked around the room. The cushions in the sofa were ripped apart and the stuffing torn out.

"What do you make of the couch?" Bliss asked.

"Maybe one of those creatures from the Alien movies was growing in the stuffing. Then it busted out."

"She wouldn't have been foolish enough to hide her money in there."

"I hope not."

There was a small bookcase in the corner and indeed there were Russian books on the shelves, including a Russian-English dictionary.

"You Magoo the closet?" Bliss asked.

"Yeah. Nothing."

"No uniforms? Work clothes? T-shirts with a logo? Company name?"

"Nada."

"Shift schedule taped on the fridge?"

"Nope. But now, observe closely as I, the great Wardino, produce out of thin air evidence which will shed some light on this mysterious case. Nothing up my sleeve. And, presto!"

Ward reached into his pants and slowly pulled out a swatch of bright red silk that became panties. Tied to them were a black bra, tied to that a red bra, tied to that were lacy white panties, which were tied to frilly red panties, tied to a red G-string with a fur patch by the crotch. Ward must have had them all stuffed down the leg of his pants.

"How long you been walking around with that?"

"Last half hour."

"Cute."

"I make her to be a pro."

"You think? A nice Russian girl? She probably works in the bakery selling babka."

"Where's her apron?"

"She leaves it at work."

"How come she ain't got day-olds in the freezer?" Ward said. "I would. Half-moons. Danish. Those little ones which are rolled up."

"Rugalah," said Bliss, remembering he hadn't had breakfast or coffee, that he'd left before sharing cereal with his kids.

"Yeah. I love a good rugalah."

"Maybe she's on a diet."

"Then at least she'd have a challah. No. She's definitely a pro. The Russian girls are all doing it."

"Where'd you read that? *The Hooker's Almanac*?"

"No," Ward said. "*Time* magazine. These Russian girls, they have degrees and everything. But they can't get jobs. So they go to Japan or to the States and become these high-priced whores for a couple of years and build up some capital in hard currency so they can go back to Russia and open stores and stuff."

"So because she's a Russian and wears fancy underwear, she's a pro. You find her fuck book?"

"No."

"So how do you know?"

"The super told me."

"He sleep with her?"

"It's a she."

"She Polish?"

"Nope. Young, gifted, and black. Beautiful, too."

Ward had a thing about black women. Maybe because he was octoroon. "I'm one-eighth Negro," he liked to say. "My dick."

Bliss left his partner alone to have a T & A epiphany and walked around the apartment, not sure what he was looking for. He had to shift gears, get the full spectrum of his detective skills up and running. This was the kind of case they called at the precinct a "Movie of the Week Murder." The kind Jessica Fletcher took on, that had a motive other than drug territory or drug money or drug-induced rage. There would be no rounding up the usual suspects on this one. It was too smooth to be a junkie's impulsive junket. The rubber gloves, the absence of forced entry, and, except for the couch, no indications of a robbery or a struggle told him that.

The apartment was extremely neat. But besides the books on the shelves, she had no personal effects. No tchotchkes, unlike his mother's house, which was full of them. His father, the cop, used to threaten her. Better take out some tchotchke insurance, he said, with double indemnity in case they are all thrown into the incinerator by your husband. This apartment felt more like a hotel room someone planned to stay in only a few weeks but no longer. No pictures on the wall. On an end table next to the exploded sofa Bliss scoped the plaster cast of a set of teeth. Hers, maybe? Someone's bite she admired? A boyfriend left behind in Russia? Some Soviet custom he didn't know about? Instead of carving your initials in a tree trunk, you carry each other's molars around with you. He left the teeth alone, figuring he'd have a brush with them later.

Remembering the grimace of the girl on the steps, Bliss went into the bathroom to get rid of the skin of crud and decay in his own mouth. While there he checked the medicine cabinet for shaving cream, razors, extra toothbrushes, prescription bottles, men's cologne—any sign of regular visitors—lovers, johns, girlfriends. Lots of pros liked other women. Two sets of makeup might give that away. An extra hair brush, two kinds of shampoo, different brands of tampons.

But it was pretty clear Elena lived alone. She used natural cosmetics. Fancy. Expensive. One of the price tags was still on

the bottom. From Barney's. Twenty-eight bucks for the base.
"Bisque" it was called. "Matte finish." She wasn't hurting. He
rubbed a little under his eyes to cover the dark circles. He
looked better. More bisque-y. More matte. As he brushed his
teeth he checked the back of the toilet, the Kleenex box, poked
through the potpourri, then dumped it in the toilet. He wasn't
sure what he was looking for. He took down the postcard that
was taped to the mirror. Some city in Russia. On the back,
Russian—and lots of it. He'd take it back to the precinct. Maybe
somebody there knew somebody who could translate it. He spit
and rinsed his mouth. He looked in the mirror. He seemed
somehow younger. He put the makeup in his pocket and walked
back into the room.

Ward was surveying his pilfered lingerie.

"I think I'll give these to Malikha."

"Who's that?"

"The super."

"What else did she say?"

"Not much. Just that Elena used to visit her in the afternoon.
Smoke a joint. Shoot the shit. You know, girl talk. Like which is
better, clitoral or vaginal."

"Clitoral or vaginal what?"

"Orgasms. Jesus Christ, what else do you think women talk
about when they get together?"

"I hadn't thought about it."

"Well, you should. Get with it, partner. This is the nineties."

"So Elena talked about her work?"

"Yeah."

"These are nice digs. Sparse, but nice. She wasn't on the
streets."

"No. She was working off the shelf."

"Who owned the store?"

"Malikha didn't know."

"Elena never mentioned anyone to her?" Bliss said.

"No."

"Anything about where she worked—complain about the
crosstown bus, subways, midtown traffic?"

"I didn't ask."

"It'll give you something to break the ice with next time you see her."

"Anyway," Ward said, "if she was with a stable, it was probably nearby. The Upper East Side is getting to be like Amsterdam. The cathouses should get together with the Chinese restaurants. The hookers could make the deliveries. Then you could have dinner and a quick bang all in one package."

"I'll talk to Ortiz in Vice. See if any of our friendly local madams had any Russian girls working for them."

"Call the madams yourself. Say 'Hello, I'm curious to know if you're currently featuring borscht on your menu.'"

"Yeah. Listen, also ask Malikha if she ever saw anyone let themselves into Elena's place with their own key."

"Oh honey, you're so good."

"I'm going to knock on a few doors. I'll try two-RF first. Maybe they heard some dancing on the ceiling last night."

Two-RF was occupied by a male couple. The one who answered the door was putting on his tie, a lush silk number that went very nicely with his plush suit. His significant other was sitting by the little breakfast table reading a pink newspaper.

When Bliss first joined the force, his simply showing up at the door would have induced instant panic in the gay couple. (Cops didn't even *use* the word "gay." Back then it was strictly "faggot.") Bliss's first partner was an old-time Irish cop who was particularly homophobic (another word they didn't use back then). One time a guy in a kimono and rollers like he had been posing for Diane Arbus answered the door and actually tried to ask if they had a warrant. Bliss's partner shoved the guy aside and made a Csonka into the room, showing his gun, talking tough, storming around the apartment until he found the lover cowering behind the shower curtain. He'd use their fear as leverage. Get them to say almost anything, not that it ever cracked a case. Then he'd sit in the locker room in the precinct at the end of the day impressing the boys, like he was telling hunting stories. "And they live in apartment Two-RF—'RF' for 'Real Faggots.'" [General laughter]

". . . and then I bagged the other one who was *hiding* in the bathtub, shaking like a scared little doe. I took a piss with him in there." [Derisive snarls] ". . . reading a *pink* newspaper. Can you believe it? They actually read *pink* newspapers." [Hoots and howls] Bliss wondered what role his father would have played in that scenario. Would he have been storyteller, one foot on the bench, one arm draped over the top of the locker door, regaling the boys with his tales like a camp counselor telling ghost stories? Or would he have been just one of the guys, baring their teeth, laughing and banging their chests in confirmation of their own power? Or would he have been like Lenny, silently staring at the floor, an empty feeling in his stomach?

But in the last few years things had changed around the precinct. Bliss knew a couple of cops who marched every year in the gay rights parade, his wife's cousin was HIV positive, and he was aware that the pink newspapers were the *Financial Times* of London and that anyone who read them probably made a fuckofalot more money than he did.

"Hi. Lenny Bliss, Homicide."

"Hi. Come on in."

The other guy glanced casually over his paper.

"How'd the NASDAQ do yesterday?" Bliss asked him.

"Down ten."

He returned to his paper.

The first guy finished tying his tie. "What's up? I saw the patrol cars downstairs."

"The press and television will be here soon. Elena, the woman upstairs, was murdered. Probably last night."

There was a moment of silence. Then the guy sitting at the table stood up and threw an empty glass across the room. It shattered against the wall.

"Damn this city! This city is shit! This city is Medea! It eats its children! Fuck it!"

Bliss waited an Art Carney beat and then deadpanned, "You knew her?"

The man in the tie responded, more calmly.

"We knew her very well. She was . . . she was a beautiful person."

"So I understand. How long have you known her?"

"Since she moved in. I work at home, so she would stop in late mornings for coffee. Always with a smile."

"Yes."

"Tell me, Dirty Harry. How'd she die?" his friend asked.

"You don't want to know," Bliss said.

"Why? Because you think I'm too delicate? Because you think I'm not strong enough to take it?"

Bliss ignored the vitriol. "She was strangled. Her couch was ripped up. She ever mention she was hiding anything? She ever ask you to hide something for her?"

"She never asked me," said the man who opened the door. "My name's Neal, by the way."

"Hi," Bliss said.

"Hi," said Neal.

Neal extended his hand. He shook it.

"Kevin," Neal said to his friend, "Elena ever ask you to hide anything?"

"No."

"You knew she was a hooker?" Bliss said.

"Yeah! We knew!" Kevin shouted. "We KNEW what she did! You gonna torment her now with that?"

"Kevin," Neal said.

"Are you going to turn her into trash?"

"Please," Neal said.

"I'm not going to work today." Kevin was calmer now. "I'm going to stay home. Stay here and protect her. I'll talk to the newspaper and TV assholes and tell them the truth. That she was gracious and beautiful. That she was the most generous person I knew. I'll keep the media whores from turning her into one of their own."

"Put on a different shirt, Kevin, if you're going to be on TV."

Kevin left the room. Neal turned back to Bliss, who leaned in the doorway.

"We didn't hear anything last night," he said. "I'm sure that's what you want to know."

"She have any regular visitors?"

"None that I knew of. As far as I could tell, we were her only friends."

"What about Malikha?"

"Yeah, I guess they hung out together."

"How long had she been in America?"

"About six months, I think. She's only lived in this building for three."

"She got her shit together pretty quick."

"She was a dentist. In Leningrad. Now called St. Petersburg."

"Wait," Bliss said. "This woman was turning tricks but she was really a dentist?"

"Yes. She came here to make enough money to go back home and start her own practice. And to buy a nice house for herself and her kids."

That explained the teeth, but little else.

"She loved her children," Neal said. "It pained her to be away from them. That was the only time I saw her sad."

"Elena ever mention anyone she tricked for? Or with?"

"Not that I remember."

He seemed to be on the level.

"She ever tell you where she worked?"

"No."

"She ever say anything about how she got to work? Cross-town bus, subway, anything?"

"I think she walked. She liked to feel part of the city. One time I saw her in the lobby with one of those little museum buttons still on her collar."

"You ever hear a car door closing before she came up? A cab, maybe?"

"Sometimes. Usually she just appeared."

"Like magic?"

"Yeah. Like magic."

"Do you remember seeing men coming in and out of her apartment?"

"Sometimes," Neal said. "We knew what she did, so we didn't look at them closely. They may have been regulars. We wouldn't want to scare them away."

"That's right neighborly of you."

"Elena was a good person."

"Mmm-hmm." Bliss motioned toward their apartment. "Mind if I take a peek?"

He walked in without waiting for an answer. The room was all Mission, with lots of chic accessories. The couch was one of those low, boxy jobs. Beautiful to look at but impossible to get up from. Bliss decided not to chance it. On the side table was a blue ceramic lamp with naked women rising out of the base. The torso was slightly chipped. Bliss thought of Elena. Then, of course, he immediately remembered Ward's remark and grimaced.

"It's Roseville. The lamp. It'd be worth three grand easy, except for the chips."

"Mmm-hmm. She ever use your phone?"

"Why would she?"

"She doesn't have one."

Bliss sensed hesitation. "No. She didn't."

The man was lying.

"I can check your phone bill. Local calls, too."

"Go ahead."

"If I need to I'll bring it by in a couple of days. You can see if any of the numbers look unfamiliar."

"I'd be happy to be of any help I can."

"You may have to bury her."

This seemed to break through his veneer. He screwed up his face slightly.

"How do you mean?"

"I mean that there's a chance no one is going to claim her body or pay for it to be flown back to Russia. If she was Jewish, the Jewish Burial Society will take her to their cemetery on Staten Island. Otherwise it'll be a pauper's grave. So you may have to bury her. Or cremate. Dealer's choice."

Kevin came back with a new shirt. "How's this?" he asked.

"Fine."

Kevin sat down at the table and whipped a laptop out of his briefcase. "I'm going to write something," he said. "A statement. So they get it right." He wiped away a tear.

Bliss headed back to the door.

"If either of you think of anything that might be helpful, give me a call." He handed over his card. "Oh, one last thing, she ever do your Tarot cards?"

"No."

"You're sure?"

Kevin looked up.

"I think we'd remember, Officer."

"It's Detective. She had a deck of Tarot cards on her bookshelf."

"She never mentioned it to me," said Neal.

"Fine. Thanks very much," Bliss said. "You've been very helpful."

Bliss met Ward in the front hall of the building.

"There's already a crowd of reporters out there," Ward said.

"Anyone we know?"

"Huntley. Brinkley. Cronkite."

"Sander Vanocur?"

"I wish."

Ward sat down on the steps and lit a cigarette.

"Ah, c'mon, Ward. Not here. There's no ventilation."

"You want ventilation? You want VENTILATION?" Ward took out his revolver and pointed at the glass front door. "I'll GIVE you ventilation."

"*White Heat,*" Bliss said. He knew the movie well. His father had taken him to see it when he was in high school, at a revival house in the Village, making a big point about that scene. Cagney locks this guy in the trunk of a car. The guy shouts that he can't breath. He needs ventilation. "You want ventilation??" Cagney screams, then he shoots some holes in the trunk. "You understand what's happening, Lenny?" his father said. "At the same time Cagney gives the guy some air, he kills him. Not bad, huh?" Ferdinand, the bull in Cori's story, would have thought otherwise. Bliss cited the scene from *White Heat* in a paper he wrote in college about existentialism. The guy in the trunk symbolized the condition of Modern Man. Cagney was God, or Fate, or Uncertainty. He'd forgotten which. Anyway, it had gotten him an A. It was one thing to thank his father for. Someday maybe he'd think of something else.

"Put your gun away, Ward."

Ward put his gun away. Bliss sat down next to him on the steps.

"We made it, Ma," Ward said.

"Yeah. Top of the fuckin' world."

For all his bravura, Bliss knew his partner didn't get his jollies discovering dead women. That it always took a few minutes for him to deal with it, to send the bile around for another circuit through his kishkes, hoping it wouldn't surface again for a long while.

"You know," Bliss said, "my grandfather was from Russia."

"Mine, too. My guess is we're looking for one of her johns."

"From Minsk. Near the Ukraine. They lived in a cabin with a dirt floor."

"Same here," Ward said. "Dirt floor. The john comes in, does his business, then she makes a crack about his teeth, too much tartar or something. He freaks out and does her."

"We have an old photo. The whole family sitting around the samovar."

"I got one of those photos, too. Sittin' roun' de ol' samovar."

"They look scared. Like they can hear the cossacks coming."

"Same here. Joe-Bob and Billy-Ray and Joe-Billy-Ray-Bob. Redneck cossack muthahfuckers."

"The problem is," Bliss said, "why would the john cut up the couch?"

"You're right. That part doesn't make sense."

"My grandfather still had his accent."

"Well, maybe you and Miss Whore-o-shevesky were related. You could be cousins. Too bad you didn't know her when she was thirteen. You could have married her, like Jerry Lee Lewis."

"She was a dentist, you know."

"Who?"

"Elena."

"Oh, we're on a first name basis now, are we?"

Bliss didn't answer.

"So what was she doing here if she was a dentist?" Ward said.

"Don't they have impacted gums in Russia? I figured that place to be the spawn pool of gingivitis."

"She came to make money. To get her practice started. Maybe she needed hard currency."

"Hard is the only currency you get being a hooker."

"Save it for the locker room, Ward."

"Maybe she filled one of his cavities, then gave him a bill. *That's* what freaked him out. You been to the dentist lately? You *know* what they charge? An hour with Elena the hooker was cheaper than five minutes of Elena the dentist. Sort of the same lingo, though. 'Open.' 'Wider.' Just matters who's doing the asking."

"Fuck you, Ward."

"Touchy today, huh?"

They sat in silence, watching the female officer outside deal with the newspaper and television reporters. The last thing either of them wanted to do was answer questions at this point in the investigation. Besides, like her neighbors, Bliss didn't want to turn Elena into a cheap, dead whore either. He sighed, and looked at his partner, who was wearing a shit-eating grin.

"How'd Malikha look in those red panties?"

"Just fine. And for your edification, she's a writer. Got herself an MFA from Columbia. She's working on a novel about this building. From the super's perspective. Each chapter is a different apartment."

"She write the one on Elena yet?"

"No. But I read the beginning. It's good. Kind of a cross between Borges and Zora Neale Hurston."

"She tell you that?"

"Yeah."

"She happen to mention anything about Elena telling her fortune, astrology, reading her cards?"

"You saw the Tarot deck upstairs?"

"I had a girlfriend in college who was into all that," Bliss said. "Tarot. Incense. Herbs. Pyramids. She put herself through school doing people's charts. She was very serious about it. We only had sex on Sunday, Wednesday, and Friday nights."

"Conflict with your love signs?"

"No. I was seeing an art history major the other nights. But the one who was into astrology, she had all these books that went with it. Lots of charts and graphs. I always had to yank them out of her hands to get her in the sack. I didn't see any books like that upstairs."

"Maybe they were in Russian."

"Maybe."

The front door opened and the girl with the bike came in. Ward and Bliss quickly got up from the stairs.

"You shouldn't be smoking in here," the girl said.

"You're absolutely right, young lady," Ward said as he took a deep drag.

"Cops," the girl muttered under her breath. She started to head upstairs, then turned back, her face suddenly full of sorrow, tears welling up.

"Please catch the bastard," she said, her voice cracking. "Please try really hard and catch whoever it was that killed Elena. Please." She continued on upstairs, her bike resting on her shoulder. Bliss and Ward watched her disappear.

"Everyone seemed to like Elena," Bliss said.

"Yeah," said Ward, taking a last drag before tossing his butt and mashing it out on the tiles with his size thirteens. "Everyone liked Elena. Maybe she cleaned their teeth for free."

After strangling Elena Koroshevesky, Johnny Tolstoy began searching for a gypsy cab to take him downtown. At least fifty yellow cabs passed by, many screeching to a halt at his feet, desperate for a fare, even someone with an iridescent red buzz cut like Johnny's. But Johnny Tolstoy was smart enough to know that a yellow cab would keep a record of where they picked him up, and that would be one of the first things Kojak would do; pinpoint the time of death, then look up the yellow cab records for that area of the city until he found a driver who remembered something. Or rather Kojak would have one of the other detectives do it. The one with the curly hair. The actor who played him was really Telly Savalas's brother, but Telly was bald so it was impossible to tell they were brothers unless you *knew*. Johnny did. He could read the credits. His English was good. Very good. So Johnny waited for a gypsy cab as he slowly walked up Third Avenue away from the apartment building where Elena lay dead.

He had to catch a cab quickly because he was scheduled to perform in less than an hour, and he still had to get to his apartment to pick up his props. Fortunately his pad was only a block from the club, so he could probably make it. They were most likely running behind anyway. They usually did at What Knot?, the club where Johnny did pretty much the same manic performance art he was doing back in Moscow two years ago, only now his audience was mostly East Village types who were even more weird than Johnny. It was New Wave Strippers' Night at the What Knot?, which meant there would be big crowds. The strippers didn't just take their clothes off. One read poetry, one wrapped herself in Saran Wrap, another dripped hot wax on her nipples while reciting recipes from the Betty Crocker cookbook. Johnny's favorite was Katrina, who dressed up like a pussycat with a long black tail. During the day she taught philosophy at a community college and at night she would strip down to her Kant. The problem with Strippers' Night was that Johnny's set might get bumped.

In the cab he thought about Telly Savalas's brother, how different he looked from Telly, and that maybe it would be a good idea if Johnny disguised himself and got some curly hair, too. Like a gray wig. Become a grandmother. Totally. *Horoshuh!* Get a shabby dress and a shopping cart and walk the streets talking to himself. And he could go into the supermarket and ask the people in front of him in the checkout line if he could cut in front of them, because he only had three items. He'd work it into his act. How in Moscow, absolutely no one would let an old lady with only three items cut in front of them in line. Because *everyone* had only three items. Johnny hooted with delight, then saw the Haitian cabdriver check him out in the rearview mirror. There goes the guy's tip. Maybe he wouldn't pay the guy at all. But he had $137 he'd taken from Elena's purse, plus the twelve $100 bills she had sewn into the couch. Her life's savings, Johnny thought. Guess the men and women of Moscow will just be walking around with a few more cavities. No, it would be better not to stiff the guy. You never want a Haitian mad at you.

When you get one of those Haitian cabdrivers, you know, in the gypsy cabs with the air freshener and some guy ranting in French on the radio, always give them a good tip. Haitians know all kinds of magic and voodoo. The guy could find something in the back of his cab, a thread from your shirt, lint from your pocket, even your smell, and do some voodoo on you and the next thing you would know, your eyebrows fall off or you get a goiter or you have pain on the soles of your feet like someone was holding a match to them. [Wait for laughter to subside.] Believe me, it's not worth risking voodoo for a three-dollar tip.

But the wig was a definite. Someone might have seen him going into or coming out of Elena's building. It was better if he disguised himself. Hide for a while. He'd go to his aunt's apartment in Brighton Beach and speak Russian again for a few weeks. Tonight would be his last show for a while, if he could get on. Then he'd go to Brighton Beach and work on the grand-mother routine. He could start the show as part of the audience. Come into the theater with the crowd. Then walk up on stage. *Ladies and gentlemen, Johnny Tolstoy couldn't make it tonight, so I, his grandmother, am going to do the show. I tell you, it's so nice to be an old woman here in America. In the supermarket, if you only have three items, people let you cut in front of them. In Russia, no one lets you cut in front, because there everyone has only three items. It's all that is sold in the store. . . . It's all the store sells is three items. . . . Three items—it's all they sell in the store. . . . It's all the store sells.*

Anyway, he'd work out the punch line. And then while the audience was laughing, as the old lady he could pull up the sleeves on his dress and show the scars on her arms where years ago Stalin's police tortured her with lit cigarettes. A little lipstick would make some convincing burns. And then he could have the old lady tell how Stalin banished her husband and finally killed him for talking to his friends about freedom and justice. Then he would put on his heavy leather construction gloves and break some light bulbs with his hands, while they were plugged in. It was something he did back in Moscow with great success. The critics thought it was a metaphor for just about everything.

It would be easy to disappear in Brighton Beach. He could become just like all the other Russian pigs who came here—acting like Russians, speaking Russian, eating Russian food, playing Russian music over the loudspeakers outside their shops. Coming here, to *America,* not to be American but to make a little Russian theme park. Jews, Ukrainians, Orthodox, atheists, Marxists, cossacks, all acting together in some pathetic display of Russian pride. It made him sick.

But in Brighton Beach at least he had a chance of finding a replacement for Elena. Johnny knew some distant cousins of his had emigrated a few months ago, and by now they were tired of cleaning apartments or baby-sitting for rich people on the Upper East Side, or waiting on tables at the Russian restaurants, where the fat Russian men and women spilled vodka on them all night and got so drunk they forgot to tip. After a few months of that, the cousins were probably ready to make some real money. It would be easy for them. Johnny figured at least one of them was turning tricks back in Moscow. Christ, it was the only way for girls over sixteen to make any money in Russia.

He also wanted to get someone younger than Elena. Even though she looked twenty-four, she was really closer to thirty. And she had that medical degree and the two kids back in Russia. Also, he was sure she cried after the men were finished with her, which maybe got her bigger tips, but Johnny knew the tears were real and that Elena couldn't help it. She was going soon. He could feel it. Back to Russia. What the fuck for? To be a dentist? Most of the people in his family had no more than three teeth left in their mouths.

Johnny had told her if she wanted to leave, she would have to buy her way out. One thousand dollars. But even though Elena was soft, he knew she would never pay him the money. He knew she was up to something. That she would leave in the night. Disappear. Like all Russians she could easily disappear in the night. A thousand American dollars would probably get her a used dentist drill. She wasn't going to just hand it over to him. But what Johnny was really afraid of was that someone as educated as Elena might get all righteous and, just before she got on the plane, send a note to Kojak, or worse, to the Russian Mafia in Brighton Beach who would ask for their 40 percent from now on, if they didn't play William Tell with his testicles first.

It felt good to be riding in a taxi. Even a gypsy cab. Like when he was working two girls. Then he could afford to ride in taxis. Shit, he could have gotten himself one of those long white Cadillacs if he wanted, like the pimp in *Kojak*, who had one black girl and one Spanish girl. They were always arguing and taking drugs, which was how the pimp, a big black guy with a wide-brimmed purple hat, kept them happy. But then one night, while this poor salesman was crying in the Spanish whore's arms because his wife died and he hadn't slept with anyone in years, the pimp bursts into the motel room and rams a screwdriver into the salesman's heart and then takes all his money.

The Spanish girl felt so bad that she went to Kojak to tell him.

Then the pimp killed the Spanish girl and then Kojak killed the pimp. But Kojak felt sorry for that Spanish girl, even though she was a whore and took drugs and tried to get out of being arrested by offering herself to Kojak. So Kojak went to her grave and placed a flower by the stone, which was about as emotional as Johnny had ever seen Kojak get. And the last shot was of Kojak walking slowly out of the cemetery with his lollipop in his mouth while the camera showed the flower on the ground with leaves blowing. Johnny saw the episode three times before realizing that Kojak never took his hat off in the cemetery. That's what made him Kojak.

But Johnny Tolstoy was too busy now with his performing to take on the worry that went with working two girls. One was fine. Two tricks a night. Four hundred bucks total. Two hundred and fifty for him. One hundred and fifty for her, plus tips. Any kinky stuff she got paid extra for was her business.

Johnny told the Haitian to drop him off on Avenue A and Sixth Street, four blocks from his house. He couldn't be too careful, even with a gypsy cab. He paid the guy with Elena's money and gave him a $3 tip, not too little and not too much, just enough so the guy wouldn't have anything to remember him by except his red hair, which would soon be covered by a wig. It would have to be a cheap one, since Johnny had to watch his expenses until, of course, he found a new girl.

It wasn't that Bliss's marriage was *falling* apart—it had already fallen. But the pieces had arranged themselves so neatly on the floor, he and his wife decided to leave them there and they and the kids just walked around them.

The kids. Julia was twelve, Cori was eight. They were both tall and thin and had sandy blond hair. Someday they'd look perfect on the arm of a surfer dude from California, where they had fled, getting as far away as they could from their sullen, detached father. From three thousand miles away, having a cop for a dad could be, like, cool. "You mean like *NYPD Blue*? Wow!" says Surfer Dude, sanding down one of the, what do you call them—dinks—on his board. Bliss hoped he'd never live to see it.

Unlike most cops, Bliss didn't live in Queens or Seagate where they could own a house with a driveway where he could wash his car. Instead, the Bliss family lived in a funky old apartment on the Upper West Side. His wife had gone to Columbia and had a lot of friends in the neighborhood and she wanted to be near Zabar's, the giant deli/gourmet shop that had incredible lox, thirty kinds of bread, and great prepared food, which meant Rachel didn't have to cook dinner very often. So Bliss was proud owner of no driveways or cars or lawns to mow on Sunday. However, they did have three bedrooms, two bathrooms, and a separate dining room in their "classic six."

But three years ago Rachel got pregnant and they decided she should get an abortion because they felt there just wouldn't be enough room for another kid.

"And I don't see you making enough in the next few years to be able to afford a bigger place," Rachel said, with intense bitterness. Of course, they could have gone to her parents for help, but it would have been too humiliating for both of them. It had been hard enough for Bliss to ask for their first down payment.

There he was, thirty-four years old, a cop for a decade already, the brave crime fighter, ready to charge into Gotham when the Bliss signal flashed in the sky, mumbling something across the table at Lutèce to his father-in-law about twenty thousand they needed to put down on the condo. Her old man nodding gravely, as if he'd expected it all along. He paid for dinner that night, too.

It was at that point that their relationship really started crumbling. Of course, he made detective a few months later, and with the raise they could have afforded a slightly larger apartment, but the baby was gone, he'd already acquiesced to a vasectomy, and Rachel had contracted a dreadful and insouciant disease—stand-up comedy.

"My friends say I'm very funny," she announced at the dinner table one night.

"You mean they've tasted your cooking?" said Julia.

"No. When I tell my stories about my life."

"*Your* life," said Bliss. For he knew there was nothing funny about her life. But *his* life, that was a different story. He knew she loved retelling his cop stories while sipping cappuccino with her friends or waiting on line at Zabar's. After all, that was one of the reasons she married him. Or, as Rachel said, quoting some Restoration comedy, why she "stooped to conquer." Yes, the beautiful, the rich, the gracefully long-legged Rachel Davis had stooped a long way when she conquered and took Lenny Bliss down the aisle. (And it was *she* who took *him,* no doubt about that.) But it was the stooping that made him so attractive. What made him stand out so dramatically, she'd told him at her cousin's wedding, against the dull, predictable landscape of lawyers and brokers. No tie, sport coat flung over his shoulder, sleeves rolled up revealing forearms clearly hardened by work. She noticed it all.

"You look weary," she'd said as they slow-danced to the wedding band's off-key version of "Sonny." He'd been up all night, he told her, driving an off-duty taxi that was really a police car looking for bad guys. "Do you really call them that?" she asked.

"Do you really call them 'bad guys'?" He was the first cop she'd ever spoken to except to ask directions. A posh young man in a sleek suit but already starting to bald glowered at them from the bar. "Who's the Prufrock?" Bliss had asked her. "Your date?" The reference to T. S. Eliot made her weak in the knees and he had to hold her up. That's when she decided to marry him, she said. The poetry-packing policeman.

And in the last fourteen years she'd never gotten tired of his stories. Often when he'd run into her friends' husbands, they would ask if stuff they'd heard really happened. They would get all giddy as they talked to him, standing on the street corner holding bags of take-out Chinese, talking to a *real* cop. Was it true, the story about the guy who was growing pot in his bathtub? How Bliss had to use the battering ram to bust into this guy's apartment? They waited eagerly for the answer, heads tilted up, eyes wide with anticipation and wonder, like Bliss was their scoutmaster showing them a fancy new knot.

"Yeah. That was true."

He'd actually heard Rachel tell that story before. He had to admit, she told it well.

"This guy had not one but *six* bathtubs in his apartment, sprouting pot plants like a herd of Chia Pets," she said. "All lined up in his living room, and there the guy was, sitting in his recliner with a sailor's hat on, like he was the admiral watching over his little fleet of tubs." This was at a dinner party made up of mostly her friends. A sprinkling of attorneys, a dash of publishing, a pinch of arbitrage, a soupçon of Broadway. "But what my husband Lenny thought was so weird about the bust was that the admiral had his Walkman playing so loudly he didn't hear his door splinter into a hundred pieces and four policemen barge into his living room." This rankled the lawyers' cockles. "And then, when Lenny comes around in front of the guy, who is now finally aware that the cops are there, he just flashes the peace sign, points to the Walkman, and shouts 'NEIL YOUNG!' " This gets Joe Theater wondering how he can use this scene in his next play. "And then Lenny, understanding brute that he is, lets him finish listening to 'Southern Man' before cuffing him and putting all the pot plants into plastic bags." And they laughed. He had to hand it to her. She'd made them laugh.

At first she was doing amateur nights and open mike nights for a month or so, but then Catch a Rising Star wanted her as a regular. After a few weeks she developed a kind of cult following. It was then that Bliss went to hear her, sitting in the back of the club, nursing a beer, and hoping nobody figured out who he was.

The audience really listened to her material—transfixed by the elegantly hip forty-three-year-old woman talking about her husband's real-life encounters with criminals, with the scum of the city. Sure they laughed, like when she described the bathtubs as Chia Pets, but mostly they *listened*, not sipping their drinks, not trying to impress their dates. It was more like a ten-minute play than a comedy routine. And when it was over, Rachel pointed to the back of the room and said, "And there sits the hero of these stories. And he's my hero, too. Lenny Bliss." Then this spotlight swung around and found first the guy sitting next to him, who pointed madly to his right, and then him. And the whole audience stood up and applauded. He remembered sort of half standing and giving a spastic bow, before the spotlight mercifully moved back to the stage where the emcee took the mike and seemed to wipe away a tear, though Bliss couldn't tell for sure.

"And how about a big hand for Rachel Davis," shouted the emcee. "Rachel DA-vis, ladies and gentlemen."

Bliss had no idea she was using her maiden name. He quickly went to the bar, where he ordered a double martini. A few minutes later, Rachel bounded over to him.

"So what'd you think?"

"I think if anyone finds out, I'll be thrown off the fucking force."

"But they liked me."

"Yeah. They liked you. You're a star." Bliss downed the rest of his martini. "Can I sleep with you?"

She settled herself down on the bar stool and gave him a coy look.

"Well, I don't usually go home with the customers, and I *do* have a boyfriend, but . . ." she licked her lips.

"I'll shoot your boyfriend, then stick a gun in his hand and an ounce of crack in his medicine cabinet and I'll get a citation."

She thought about it for a moment. "Okay," she said.

She ran her hand up his thigh. He threw down a sawbuck for his drink and led her out of the club and into a cab. They kissed passionately the whole way home.

When they got back to the apartment, Cori was screaming, Julia was throwing up, and the baby-sitter was sitting in the middle of the living room floor in tears. It took an hour to get everything settled down. When they finally got in bed and were getting warmed up again, the phone rang—the baby-sitter hadn't arrived home and her mother was in a panic. It turned out she had gone to her boyfriend's house, which took another hour to get straightened out. By then, the mood had disintegrated, and the next morning most of the curt tolerance that characterized their marriage had returned.

On the day Elena was strangled, Bliss didn't get home until about 8:30. Rachel was waiting by the door when he walked in.

"Thanks, Lenny. Jesus. You completely forgot my parents are coming to see me tonight and I open the nine-fifteen set. I'll just make it."

"Sorry."

"Julia is doing her homework. Cori has a slight fever, but I think she's okay. I'll be home by eleven, unless they need me to emcee the late show."

"Take a cab down there."

"Of course I'll take a cab."

"I didn't forget to be home. I was on a case."

"You should have called. The elevator's here. 'Bye."

"'Bye."

This would be the first time both her parents had watched her act. Her mother had been already, even offered a few punch lines of her own (what's a mother for?) and then wanted to take Rachel to Bergdorf's to celebrate by buying a new outfit, until Rachel reminded her the store had closed five hours ago. But her father, scion of a commercial real estate empire in Queens

(Rachel had a strip mall named after her off the Clearview Expressway) had yet to join the crowds of college kids and cretinous young rich white assholes from Jersey and Long Island to hear Rachel's routine. Tonight was the night he would finally witness for himself the complete depths of depravity to which his precious daughter had descended. Between private school and college he had spent over a hundred grand to educate her, plus another ten large for tutors, summer camps, and edifying programs abroad. Now, instead of her picture being in the Sunday *Times*, resplendent in a long black gown, hanging on the arm of her philanthropist husband as they welcomed guests to the charity ball they were hosting, Rachel was spending her evenings working smoke-filled toilets for a hundred bucks a night telling stories about her husband's job.

However, she was no longer recounting his exploits verbatim. Bliss really would have been thrown off the force if she did. Instead she talked hypothetically about being a policeman's wife—about seeing the world through his tired, jaded eyes. She was a kind of cross between Lenny Bruce and June Cleaver. Rachel Davis, Policeman's Wife—and the crowd loved her. And tonight, hopefully her father would, too.

Bliss checked on Cori. She felt a little warm, but not much. Julia was in her room reading *The Shining* by Stephen King. She didn't look up.

"Don't you have homework?"

"I finished it."

"Oh. Aren't you a little young for that book?" he asked her.

"I'll read it again when I'm older," she said. "To get the parts I missed."

Bliss left shaking his head and went to draw himself a bath. On a case like this he liked to spend a little time in the tub, to sort out the information. He let the warm water fill up around him. At six feet four inches he had to bathe in sections. With his knees up, he could get his stomach and chest covered. Sitting up, like he was in a bobsled, he could get his legs. He dreamed of long tubs.

He and Ward had spent the day canvassing the street, talking to shopkeepers, supers, Social Security types who spent the day sitting on their stoop or looking out their window. Some recognized Elena from the description. Some knew her by name. No one knew much more. She didn't seem to talk about herself. Only the dry cleaner offered anything like a clue—that she had recently brought in what he remembered her saying was most of her clothing because she wanted them clean for a trip she was taking. Bliss thought she was maybe getting ready to leave town. Ward agreed.

They had to wait until 6:45 before the other tenants got home. And again, no one seemed to know many details about the young Russian woman. Some didn't even know she *was* Russian. Bliss was pretty sure that one guy, a jazz saxophone player who lived on the first floor, had paid the price to sleep with her, but he didn't admit it. Bliss had woken the guy up at ten in the morning and watched him mix a Bloody Mary for breakfast. He was definitely living the jazz life. Bliss broke the ice by asking if he had any Don Byas sides. Byas was the saxophone player's saxophone player—with a razor sharp tone and incredible chops. His Town Hall duets with Slam Stewart were seminal tenor. They talked for an hour about other swing players—Prez, Hawk, Ben, Chu, Jug, Flip, Jaws, Gonsalves, Arnett, Jacquet.

The kid got excited. He started pulling out records—disks Bliss remembered from when he was in college. He touched the covers with reverence. The heavy cardboard and lurid colors of the Emarcy jackets. The dark moodiness of Blue Note and Prestige. The angular drawings on the old Verves. They spent twenty minutes in silent reverie listening to *Ben Webster Meets Art Tatum*. Then, regrettably, Bliss had to ask him about Elena. The kid blushed.

"I knew her a bit," he said, mixing himself another drink. His eyes were already jazzwise and weary. "She liked the music. Jazz is big in Russia, you know."

"Yeah. I know."

"Once we came home at the same time. She stopped in and we listened to Gene Ammons for a while."

"What time was that?"

"The last set ended at one-thirty. I had a couple of drinks at the bar, so it was probably two forty-five when I got home."

"Was she coming out of a cab?"

"No. She was walking down the street. She was halfway up the block when I heard her footsteps. I waited for her at the front door. She came in, had a drink, listened to some music, then she left."

"Gene Ammons plays pretty soulful tenor, suggesting a certain mood, like you might have wanted something from Miss Koroshevsky."

"Koroshe-VESS-sky."

"Right."

"It was late. I played something soft."

"What about Kostelanetz?"

"Andre's L-seven, man."

"Square. I dig. You ever see her again?"

"No."

"Go to her apartment? Borrow a cup of sugar? A can of tomato juice to make breakfast?"

"No."

But his voice lacked conviction here. Bliss knew the kid was harmless, but he didn't like that he was lying.

"She ever talk about her work?"

Again he blushed.

"No."

"Who she worked for?"

"She was pretty reserved."

Bliss was getting pissed. Everyone talks to her, but no one knows anything about this woman.

"She ever talk to you about your sign? Read your palm? Do Tarot cards with you?"

"No. Really. Nothing like that. But there is one thing I should tell you. I once saw her outside the building."

"On a date?"

"No."

"Then where? And please don't fucking blush again."

"Okay. I know this guy, plays this really out-there music. Writes it all himself."

"Like Sun Ra?"

"No. I mean like way out there. He's classically trained and everything, but he plays like from Mars or something. He's got this huge trust fund, so he pays his sidemen like scale, which is unheard of for a gig in one of the East Village places. I think he also pays the club to let him play there."

"And that's where you saw Elena?"

"Yeah. I glommed her from the stand. She was sitting at the bar—waiting for someone it seemed like. Kept looking at her watch. Then I had to play this bizarre solo while the guy whose gig it is puts this raccoon in this oil drum along with a microphone and you hear this raccoon going crazy with these squeals and high-pitched scraping trying to climb up the sides of the barrel. And I'm playing like a duet with this trapped raccoon, and when I'm done, I look up and Elena's like split."

"So you never saw her talk to anyone."

"No. This going to take much longer, man? I've got to practice."

"It takes as long as it takes," Bliss said. "You remember the name of the club?"

"It was Visiones."

"Visiones isn't in the East Village."

"Oh. Yeah. You're right."

Bliss did one of his quick draws, where his gun seems to come out of nowhere. An ex–Secret Service guy he'd met had shown him how. The sax player was now staring at a .38 pointing straight at his lip, ready to permanently screw up his embouchure.

Keeping his arm steady, Bliss cleared his throat and started singing softly in his raspy tenor, which, he'd been told on more than one occasion, sounded a lot like Chet Baker.

> *You promised me*
> *That you'd care a lot*
> *But you forgot*
> *To remember.*

"What Knot?" said the sax player, his voice shaking.

"'Whatnot' shit. Don't play me no cadenzas."

The sax player swallowed hard. "That's the name. Of the club." His voice was just a whisper. "Where I saw her. *What. Knot?*" He was barely audible. "With . . . a . . . ques . . . tion . . . marrrrrrrrr . . . k."

Bliss holstered his gun.

"Two things. One, I never keep a round in the first chamber. Two, you should be proud you didn't shit your pants. "

Having taken the last chorus, Bliss closed the door, leaving the sax player to finish the tune and close out the set.

Back in his tub, Bliss used his toes to turn on some more hot water. He was good with his toes. Especially the right one. Wedge a brush in there, he could probably paint a picture of a clown. Good enough for Ripley's. Something he could do in Florida when he retired. Keep him busy. Sit on the beach and let the tourists gawk. Sell a few canvases. Pay for his stone crabs at Joe's. Pay for his quarts of Thunderbird. A girl in college used to like what he did with his toes. The art history major. Made her purr. Rrrrrrafael. Made her moan. Mmmmmoan-drian. Great breasts. Like a Renaissance Madonna. There was that art critic she told him about, something Steinberg, wrote that Jesus was the pinup boy of the fifteenth century. That's why he always had his clothes off, muscles rippling, scanty loincloth. The original Chippendale. And as a baby, the Jesus boy was no fool, with his lips to Mary's nipple, a sly grin on his face. Not just sipping the milk. Something else on his mind. "Not bad, huh?" That was Bliss, his mouth on the freckled breast of the art history major (could her name have been Mary?) posing for a soft-porn altarpiece. And oy shit, there it was again, his johnson like a turtle's head poking up through the surface of the pond. The girls were still awake and the door had swung open. He hooked a leg over the tub and tried to close it with his foot but he slipped and fell under, taking in a mouthful of suds. He righted himself and looked over the side—a large puddle was inching its way across the tiles. Shit. If it got to the corner it would start seeping through the floor and down through Mrs. Kramer's ceiling below him. Then she'd threaten to sue him and he'd have to call the desk sergeant's brother-in-law the plasterer again to come in and fix it.

He climbed out of the tub and threw a towel on the water and instantly realized it was the only one around and that he'd have to call one of the girls to get him another one to dry himself with, sticking an arm through a crack in the door and throwing it in his general direction. He'd deal with it later. He climbed back in the tub and started going over the rest of his day. Anyway, his hard-on had gone away. Another small favor. If the bad guys could see him now.

He and Ward also spent part of the afternoon on the phone to Immigration and the Russian consulate, with no positive results. There were three Elena Korosheveskys who entered the country in the last eight months, and three others with similar last names.

Ward spent most of the day whistling the Beatles' "Nowhere Man"—always a bad sign.

"All we got is the name of this weird downtown club," Ward said. He was clearly not very keen about following any leads down there.

"I'll have a photo of Elena tomorrow," Bliss said. "I'll go down there and show it around."

"Make sure the tape they use to keep her eyes open doesn't show in the picture," Ward said. "People see that and they can't concentrate anymore."

"I'll check it."

"Good. I'm going to work on Malikha tonight. I think she's holding something back. But she won't be for long." Ward gave his Al Green under-his-breath laugh, and headed out the door. Bliss headed home.

Which brought him to his bath and no closer to figuring out who was the killer and who, exactly, was the kill-ee. This lack of information about just who it was who was dead was the new wrinkle in homicide work. Used to be a body turned up and if it was a regular person—robbery victim, accidental shooting, hit and run—there would be a grieving relative not far behind to tell you what you needed to know about the deceased. If it was a criminally related homicide, some wise guy getting whacked, some known dealer getting his territory taken over, you'd run the prints through Albany and in an hour you'd get a printout of a yardlong rap sheet on the deceased like a W. C. Fields prop. Either way, once you knew who it was who was dead, it was a lot easier finding out who killed them.

But in the last ten years it seemed like every other stiff was a John or Juan or Jean Doe. They were tripping over the dead bodies of people who hadn't been in New York long enough to get over jet lag. Haitians, Jamaicans, South Americans—usually drug related. No ID. No passports or visas. No notes from home pinned to their jackets. Their luggage didn't have baggage claim stubs. There were no used bus tickets crumpled in the waste-baskets. It was like the Starship *Enterprise* beamed them into a seedy hotel room just in time for them to catch a bullet in the base of the skull.

Sometimes there would be a group of them, a tableau, lying in the living room, like they were having a sleepover. Bliss half expected to see a game of Twister set up, punch and chips, and a bowl of M&M's. But this party was dead. The guests' necks were all bent a little too far over to be sleeping, and besides, there was usually some indication of blood or vital organs on the sunny side of their skin. Chopped liver had a whole new meaning at these gatherings. And those weren't little toys you scattered across the linoleum with your shoe when you walked through the kitchen. Not jacks or Matchbox cars. Those were shells, from Uzis or 9mm automatics. The apartments seemed to belong to no one; there weren't any photos of the deceased when they were alive, so they had to prop the dead bodies in a chair and tape their eyes open. They looked like publicity stills for *Night of the Living Dead*. People who were shown these photos for purposes of identification either looked away in horror or laughed. Bliss sighed. Some are born great; some achieve greatness; and some have greatness thrust to the back of their head and then the trigger is pulled.

As for Elena Koroshevesky, Bliss knew only that she was about twenty-eight years old, that she had emigrated six to eight months ago from St. Petersburg, where she had been a dentist with two children and presumably no husband. She had come to the States to work as a prostitute so she could make enough money to set up her own practice back in Russia. She paid a large enough rent to suggest that she didn't work the streets but rather had some high-class private clients. That she was very pretty and everyone who met her seemed to like her. Except the person who strangled her to death. The sofa suggested that robbery was part of the motive, though it could be someone was trying to throw them off. But if that were the case, they probably would have made more of a show of trashing the place. She had also been seen briefly at a club in the East Village. Bliss also knew she had been dead almost twenty-four hours and that the lab had found no prints, no skin under her fingernails, no semen stains, no fibers, no phone calls to trace, no diary, no paycheck stubs, bank account, or charge receipts and that unless someone walked into the precinct, held out his hands to be cuffed, and said, "I killed Elena Koroshevesky and I want to be arrested," the case would most likely go unsolved.

Bliss didn't want that to happen. Here was a woman who came to America to help realize her dream, to make a life for herself and her two kids. Just like Bliss had two kids. She was making the ultimate sacrifice—leaving her children and selling her body. And that seemed noble to Bliss. He didn't want this one to go unsolved.

But the sad truth was, there wasn't much to go on. Maybe the set of teeth in her house belonged to the killer. He left them out of courtesy, so the good guys could quickly track him down through his dental records. A killer who wanted to get caught. Nothing new. But somehow Bliss didn't think so. Not this time. The teeth were just a grim reminder of what might have been.

He pulled the stopper and felt the water and warmth drain out, and much of his hope drained out with them.

Johnny Tolstoy had a theory that this generation of Russian women were the first in at least a hundred years to enjoy the pleasures of sex. Take the girl he had been with that night. Tatyana. Her orgasms were ridiculously flamboyant—waving her arms like she was drowning, sending out wild shrieks and yelps as if she were making up for the millions of women peasants with faces like Fred Flintstone who had never experienced a moment's passion in their lives. At one point, when Tatyana was moaning deeply and clapping her hands, he thought he had the Red Army Chorus in bed with him. But instead of singing about the glories of collective farming, she raised her voice in rapture as Johnny's index and middle fingers played with her dexterously. "Now we can do this!" her shouts of passion declared. "This is Gorbachev's great gift to the Russian people! Oh yes! Yes! Oh Johnny, *perestroika* me, baby. From behind! Oh, take me now, through the Ukraine! Yes! I want you inside me NOW!"

No, it was unlikely Russian women had ever spoken this way. Johnny, however, wasn't swayed by her entreaties, and, like a veteran safecracker working while the alarm wailed, he continued his calm and precise digital manipulations until Tatyana collapsed from exhaustion on the bed. When she caught her breath and regained her composure, she wanted to do him. With her mouth, her hand, her crack, anything he wanted, but Johnny calmed her. He didn't need it, he told her. He was fine.

She protested.

"Please. I want to," Tatyana said, and she began foraging under the sheet until she felt a viscous hand grip her wrist, squeezing with machinelike strength, until it felt like the two bones in her forearm were bending together, then he let her go.

"I'll take care of both of us," he told her. "I'll take care of you

50

and I'll take care of myself." Then he gently kissed away the tears that were now flowing freely down her cheek. He lay on his back in the bed, guided her down next to him, so her head rested on his shoulder, and as she sniffled quietly, he sang her a lullaby in Russian until she fell asleep.

She was twenty-two, she said, tall, and quite beautiful. Her lips parted slightly when she smiled, which was very enticing. She was going to make him a lot of money, as long as she didn't fall asleep afterwards. Even in America, you can't make money sleeping.

Her parents were in the room next door and had probably woken up from Tatyana's ecstatic vocalizing. He wondered if they knew what was going on. The father had probably never heard a woman make those sounds. Maybe he thought Johnny was casting some kind of strange spell over his daughter, after which he would hopefully take her away, so he wouldn't have to feed her anymore.

Johnny Tolstoy didn't want to think about it. For the moment he was almost happy. His day went exactly as he had planned, which was starting to be no surprise, now that he was getting the swing of things—the American Way. Holding the heavy, listless weight of Elena's head on his shoulder, Johnny knew all he needed to do was plan things well and they would happen.

Johnny stared up at the dirty ceiling in Tatyana's bedroom, four different patterns of tin nailed overlapping each other like some kind of showroom. The paint peeling from the walls. The steam pipe in the corner was veined with rust. Her closet was fashioned out of a refrigerator box with a broomstick stuck through it. She'd probably never seen a box this big in Russia. Lying on the worn rug on the floor next to the bed were a bunch of stuffed animals—a baby tiger, a few bears, an elephant. She was probably allowed one suitcase for the trip to America. She chose to fill it with her animals. Tatyana's ark.

It wasn't the first decrepit ceiling he'd stared at that day. The other was at his aunt's house, just a few blocks from where he was now. He had arrived there early that morning, after cleaning out his apartment and packing his few belongings in a suitcase.

He had taken the F train to Brighton Beach and tracked down his aunt, making sure to bring her an assortment of pastries, a pumpernickel bread, and a bottle of Prince Matchabelli perfume he bought off a kid in the subway for two bucks. His aunt loved to get little presents. He felt it best not to be anywhere near his own apartment for a while. Even though Elena didn't have a phone, which meant Kojak couldn't trace any of her calls to him, he felt safer disappearing into the Russian chaos of Brighton Beach. His aunt's apartment was the first stop. He would stay with her only as long as he had to.

When he arrived at her building, she was just getting back from the butcher. She got up every morning at 6:00 to be the first on line. Johnny had once tried to convince her there were no lines in America, but she did it anyway, watching the sun rise through the cracks in the giant shadow of the elevated subway, chatting with the shopkeepers as they opened their stores.

Like Johnny, she had come to America two years ago. She arrived with her husband and son. Since then she had lost them both. The son was Johnny's age, a cousin he knew as a kid. They'd play King of the Hill on top of a giant black mountain of discarded tires that loomed at the end of their block. Sergei, his cousin, was always quickest to the top, dropping the bald, patched tires down on the heads of the rest of the kids to ensure victory. Here in America, he also started looking for a quick way to the top and fell in with some fast Mafia types who liked to drop tires too, only theirs were filled with cement and had Sergei's feet stuck in them. They sent his St. Christopher medal back to his house and the twenty-three bucks and change he had in his pocket. The next day, Sergei's father took most of their savings from the bank and bought himself a ticket back to Russia.

It was a lesson to Johnny, what happened to his cousin. How you couldn't expect to succeed here unless you had a plan. And that you definitely had to watch out for the Russian mob.

His aunt, however, as soon as she was on her own, began to flourish. She sewed lace on panties for one of the lingerie shops and worked Sundays in a bakery to make ends meet. The rest of the time she walked along the boardwalk, arm in arm with her new friends, other old women just like her. In summer they wore floppy hats festooned with plastic flowers and bathing suits that revealed far more of their jiggling bodies than anyone would ever want to see, but they didn't care. In winter, they sipped tea in bright red and pink overcoats they bought in the Salvation Army. Russia to them became a strange dream they had somehow shared, most of which was fading away, washed into the sea by the Brighton Beach tide. She still lived in a hovel of an apartment, she still got to the butcher two hours before he opened, but she was definitely becoming an American. Because the truth was, everything else was gone—left behind in a country that no longer existed. One day she took all her photos and the trinkets she had from home and put them in the broken suitcase held together with string and tape (*Russian* string that broke when you tied it, tape that wouldn't stick) that she brought with her in the plane and threw it all away. Johnny liked his aunt. They thought alike. She was starting over. Reinventing herself. Which Johnny knew he had to do as well.

She was happy to see her nephew.

"What happened by your hair?" she asked. "Where is the red? I liked this red. My friend was going to help me to do mine this way."

"I got tired of red," he told her. "I'll do something else with it soon. Maybe white."

"White's nice. Like this basketball player. What's his name . . . Rotman?"

She ate three of the danish he'd brought and put the rest in the freezer. She placed the bread in the bread drawer and the perfume on the counter.

"I hope you didn't pay more than two dollars for this," she said. "I get it from the man on Ocean Boulevard sells it from the trunk of his car."

"That's what I paid."

"Good," she said.

He didn't protest when she offered to sleep on the couch so he could have her bedroom. He needed to be alone, to carefully formulate his plans. Everything depended on those plans.

"I got liver today from the butcher," she said. "I was lucky. And there were still potatoes at the market. But I bought only two little ones. If only I had known."

"I'll go out later and get two more."

"You think? You think you can find some?"

"I know a guy who knows a guy can get me a couple of potatoes."

"It always helps to know people," she said. "Just make sure you don't double-cross them. Just make sure you don't keep one of the boxes that fell off the truck for yourself. Like my son. Just don't get greedy."

She was making sense.

He left his aunt in the kitchen making tea and went to lie down on her soft bed and plan his day. He would get his wig and begin practicing his act. Russian Woman Tells All. He'd shout about the shortages, the pain of raising children on bean soup twice a day, of being crowded three in a bed.

We were packed so tight, when my brother thought he was jerking off, he was really giving me a hand job. I had no problem sleeping. Then my sister wanted to get into the act.

That was from his old routine. He'd find a way to adapt it. He'd become his mother, raging the way she never could at the system that denied her a life.

Chicken feet, half-rotten potatoes, lima beans, beef hearts, blood sausage. That was the featured omelet, the soup of the day, and the blue plate special all rolled into one. My kids ate so many beans, I thought they'd blow the roof off. If they slept on their stomachs, I could see the blanket puff up—like little grenades going off.

He'd shuffle around in a tattered housecoat, his stockings rolled down below his knees, glasses taped together. He'd do his mother's voice, ragged and raspy from years of smoking.

In New York, people wait on line five minutes, they get upset. In Soviet Union, we lived on line. Women gave birth, children played doctor, kissed, got married, made babies. Died. But no one gave up their place.

Maybe this would be the act that would make him famous. So far Yakov Smirnov was the only Russian comic to make it, and

Johnny wasn't even sure Yakov was born there. Probably New Jersey. These dives, the dumpy clubs were just the beginning. He'd rise up—like Sandra Bernhard. He'd do MTV. He'd be the symbol of the end of the Cold War, harbinger of the New World Order. Johnny Tolstoy, ladies and gentlemen. Johnny Tolstoy!

After he got the wig, he planned to find himself another girl. Visit a few coffee shops, maybe get a manicure, the Russian bookstore, see if any young girls were tired of their four-dollar-an-hour jobs. Maybe he could pry one loose, one who had a little adventure in her, a little daring. She was out there, newly arrived in Brighton Beach, just waiting to be set free. Sex wasn't a sacred thing anymore in Russia. Sex had become like a souvenir. Something a tourist picked up, along with a postcard from the Hermitage and a bottle of vodka.

And wouldn't you know, his plans paid off. After a glorious dinner of liver and potatoes, he left his aunt's apartment, and later that night he met the very thing he needed—the oh so talented Tatyana, who was now curled up next to him, hugging a stuffed tiger and making soft smacking sounds with her lips.

Johnny felt like he was back in action. Planning is everything, he thought.

Elena is a danger, certain to betray him, certain to ruin everything with her selfishness. So he makes a plan, executes it, and alleviates the danger.

He is then left without a girl to support him, so he makes a plan, follows it, and now he has Tatyana, who will do for the Japanese businessmen what she wanted to do for Johnny. And best of all, he didn't have to sleep at his aunt's. It was all working out fine. *We're just going to take a short break and be right back to talk some more with tonight's special guest, Johnny Tolstoy.*

He got up from Tatyana's bed and watched as her thumb slowly made its way to her mouth where she started sucking it like a two-year-old. Johnny's eyes almost popped out of his head. Christ! He'd have to charge extra for her—at least for the first few months. He put on his boxers and went into the kitchen for a glass of water.

A sorry old man sat at the kitchen table. He hadn't been there when Johnny came in. He wore a torn sleeveless T-shirt and two-day-old beard. He had a bottle of vodka on the table. Most of which was now in a water glass, which the man seemed to be holding on to for dear life. He looked like shit.

"You Tatyana's father?" Johnny asked him in Russian.

The man grunted.

"You got a clean glass somewhere?"

He might have nodded toward one of the grungy cabinets by the sink.

"You get some of these cockroaches trained, you'd have your whole place spick-and-span in a week."

Have to work that line into the act. Johnny opened one of the cabinets. It was filled with cat food. When he was a kid he knew a family that had cat food once a week for dinner. He remembered once seeing the mother on all fours in the kitchen drinking the milk out of the cat's bowl. The next cabinet had some cans of soup and a half-empty jar of herring.

"Shouldn't this be in the refrigerator?" he said, holding out the jar.

The old man was crying. Just like a fucking Russian. Every time they drank they either got ugly and violent or maudlin and comatose. Give the whole country to the Jews. At least they don't drink.

He found a glass in the sink and washed it out. He let the water run for a while until the cold pushed its way through the pipes. New York water tasted almost sweet. He looked again at the old man. In Moscow he could understand it—it was a way of life. But *here!* I mean, you'd have to work *hard* to wind up so destitute.

"You should be ashamed of yourself," Johnny said to him. "Traveling so far to piss away your life. You could have stayed in Moscow and saved yourself a trip." He filled the glass again and took another drink. "I'll give a little tip. What you need here in America is a plan. In Russia, they make one up *for* you. But here, you have to decide your own. That's what I do every morning. I wake up and make my plan." The guy clearly wasn't listening. He barely blinked. Another dead Russian.

Walking back into her bedroom he decided he'd have to find Tatyana a place of her own as soon as he could. Somewhere in the East Sixties this time, closer to the hotels. Maybe he could work out a deal with one of them, have them charge Tatyana to room service. Elena's twelve hundred dollars would help him get a place, but first Tatyana would have to prove herself. He'd get back in touch with a few of the doormen he knew on Park Avenue. The ones wise to which doctors like to take a little time off in the afternoon, to give a full examination to a special patient like Tatyana. He could also set her up with some of Elena's johns. They'd probably like the change of pace.

He slowly pulled the sheet down from the sleeping Tatyana, revealing her fabulous white breasts. Worth a twenty-dollar tip each. She purred again. Johnny gently rubbed her nipple until it was hard and erect, then he clamped it with his thumb and middle finger, squeezing it as tight as he could. Tatyana smiled for a brief second, then woke up with a start and began screaming and crying, writhing, flailing her arms and legs against the bed. Sobbing. Begging him to stop. After about a minute he released the pressure. She immediately curled up in a ball and wept. But she didn't hit him, and she didn't try to pull his hand away. That was very encouraging.

"Most of us have been pulled over by a cop. And some of you out there in the audience have been *arrested* by a cop. But if you think that's bad, how would you like to be *married* to a cop? Well, this woman is, and she's here to tell us all about it—every gory detail, right, Rachel? Right. So put your hands together and welcome Rachel DAVIS. C'mon, give it up. Give it UP for Rachel DA-vis!"

"Thank you. Thank you very much. Yes, I am married to a New York City cop. I won't mention his name, to protect the innocent. It's fun being married to a cop. We have two kids and a police dog and a police parrot who says 'Up against the wall and spread 'em.' Our kids both go to a fancy private school, which isn't easy to do on a cop's salary, but my husband got the head-master a clergy sticker to put on his car, which lets him park any-where in the city, so they give us a break with the tuition.

"It's a little different for our kids, having a cop for a dad instead of a CEO or a broker or a lawyer or some famous movie star like most of their classmates. For show-and-tell, instead of bringing in a poster for a film their mom starred in or the names of the companies their dad took over and closed down, or a pic-ture of the horse their family owns winning the feature race at Belmont, my kids bring in things like fiber samples and knives with latent fingerprints. But once, when my oldest was in fifth grade, it just so happened my husband had made a collar the very morning Julia had show-and-tell. So Julia got to bring in José Morales, who'd shot a fellow drug dealer in the head the night before. The kids got to ask José all kinds of questions, like did his being deprived as a child—not having a maid or a cook or a house in the Hamptons—turn him into a criminal. They also got to practice their Spanish. *Como estás, José? Cuantos años tienes?* They start languages early in private school.

"But sometimes I think our kids feel a little deprived. Like I remember one night we were sitting around the dinner table having dessert and Cori, my youngest, asked why we don't have a country house. All the other kids in her class had them and they go away on weekends and take tennis lessons and tree climbing lessons and go swimming in the pool in their backyard.

"There was silence for a moment, then my husband said, 'But we *do* have a country house, Cori. It's called the Big House and it's just an hour north of the city in Ossining. We can visit there anytime and they have a really great yard and a terrific weight room. You wouldn't be able to take tennis lessons there, but I know some guys can teach you girls how to pass paper and nick someone's wallet without them knowing. Oh, and guess what? We could see José while we're up there. Wouldn't that be fun?'

"That seemed to make the kids happy. So then Julia asked for a second helping of pie. 'Daddy, I'd just like a little piece,' she said. Next thing I know, he's reaching down to his ankle holster and he's handing my daughter a twenty-two caliber pistol. His throw-down gun—you know, in case they shoot an unarmed suspect, cops have an extra gun which they can put in the perp's hand to make it look like he was carrying. Not that *my* husband ever did such a thing. But it happens.

"'That's neat,'" Julia said, holding the gun. 'It's just like the one my friend Max's bodyguard has.' A lot of the kids have bodyguards. Not so much for protection, but in case one kid picks a fight with another, he can say, 'Have your bodyguard meet mine at the flagpole at three o'clock.' This way the kids can fight without messing up their teeth, which have already cost the parents ten grand for braces.

"But I don't want you to get the wrong idea about us. Basically we're just a regular American family—dreaming, planning for the future. The other night we were spending a quiet evening at home—my husband was watching *America's Most Wanted* while I was darning a little hole in his bullet-proof vest, when we heard this sound coming from outside the front door of our apartment. A curious little sound. So, while my husband covered me, I opened the door, and there, in a little wicker basket, all tucked up in a soft cotton blanket, was a stray bullet. Yes, it was so touching. Someone had left a stray bullet on our doorstep.

"I said we should look for its owner, but my husband insisted we keep it. 'I have just the place for it, in that twenty-two I gave Julia. She can take care of it until someone comes back to claim it. Otherwise, it's ours. After all, this is New York.'

" 'But we have so many bullets around the house already,' I protested.

" 'So then what's one more? Besides, I had a little shoot-out two nights ago and I spent a lot of cartridges.'

" 'I suppose that's where you got this,' I said, pointing to the hole in his vest.

" 'Shucks, I just plum forgot,' he said.

" 'Well, I still think it's not a good idea for us to keep it.'

" 'Awww, honey,' he said, spinning me around so I faced the wall and kicking my feet apart while the parrot screamed, 'Up against the wall!' 'You know I always have a soft spot in my heart for a stray. Pleeeease can't we keep it? Pretty pleeeease?'

" 'Oh all right, ya big lug,' I said. 'We'll keep it. You know I can't resist those police dog eyes. Now get my hands out of these cuffs so I can finish my sewing. Otherwise I'll tell the guys at the precinct you were whining again!'

"I tell ya—thank you, thank you—I tell ya, it's always something with this guy. The other morning I woke up and there was this sixteen-year-old hooker in bed with us. I said to my husband, 'Honey, you just have to learn how to not take your work home with you.' She was a very nice Puerto Rican girl. She stayed with us for a few weeks and worked out of our house. You know, my daughters were in school all day *anyway,* so it's not like they were *using* their beds. And we sure needed the extra income. She cooked fabulous rice and beans and menudo for us and helped the kids with their Spanish. But after a few weeks she took off, leaving us a nice present for the house—the crabs. But she *did* take the stray bullet, and I think she'll give it a very nice home.

"Thank you. You've been a wonderful audience. Thank you and good night."

"Rachel DA-vis, ladies and gentlemen. Rachel DA-vis!"

The next day—nothing. He made a few calls, bugged Immigration again, just for something to do. The desk sergeant's sister-in-law knew Russian. She stopped by the precinct and translated the postcard they'd found. It was from Elena's mother. No return address. The card had evidently fallen on the sink, so the ink was smudged in several places, including the postmark. It announced that Elena was an aunt again. The girl's name was Anastasia. It said Elena's children were fine and missed her a lot. The picture on the card was of a church in St. Petersburg. It offered no clues. Bliss taped the card to the side of his computer. A memento mori.

That afternoon, after sitting in court for three hours to give testimony, he went back to Elena's apartment and walked through it again, thinking maybe he missed something. It wasn't the home of a mother with two kids. She must have left that part of her behind in Russia. Here she had another name, what the johns called her. Veronica or Cassandra or Tiffany. This life, like her new name, was temporary.

He looked at the way the cushions on the couch were shredded. Clean. Like the cuts on her belly. A razor, maybe. Or a homemade shiv, like something someone would use in a prison yard. Maybe the perp did time. He could ask around, see if anyone remembered a case involving someone Russian. Or part Russian. Hell, maybe he was a gourmet chef and he used a paring knife.

He took the Tarot cards off the shelf. Could be they were arranged in some kind of order, spelling out a secret message. The Tarot Card Killer. The card on top said "The Fool." He was standing on a mountaintop staring off into space. Dreaming. That was Bliss. Dreaming on the mountain. The mountain—that was the real part. The indisputable truth of Elena's death. The dreaming—that was him in the tub, imagining scenarios, possible suspects. Bliss tried to remember what sign he was. In college he always replied "*catcatore.*" He put the deck in his pocket, being careful to keep them in order. He'd find someone to look them, see if anything was odd. If it meant anything that the Fool was on top of the pile. Maybe he'd try and get in touch with his old girlfriend. She lived in Greenwich Village somewhere. Telling fortunes—probably making more money and getting laid more often than he was.

Bliss put the Tarot cards in his pocket and found the makeup he had swiped the day before. Supposed to give it to Rachel, but he forgot. Forgot, or didn't want to. He wondered why he was so taken with this dead woman. It wasn't his first comely stiff. There was the young hooker he and Ward found in a Dumpster a couple of months ago after an anonymous phone call.

"Jesus, she's young," Bliss said after they had found her. "What do you figure? Fourteen? Fifteen?"

"Tops."

Ward took a thoughtful pause.

"Not much older than your kid. Julia. Kind of looks like her, too. Don't ya think?"

Then Bliss exploded.

"Who the fuck do you think you are?" He punched Ward as hard as he could in the arm—like he used to do to kids in high school. "You can't just *say* shit like that." He hit him again. "It stays with me!" He hit him harder. "I have to go home and think about what you just said every time I see my daughter!!"

Ward took the punishment until Bliss chilled. Then Ward rubbed his arm and looked strangely at his partner of six years, trying to decipher what was wrong, like when someone you know has just gotten new eyeglasses or recently shaved off their mustache.

The Dumpster was behind a French restaurant and smelled of fish. The girl was pretty well wedged in. When the crew came to bag her, they had to dig down to get to her through layers of trout bones, lobster shells, crab claws, and shrimp tails, like culinary geologists. Her face was a hideous mask of cream sauce and onion skins. Pulling her out a bit further, they discovered that a

stale baguette wedged between her legs had given her something that resembled a giant hard-on. Ward and the patrolmen at
the scene broke down in convulsive laughter. It took them several minutes to regain their composure. They were careful to
leave the bread in place when they put her in the body bag and
carried her to the ambulance with unprecedented care and tenderness. Not because she was a pretty young girl whose murder
and subsequent humiliation in the garbage had moved them,
but because this was going to be one fucking big surprise for the
guys in the morgue and, shit, they wished they could be there
when they unzip *this* one.

Apparently it had caused quite a sensation, because two
weeks later, guys still talked about it down at the precinct—
grilling Bliss about whether it was really true. Because he was
there. Because he had *seen* it. Something about the job that
would make them laugh and it was his responsibility to share it.
It went with the territory, like a traveling salesman regaling the
showroom with tales of bored, despondent housewives escort-
ing him to their bedrooms with nothing on but a pink chemise.
So every time Bliss recounted the tale of "The Girl and the
French Bread," because of Ward he could only see his oldest
daughter in the Dumpster, blond, blue-eyed, dead, covered in
shrimp guts and garlic—béarnaise dripping from her nose, an
apple stuffed in her mouth.

The girl in the garbage was from Indiana. A runaway, working
the streets. The parents came and took her back. Faces blank.
Church and booze might ease their pain. Maybe. No one came
forward. No one saw anything. The hookers they knew hadn't
recognized her. Maybe she hadn't even gotten that far, never
made it to the streets. Maybe some sicko was out hunting in Port
Authority and got her in his sights, just off the bus, dazzled by
the lights. There were men who could track these girls as well as
any Indian brave ever hunted deer. Silently, moving on padded
Nike feet, they sniffed out the young and vulnerable, boys *and*
girls, from the thousands who passed through every day. Bliss
thought they should make a documentary about them, with one
of those English guys narrating. "The Hunters of the Port." Run

it on PBS. Lots of hand-held camera, showing how he could silently sneak up behind his prey on the escalator, sweet-talk her into his broken-down van parked a few blocks away, drive her somewhere, rape her, and kill her. Then they could break from the film for a few minutes so they could do some fund-raising, and come back with Part Two, showing how the brave hunter tossed her body in the Dumpster and kept her knapsack, stuffing it and mounting it above his bed—a trophy. Such a noble hunter. Only there was no limit on young girls and no season and you didn't have to sign up for a permit.

But that case was as cold as the shrimp skins that had covered her. No leads. No witnesses. The only prints they found belonged to the bus boy. Now, two months later, Bliss wasn't thinking about the girl in the Dumpster. He was thinking about a dentist with two kids who was murdered right here in her own apartment.

A dentist.

He sat on her sofa, its guts symbolically spilling out, thinking about her. He couldn't stop. Because she was from Russia, maybe? Because they had that connection and could have been, like Ward said, cousins? But how connected was he to Russia? One grandfather, his mother's, who left when he was eighteen to avoid the draft, changed his name, and wouldn't eat at a restaurant that served borscht or listen to a radio station that played Prokofiev. "Scratch a Russian, you get a Polack," he used to say. "Scratch a Polack, you get a Nazi." So it wasn't exactly the Russian connection. Was it because she was a dentist? A professional? Was it because she knew what she wanted and went after it? Didn't just wind up doing what her father did, but had a dream and fulfilled it? It was the thing Bliss never managed to do. Sacrificing everything, working hard to make a dream come true. Whereas Bliss was doing what he did because he never decided on anything else. Maybe he wished he'd been married to her, the dentist. He would have stayed home and cooked and cleaned and taken care of the children while she was in the office. Have a platter of stuffed cabbage waiting for her when she came home. He couldn't figure it out.

Later that night he'd go down to that club in the East Village—the What Knot? Club with a question mark—to see if anyone there knew her or remembered who she spoke to.

He went into Elena's bathroom and looked at himself in the mirror. He was starting to resemble his father—nose hairs, ear hairs. Pretty soon he'd have a dead stogie growing out of the corner of his mouth and he'd be playing pinochle until three in the morning. But who did Bliss know to play pinochle with? He found Elena's tweezers and yanked out a few hairs. He pulled down his lip. His gums were retrenching, packed up for the night, like shopkeepers who pull their gates down halfway to show they were closed. He remembered floss on her sink. Of course she'd have floss. She was a dentist.

He flossed.

She would have been disappointed with his dental hygiene. Reprimanded him. He'd cut out the candy bars, brush twice a day, floss more often. If he couldn't find her killer, at least he'd keep his teeth clean in tribute. Bliss brushed. Bliss rinsed.

He went into her kitchen area and made himself some coffee. He sat at her table and thought about what Kevin downstairs had said. How he had blamed the city for her death. Was that right? Was it the city's fault? Or the fault of an individual within that city? Philosophers spent their whole lives thinking about that kind of stuff. Mill on Liberty. Rousseau, the Noble Savage. Spinoza on everything that no one could figure out. They busted their brains getting the skinny on the Nature of Man—the forces that influenced people. Bliss looked at the outline of Elena's body on the floor. *Was* it the city that did this to her? Some kid who got lost in the school system? Whose spirit was broken by bad foster care? Drugs? If a young black kid kills someone, they blame society. If a cop kills someone, they blame the cop. If a young black kid kills a cop, they hunt him down like a dog.

He left the apartment, walked down one flight, and knocked on the door of the taut, sexy girl with the bike. A young man answered. He had no shirt on. His stomach looked like a braided challah.

"You should always ask who it is before you answer the door,"

Bliss scolded him. "And you should look through the peephole. A woman was murdered here last night."

"I heard she was a whore."

This prick came from money. Bliss could hear it in his voice. The telltale lilt that belies a trust fund. And the way he cleared his throat, as if he were reading a cue card—"Ahem." Rich people did that. When they sneezed, they said "Ah-choo." Their dogs went "bow-wow." Their pee-pee tinkled when it hit the toilet.

"Ahem. What can I do for you?"

Bliss wanted to tell the mincing little sub-yuppie to go get some Crisco and pull down his khakis, so Bliss could cornhole him right there in the doorway.

So Bliss told him exactly that.

"I don't have to listen to this! Who the fuck are you?!" He said "fuck" like he'd learned it at the movies. De Niro in *Mean Streets*. Keitel in . . . just about anything except *The Piano*. The guy started to slam the door. Bliss got a foot in it and whipped out his badge.

"Homicide. Detective Bliss. I need to ask the girl who lives here a few questions."

"Courtney's not here."

Courtney. He should have *known* she was a Courtney. He wouldn't have sought passage, even on such a sleek ship, if he'd known she'd been christened with such a pretentious moniker.

"Well, please tell Miss Courtney to give me a call. Pretty please. I need to ask her more questions about Elena Koroshevesky's murder. She already has one of my cards, but here's another one. You can call me too, Prince, if you get lonely." Bliss blew him a kiss.

The guy sneezed.

"Ah-choo."

"You should put a shirt on. You'll catch your death."

He stopped by the precinct. There was a message for him to call Alexa Gurevich—RE: Elena Koroshevesky. He quickly dialed her number. He Buddy Riched his pen on the edge of his desk, waiting for someone to answer.

"Hello." It was a woman's voice. With a slight Russian accent. Bliss got to the point.

"Is Elena there?"

Silence. She stopped talking. What kind of game was this? He didn't need jokers right now—sixth grade pranksters who read the *New York Post* instead of doing their homework or watching MTV.

"Is *Elena* there!!?" he shouted.

As she hung up he realized his mistake. He hit redial. The woman answered.

"Please," she said, her voice quivering. "It's not nice what you're doing. Taunting me."

"Is this Alexa Gurevich?"

She swallowed hard.

"Yes."

"I'm Detective Bliss. Homicide. I'm sorry, I . . . I asked for Elena. Instead of you."

"Oh."

"I'm sorry. I was confused."

"It's all right."

"I got a message that you had some information."

"The man who lived downstairs from her gave me your card," she said, her voice becoming more assured. This is Elena talking. This is how she would have sounded, informing him his gums were in trouble, telling him to brush better. Concerned about his molars. A stake in his tartar. His plaque on a plaque.

"Good," he said. He was up from his chair now, pacing by his desk.

"He said you were doing the investigation."

"I am. Do you know anything?" he was almost whining into the phone, like one of his kids. "Do you *know* who killed her?"

"No. I don't."

His daughter Julia used to read *Encyclopedia Brown—Boy Detective*. Bliss wanted her to search for the clues, to be a good detective. But she always looked in the back for the solution. Now *he* wanted to do the same thing, to turn to the last page and read the name of the murderer and then go out and arrest him. He felt foolish.

"But you knew her."

"Yes. She was my cousin."

"Do you know where she worked? Who she worked for?"

"No."

"But you knew she turned tricks." No response. "That she was a prostitute. That she . . ."

"Yes. I knew."

"When was the last time you saw her?"

"About a week ago. I came by for Sunday dinner. She didn't work on Sunday. At least in the evening. I made potato piroshki. We always together spoke in Russian. So she wouldn't forget."

"Did she plan on going back?"

"Yes."

"Did she say she was in any danger?"

"No."

"Did she mention feeling threatened by anyone?"

"She was getting ready to leave. She wanted to be home."

"She had a ticket?"

"No. But she told me she was getting ready. That she wouldn't have to do much longer this . . . this . . . business."

"Did she ever do Tarot cards for you?" No response. "Tell your fortune? Anything like that?"

"The Tarot cards are mine."

"The ones I found in her house?"

"Yes."

"On the bookshelf?"

"Yes."

"Oh."

"I'm sorry if . . . if they confused you."

"Can I see you sometime? I mean, can I come by and talk to you? In more detail. About Elena."

"Certainly. You can . . ."

"Maybe there was something she said."

"Yes. I . . ."

"Just in passing. Something that might help me track down this person."

"Of course."

"What's your address?"

She told him. In the Eighties off Central Park West. Not a bad location.

"Later today okay?"

"I have appointments all afternoon."

"Appointments?"

"Yes. Readings. And massage."

"Massage?" Meaning what, Bliss thought.

"Yes. But not like . . . Swedish. It's not what . . . I have table to set up in people's house. For the massage."

"This could be important. The sooner the better, Miss Gurevich."

"Tomorrow after lunch would be all right."

"I'll come by at two," he said.

"Okay."

"I'll bring your Tarot cards."

"Thank you."

"Oh, by the way, the card—on top. The Tarot card on top was of The Fool. Is that the one you left there? Is that how you left the deck?"

"The Fool?"

"Yes."

She thought for a moment.

"Yes. When I left Elena it was there. On top."

"You're sure?"

"Yes, I must have."

"Why?"

She thought for a moment.

"Perhaps for you."

The wig Johnny finally decided on was silvery blue with lots of curls. It wasn't quite as puffy as he would have liked, but the young black girl who sold it to him suggested he buy a can of Adorn hair spray. She told him he could treat the wig just as he would his own hair. She had no idea how he *did* treat his own hair. She threw in a special styling comb and said if he followed the directions on the can he'd have no trouble teasing it up.

"You picked out a nice one," she said. "The color's just right."

"My hair was red up until a couple of days ago."

"Oh, I think red would be too harsh for you."

She had to shout the last few words because the subway was thundering by on the elevated tracks.

"I thought so, too," Johnny said.

"I think you'll be very happy with that one," she said, pointing to the wig. "It's not one of our more popular models, but the popular ones are the most tacky. The older Russian ladies like the blond ones the best. They think they're Marilyn Monroe. Makes them feel more American, I guess. Some even give themselves little beauty marks. Then they walk around in two-piece leopard-print outfits like they've escaped from some kind of weird zoo or something."

Johnny wanted to tell her that anyone who left Russia *had* escaped from a weird zoo, but he was too busy thinking about how he could use this in his act.

Then she leaned toward him and whispered, "I'm not supposed to say this, but if you don't like it you can bring it back. The wig, I mean."

"Thanks."

"Oh, and remember to close your eyes and cover them with your free hand when you're using the hair spray."

"Okay. Thanks again."

As he left the store it dawned on him that the girl had assumed the wig was for him, and that she was completely at ease talking to him about it. He probably wasn't the first young man she sold a wig to. In fact, there was probably someone in New York at that very moment working on a comedy routine where they dressed up like an old woman and complained about their life. He rushed back to Tatyana's house, anxious to get things started.

She was in bed waiting for him when he returned, wearing the black bra and panties Johnny had bought for her. Johnny wished he had grabbed the ones from Elena's top drawer before he left, but it had slipped his mind. He looked her over.

"Nice," he said. "Now try on the red ones. The Japanese men like red. When you bend over, your ass reminds them of their flag."

"Okay."

She stood on the bed, bouncing a little bit as she took off her bra. Her breasts shook gently. She giggled. Johnny was trying to act cool, but he was barely able to control himself, she was so alluring—four generations of lust drawn back like a slingshot, ready to explode at his fingertips. Maybe he would give himself to her. If she proved worthy, wasn't selfish and moody like Elena, as a gift, he would let *her* be his first. At least with her hand. Maybe he could get used to that.

She now had on the red ensemble. Red looked good on her.

"Wear that," he said.

"Now?"

"Whenever you're with me."

"Okay."

He climbed on the bed and knelt at her feet. He reached up and scooped one of her breasts free. She shuddered, remembering how he treated her the last time. But now Johnny kissed her—very tenderly. He kissed her over and over, until her nipple hurt again, but this time she didn't mind.

Johnny was proud of her. She had turned her first trick that morning. A plastic surgeon on Park Avenue. Johnny had chosen him carefully. He was one john Elena had said was always very gentle. Elena had probably fallen in love with him. The two doctors. Talking about medicine. Comparing anesthetics. Showing off the special knots they used for stitches. Miss Know-it-all. He was happy to be free of her.

Johnny had called the plastic surgeon the day before, using a code name they had worked out. He personally fit Tatyana in for a one-hour consultation. There was a couch in his office. Tatyana said he only took about twelve minutes. She was probably too much for him. A dream come true. And she hadn't even worn the red panties.

"It didn't bother me," she had told him, snuggling up next to Johnny as she told him that afternoon about the doctor. "He seemed so grateful. Like in Russia when we used to give the old man next door an extra sugar ration coupon." She handed Johnny an envelope with the cash and he counted out her share.

She was good. She didn't know much—didn't ask questions. She was working out just right. He wasn't sure about it when he'd first seen her that night at the St. Petersburg restaurant. Johnny watched her from the bar as she deftly slipped the wallet from a purse hanging off the back of a woman's chair while she was dancing with her husband. She had a beautiful face, but, to be honest, in her ill-fitting waitress outfit, Johnny had no clue as to her body. He knew the Japanese liked thin girls with big boobs. Thin, tall, and blond. Great Saxon Venuses for them to conquer. Given her sweet face and blond hair, Johnny figured she was definitely worth a try. He waited until she passed near the bar with a tray of dirty dishes and called her over. He whispered in her ear that he would split her take from the wallet in exchange for keeping quiet. Johnny had to act quickly to save her from dropping her tray. She didn't say anything, just stared, then walked away, avoiding him the rest of the night.

Johnny waited patiently. Every half hour or so she would glance over to see if he was still there. He just smiled, lifting his glass of seltzer in salute. Tatyana was now waiting on a table of rich and beautiful Americans, boys and girls in their twenties, dressed like models, laughing and toasting. "To us, comrades!!" they shouted and crashed their glasses of vodka. "To Stravinsky! To Stanislavsky! To Rimsky-Korsakov! To Roxana Bayul!" They hooted and shrieked. "More borscht!" they said. "More peero-geez!" The women were in low-cut dresses, their hair soft and luxuriant. Their glowing cheeks free of spots and moles. Five years ago these girls were on a farm in the Midwest, finishing high school, hay in their hair, braces on their teeth. Now they were here in New York, living the fast life, which apparently included imagining they were drunken Russians. One of the boys squatted down to dance like a cossack. The others clapped their hands in rhythm. "More vodka!!"

It was the most remarkable thing about America—a person could *imagine*. Yes! You could imagine things—things you wanted to own, people you wanted to know, places you wanted to visit. And if you were smart and worked hard and cheated a few people, you could get what you imagined. In school they taught him that what separates humans from farm animals was that we can imagine. Which meant once Lenin, then Stalin destroyed everyone's imagination, there were no more human beings left in Russia.

"I grew up in a lifeless country," Johnny thought. "Deadsville."

"To Lenin!" the rich Americans shouted, toasting again. "To Comrade Stalin!" One took off his shoe and banged on the table. "To Comrade Khrushchev!"

At two in the morning she strode past the bar and shoved open the front door. She now wore a pair of tight black stretch pants and a man's white shirt with only the center two buttons buttoned. Johnny still couldn't see much, but he had a very good feeling about her.

Johnny paid his tab and headed outside. She was waiting across the street in the shadow of the elevated subway, her hands up by her chin, nervously picking at her nails. He crossed the street and leaned against one of the steel supports holding up the subway tracks. He could hear a train approaching in the distance and waited for it to pass. The supports swayed and the street shook as the train arrived. The brakes sent out a piercing screech that echoed off the buildings. Johnny gave her his best, most irrepressible, shit-eating grin, holding it until she couldn't help but smile back. The train finally pulled away.

"I didn't mean to," she said in Russian. "I . . . my father doesn't
. . . can't find a job and the people get so drunk they forget to tip.
If I didn't . . . you know . . . then we wouldn't have enough for the
rent."

"Hey," Johnny said, "I was just fooling with you. I don't want
your money."

She breathed a sigh of relief.

"And you won't say anything to Mikhail?"

"Who's he?"

"The manager."

"Mikhail's doing the same thing you are, charging people for
stuff they didn't order."

"I know."

"And since the customers *are* too drunk to tip, you're only taking what is rightfully yours."

"I guess so."

"What's your name?"

"Tatyana. What's yours?"

"Johnny."

"Hi."

"Hi. You sure look prettier when you're not in your uniform."

"Thank you," she said.

"You'd get larger tips if they let you dress like that."

"Mikhail says it's bad for business if the waitresses are much
more pretty than the lady customers."

"You could wear a potato sack and have a mop on your head
and still look prettier than those cows."

"You're funny," she said.

"Instead of giving me half your take, let me walk you home,"
Johnny said.

"Only if you make me laugh."

"I didn't know Russian women knew how to laugh."

"But we're not *in* Russia anymore," she said coyly. "Are we."

She took his arm and led him down Brighton Avenue, under
the subway, to Utrecht, where she lived. She stopped at the
steps in front of one of the decrepit four-floor dumbbell apartment buildings that lined the street.

"My parents are upstairs asleep," she said.

"Do you have your own room?" he asked her.

"Yes."

"Let's go up," he said.

A few minutes later he unleashed the ecstasy and passion that had been coiled inside her, waiting to explode.

Now, two nights later, she was holding her pay for twelve minutes' work, more money than she'd make in four nights of waitressing. Johnny knew they wouldn't all be this easy, or clean, but now that she'd started, there'd be no turning back. The Japanese men would go crazy over her, hocking samurai swords that had been in the family for five generations just to have an hour with her.

Johnny sat on the edge of the bed and took the wig out of the bag.

"Come over and help me with this." He put it on and looked at himself in the mirror. Ridiculous. No amount of Adorn, no amount of teasing would make him look like anything other than a weird creep in a cheap wig.

"Go get me some clothes."

She went to her dresser.

"No, not yours. Something from your mother. A dress. Shabby. Your mother has a shabby dress, doesn't she?"

Tatyana laughed, and headed toward the door.

"Get me some stockings, too," he called to her. "And some shoes."

She came back with an armful of clothes. They spent the next half hour trying things on. He practiced his walk. The shoes were much too small, but Tatyana had swiped her mother's pink fuzzy-toed slippers, which Johnny squeezed into.

"She actually wear these?"

"Every day. Now you need some shopping bags," Tatyana said. Laughing, she ran to the kitchen and came back and stuffed them in his hands. "Good," she said. "Now for some makeup." She started with mascara, drawing thick black lines under Johnny's eyes. Then she did Johnny's lips with the new red lipstick he'd gotten her. She also put a few dabs on his cheeks and then rubbed them in.

He looked at himself again in the mirror. He saw his mother looking back. He was scared.

" 'Ladies and gentlemen' . . . go ahead, say it."

Tatyana cleared her throat.

"Ladies and gentlemen."

" 'Catch a Rising Star' . . ."

"Catch a Rising Czar . . ."

"Not 'czar.' 'Star.' "

"Catch a Rising Star . . ." She wanted to laugh, but Johnny looked so deadly serious, she was afraid to.

"Good. 'Is proud to present . . .' "

"Is proud to present . . ."

" 'One of the funniest guys around . . .' "

"One of the funniest guys around . . ."

" 'Johnny TOL-stoy.' "

"Johnny Tolstoy."

"No. No. TOL-stoy."

"TOL-stoy."

"Excellent."

Tatyana had brought her mother and father in to watch. They were all sitting on the bed. Johnny was working the room from in front of her dresser. He started his new act the same way he did the old one, except he substituted his mother's name for his own.

"Hello, ladies and gentlemen. My name is Anna Kropotkin. For sixty-two years I live in Russia, but now I live in America and have hot dogs for breakfast."

Johnny paused for a laugh. Tatyana smiled on cue. Her mother continued knitting sullenly. Her father took a drink from his vodka bottle, staring coldly and intently at the door like he was auditioning for an Ingmar Bergman movie. "Your boyfriend's fucking crazy," he said in Russian, under his breath.

Johnny continued.

"I raise three children in Russia. I work every day in meat-packing plant. I was specialist. I cut out tongues from cows' heads. I cracked skulls and scoop out brains. I separated hearts and livers from the ribs. And this was for *gourmet* restaurants. I cut from cow parts cow not know she had. I hold muscles and organs all day long, but at night I have nothing to put on family table but beans and cabbage. Three kids eating beans and cabbage, it was like siege of Leningrad."

Tatyana's mother laughed. She was getting into it.

"Laundry by hand," she said.

"Right," Johnny said. "Forty years washing underwear and socks. They make meat factory look clean."

Loud laughter. "Bugs!" Tatyana shouted.

"Bugs everywhere," he said. "You can train them to bring food to table. Only place we *don't* have bugs was in our bed—because there wasn't enough room."

Tatyana's mother was starting to lose it. Huge belly laughs. Johnny stared at her with pity and contempt. He continued, his voice tinged with anger.

"So this is why my boys were messed up," he said. "My oldest, dead. Killed outside our door, his throat slashed. 'Can't you keep your boys from messing up the hallways?!' the neighbors shouted. And my middle one, in jail because he forces himself on young girl. Then, since he is soft in head from eating too much cabbage, he falls asleep in her bed. He is lucky the girl's father didn't kill him. They execute him soon. But at least now he won't die a virgin. And my youngest, the one I had hopes for him—giant hopes for, he is in America. He calls himself Johnny, like an American. But like a Russian he is still sad." Johnny was starting to cry. The cheap mascara made black tracks down his cheek. "So very sad. He wants to make people laugh, but people just turn sad and die around him. His jokes just make people weep."

He dropped to his knees and leaned over the bed, burying his head in his arms. Tatyana shooed her parents out of the room. Then she helped Johnny out of his costume, washed his face, and tucked him into bed. She lay down next to him and gently rubbed his back until he calmed down.

Later that night he let her do him with her hand.

Bliss was holding a fork to his younger daughter Cori's face.

"Eat your asparagus," he said. "C'mon. Just two pieces."

"That's two too many."

Julia piped in. "Read Cori her rights, Dad." Julia liked asparagus. It didn't have any fat. "Cuff her," she said.

Bliss tickled Cori's lips with the spear.

"C'mon. Open up. Just take it."

"No way."

"She doesn't want stinky pee," Julia said. "Hey, that could be a good clue for you. You walk into an apartment with a dead body. You smell that smell. The killer must have eaten asparagus. I can see the headlines—Asparagus Killer Strikes Again. No, wait . . . Asparagus *Stalker* Strikes Again. Do you get it?"

"I get it."

"Then how come you're not laughing? What're you, a father or an oil painting?"

"You've been talking to your mother too much."

"You mean I'm *not* supposed to talk to my mother? Oh. I'm sorry. I thought children were *supposed* to talk to their parents."

Bliss tried one more time to get Cori to eat the asparagus, pushing the tip between her lips.

"I hate it," Cori said through clamped teeth.

"Please," he said. He sounded pathetic. "Pretty please."

She shook her head defiantly. Did Rachel get them to eat their vegetables? he wondered.

"Wait," said Bliss. "Did you say the Asparagus *Stalker?*"

"Yeah."

"That *is* funny. Sorry, I should have laughed."

"It's okay, Dad. Are you thinking about a case?"

"Yeah."

"Tough one?"

"Yeah."

"Can you tell us about it?" Cori asked.

"You know better."

"I'll eat my asparagus," she said sweetly.

"Cori!!" Bliss shouted, startling them all. Silence. Shit, Bliss thought. I treat suspects better.

"Sorry," he said.

Cori nodded—mumbled something—then more silence. He thought about Rachel's comedy routine, what a joy it was to be married to a cop.

"Hey," Julia said, "Dad. I'll give you another chance. To laugh, I mean. You walk into an apartment, you see a dead body, only this time there's a bowl of Cheerios on the table. What's the headline?"

Julia looked at him with her mother's same inscrutable gaze.

"I don't know."

"Cereal Killer Strikes Again."

Bliss checked his watch. He had left himself just enough time to go home and see his wife and kids before he headed down to the club in the East Village. He wanted to get there early, talk to the waitresses . . .

"Dad."

. . . bartender, anyone who might have . . .

"Dad."

"Yeah?"

"You forgot to laugh again."

"Oh."

He looked across the table at his two daughters. They were clearly worried.

"How's school?" he asked weakly.

They let out a collective sigh. Cori starting eating her asparagus, looking up at him, smiling hopefully, as if that would make everything okay.

"It's all right," he told them.

They nodded in unison and starting cleaning off the table.

"We'll do the dishes, Dad," Julia said. Cori took one last bite of asparagus and patted her stomach. "Mmmm, good. Yummy."

He sat alone at the table sipping his coffee, thinking about his

kids. Julia seemed fine, smart as a whip. Like her mother. It was
Cori he was worried about. She seemed more like him. Keeping
everything inside. Cursed with sullenness. He wondered about
Elena's kids, if they were both girls, if they missed her, if they
knew she was dead. He wondered how she could have left them,
traveling so far. He knew many of the women from Jamaica and
the Philippines who did baby-sitting in Manhattan left their
children behind, seeing them once a year, watching them grow
in the snapshots they received in the mail. How could they stand
to do that? But then Bliss wasn't much better. His kids were
growing up right in front of him and he wasn't paying attention.
Instead he shouted at them. Asked about school. Pathetic. Julia
had two funny lines tonight, and where was he?

He checked his watch again. It was getting late and Rachel
wasn't back yet. She'd been working with weights since her comedy started clicking and was looking trim. He'd noticed definition
on her biceps. He wasn't prepared for this. He knew she was sending him some kind of message. "Play me or trade me, but I'm not
sitting on the bench anymore." To be honest, he never believed she
would stay on the bench as long as she did. If anyone was ever
born to be a star, she was. That's why her family hated him. She was
their butterfly, their fabulously colored butterfly who should
have flown off into glorious fame long ago. Instead she was nailed
to the wall, like a display, a souvenir. Like in "Prufrock." "When
I am pinned and wriggling on the wall." Bliss was the pin. But he
knew that he had better figure out what she wanted, because soon
she was going to use her newfound muscles to wrench herself free
from the pin. And take the kids with her.

Then the phone rang.

"Is this the home of Detective Bliss?"

Bliss didn't recognize the voice. Sounded like a broker, going
to pitch him some startlingly productive mutual funds. But why
"Detective"?

"Yeah. This is Bliss."

"Oh good. I wanted to help you with your case. The death of
that girl. I think I saw something that could help."

"You knew her?"

"No. No. I didn't *know* her."

Bliss heard clinking glasses in the background. Cash register. Low crowd murmur. Like on a live jazz album. Restaurant? Bar?

The man continued. "I just saw something."

Bliss registered "flake" and went for an ID.

"Who am I talking to?"

"Well, I'd rather not give my name."

The voice was deep and clear—a little fey, but cultured, like a classical music deejay. Not the usual doltish crank. Bliss tried to sound intelligent.

"It would behoove you to identify yourself," he said, and immediately wished he hadn't.

"Did you say 'behoove' me?"

"Yes."

"Oh. I see. But Officer . . ." More fey now, but confident, like he was used to getting laughs at a power lunch. "I'm not sure I *want* to be behooved."

Bliss was sure the guy was batting his eyes.

"Just tell me what the fuck you saw," he said.

His kids looked up from the table. Julia giggled. Bliss put his finger to his lips.

"Whatever you say, Officer."

"It's Detective."

"Oh dear. Excuse me, Detective." The man laughed.

Maybe he was one of Elena's johns. He heard the news and he's feeling guilty. Could be he's a steady customer. A regular, like a guy at the deli. Came for his special sandwich every Thursday. The rest of the week he was with his Trophy Wife on Park Avenue, who stopped putting out the minute her name was on the deed to the house in the Hamptons.

"So. Talk to me, Mr. Anonymous-Yet-Concerned New Yorker. Tell me something I don't know."

"I saw a car."

Bliss pounced.

"Where?! In front of her house? What time?"

The man stopped. A woman laughed in the background.

"Whose house?" He sounded genuinely confused.

"Elena's. The Russian girl."

"I'm afraid you've lost me, Detective."

"You saw a car. At Thirty-five-eighty-nine Third Avenue. By Ninety-second Street."

"No."

"Then where was it?"

"By the Dumpster."

"Oh." Shit. *Girl Found in Dumpster.* Front page of the *Post* for three days. Phone ringing off the hook. Every nut case in the city called with a tip on that one. Where to find her buried clothes, her pawned jewelry. They should have put in a 900 number. Would have made a mint. One guy claimed to have her missing pinkie finger. (It wasn't.) He wanted to send it in an envelope. He did. Three women turned in their husbands. Everyone wanted a piece of her. But the calls stopped six weeks ago. Now here's Mr. Suave on the phone. Not the kind of guy who would waste his time on a prank. Take him more seriously, Bliss thought. There's something here.

"Silly," the man said. "You thought it was about some other case, didn't you?"

"I did. I *am* silly. You're not the first to say it."

"Mrs. Detective?"

"How'd you guess?"

"Oh stop."

Julia and Cori started arguing over something. *Now* they argue. He gestured wildly for them to be quiet. He didn't want this sick fuck to hear kids in his house.

"You have to *rinse* them before they go in, Cori," Julia shouted.

"Are those children I hear?" the man said.

"No. It's the TV."

"It sounded like the laughter of little girls."

"It's a Barbie commercial."

"She said 'Cori.' "

"That's Barbie's new friend."

"I see."

"How'd you get my number, anyway?"

"Because it's unlisted?"

"Yeah."

"The tricky thing is not how I got your number, which was easy, but how I found out your mother's maiden name."

Shit. This wacko was for real.

There was some clicking on the line. The guy's quarter ran out. He put in another one. Local call. Otherwise he'd need more than one coin.

"So, anyway," Bliss said—casual, in the know, "you saw a car."

"Yes."

"By the Dumpster."

"Mmmm-hmmmm."

"Can you describe it?"

"Yes. It was blue."

"Sky or teal?"

"Actually, it was meridian."

"Good old meridian. My favorite shade of blue."

"You have a right to sing the blues, Detective."

"And to moan and cry?"

"And to sit and sigh down along the river."

"Anyway, do you know whose car it was?"

"I do."

"And who may that be?" Bliss had his pencil ready, but it was just wishful thinking.

"The car by the Dumpster belonged to the same person who was foolish enough to throw away a perfectly good young blonde."

"And that was?"

"Me."

A short giggle. Then a click. Then the line went dead.

Notes. Write them now. Now!

"Dad, Cori won't listen to me! She . . ."

"Shut the hell up!" he screamed at his kids. Then he started writing.

1. A soft *click on the hang-up—used his finger—didn't slam the receiver. Not angry. Why? Genteel. Maybe someone behind him, waiting for the phone—didn't want to call attention? Definitely likes being in control. Playing a game.* A game! *Wants to get caught.* (Bliss underlined it.)

2. *"Right to sing the blues." Knew the words. Obscure tune. Obvious jazz fan. What does that mean?*
3. *Call came from a pay phone, but was very quiet. Hotel? Classy restaurant? Somewhere expensive?*
4. *"Silly." Possibly says this on a regular basis. Odd, effete word—something someone would remember. But WHERE! Could be useful if we get closer.*
5. *"Meridian." Knew the exact color. Where's it from? Car showroom? Salesman? Sales pitch?*
   SALESMAN: Here are the new colors for this year.
   CALLER: I like the "navy."
   SALESMAN: Actually, sir, it's "meridian."
   CALLER: Oh. Silly me.
   Check showrooms. Benz. Jag. Infiniti. Beemers. Any "meridian." Any "silly."

"And . . ?" Ward said. It was an hour later. Ward was having his dinner and a few beers at the Corner Bistro, a cozy spot in the West Village that had the best burgers in New York. Bliss sipped a cranberry juice.

"Nothing."

"You checked the showrooms?"

"I checked. I checked."

"Results?"

"Ventures."

"'Wipe out'?"

"Yeah. Jaguar had Mediterranean, but no meridian. Mercedes had deep blue."

"Pedestrian."

"Infiniti was closed. BMW had royal."

"Of course. For Daddy to buy his little Princess."

"I could try GM and Ford."

"Not likely, if he's as much of a piece of work as you say he is."

"Maybe Saab."

"Yeah." Ward scoped Bliss's notes. "You think he has a wife and kids?"

"Possibly."

"Try Volvo. Check it out tomorrow. Especially the station wagon. Carries a dead sixteen-year-old with plenty of room for the groceries."

"Shit."

"What?"

"I forgot to call home. See if Rachel got there."

"Better do it now, partner."

Bliss found a phone booth and called. His older daughter answered.

"Hi, Julia. Mommy get home?"

"Oh, hi, Dad. Hold on." Then she shouted "Mom! It's Dad on the phone! Do you want to tell him about the divorce or should I?!" Pause, then back into the receiver. "Just kidding, Dad. Okay, you walk into the apartment, body on the floor, you look in the kitchen, the stove is missing. What's the headline?"

"I give up."

"De-ranged Killer on the Loose. Get it? De-ranged? The stove is missing? Range? Stove? Here's Mom."

His wife got on.

"Hi," she said.

"Hi. Everything okay?"

"Yeah. Working late again?" she asked.

"Drumming up material for your next routine."

"Thanks."

"Got a guy who's playing games with me in the Dumpster case. Says he did it."

"He tell you his name?"

"No. But he's a game player. I think he wants us to catch him. So we will."

"Good."

"The thing is, he called me at home. I want you to be careful. I'll talk to the doormen and the super."

"Okay."

"I'm going to get a caller ID for the phone."

"All right. It'll help us keep track of Julia's suitors."

"Make sure there are no Montagues."

"Right. What about the Russian woman?"

"I'm working a lead now. Over at the What Knot? Club. I'm late already."

"That pit? Well, do us a favor and put your money in your shoe and don't touch the toilet seat."

"That bad?"

"Yeah. They wanted me to work there once—part of an all-female comedy night 'Pamplona in New York—The Running of the Bull Dykes.' I explained that I wasn't a lesbian and that even if I *was,* I'd be one of the pretty ones."

"That's reassuring."

"What time will you be home?"

"I hope by eleven. I'll walk the kids to school tomorrow. You can sleep in."

"Okay. Take care of yourself, Lenny."

"I will."

"And if you hear any funny lines, steal them for me."

"Okay. 'Bye."

"'Bye."

"Ummm . . ."

"What?"

"I . . ."

"What."

"I miss you."

"So hurry home," she said.

"Okay."

Ward was paying their tab when he got back to the bar.

"I've got to go see Malikha," he said. "She's wearing the red ones tonight." Ward downed the last of his beer. "You leave the tip."

"You sure you won't come down to this club with me?"

"Listen, you *know* I bust down doors. Right? You *know* if there's a crack house door to be busted down I'm point man on the battering ram. And you *know* I've slept with Puerto Rican women—married ones, too, while their husbands were outside playing dominoes. So I don't lack *cojones.* But I don't *like* those places—those people. After nine o'clock I just want a cold beer and Sam Cooke on the turntable. Or Jackie Wilson. Or Marvin Gaye.

Because I'm too busy thinking about my baby, and I ain't got
time for a bunch of ugly, smelly, green-haired, cheap-tattooed,
ugly—did I already say 'ugly'?"

"Yup."

"Brainless, pseudo-assholes who probably have more money
in some trust fund than I'll make in my life and if they *don't* then
they're *really* assholes, pissing away the best years of their lives.
And piercing away the best years of their noses. If you want to
break into the joint after it closes, give me a call. Otherwise,
you're on your own."

"Fine. Be that way. But while Malikha's slipping out of her
purloined frillies, check the labels. Let me know if they're from
a specialty store. A place where someone might remember the
person who bought them."

"I'll try. But I imagine I'll have other things on my mind."

Ward left, singing Otis Redding's "Try a Little Tenderness" in
his raspy baritone. He sounded pretty good.

He decided to take Bleecker Street through the Village, past
John's Pizza, where he and Rachel had gone on one of their first
dates. And there was that pastry shop she took him to, with the
sfogliatelli. After dessert, they walked up Seventh Avenue to the
Village Vanguard to hear Bill Evans. Later they went to Caffè
degli Artisti for cappuccino, *before* it was the rage. "Hurry
home," she said. That was a good sign. That she wanted him
there. That she wasn't too hung up on some sculpted Adonis she
met at the gym.

He stopped just before he came to Sixth Avenue and looked
down Carmine Street. The fourth building down, past the used
record shop where he picked up that rare Ellington, which of
course wasn't rare anymore since everything had been reissued
on CD, that building was where they lived right after they were
married. It was Rachel's apartment. Squalid splendor, she used
to say. He knew the Village only through the jazz clubs. She
seemed to know every inch of it. Her father came to visit only
once, thinking how for another hundred bucks, the interest off
the interest off the interest, he could get us into a doorman

building on the Upper East Side. But then he was still reeling from the wedding.

The ceremony had been closer to Damon Runyon than Martha Stewart. The left side of the aisle belonged to Bliss, mostly a sea of blue, his father's buddies from the precinct, of which he ignored not a one, all in full dress, resembling an ocean not just in color, but in their gentle rise and fall like small swells as they tried to keep steady after the bachelor party the night before, where, it seemed, every hooker in the city showed up, looking for a few hassle-free months on the street in exchange for services rendered in celebration of Monty Bliss's one and only kid getting hitched.

Scattered among the blue tide, like bits of flotsam, was his father's bookie. And his *other* bookie. And the Chinaman who'd been pressing his uniform shirts for the past twenty-eight years, along with his wife. And the Greek barber who had a chair near the window from which, using binoculars, you could monitor the tote board in the OTB across the street. Every New York character that Joseph Mitchell or A. J. Liebling ever wrote about, every four-flusher, telephone booth Indian, or bootblack philosopher seemed to be on hand, most of whom got their invitations on the inside of a matchbook or a damp cocktail napkin on which his father scribbled the date and time. Needless to say, they weren't on the official list. But there they were at the synagogue, all the regulars that his father knew from his twenty-eight years on his beat. That was his real family.

On the other side of the aisle, the Davis clan and associates. Clean-shaven, socks that matched, ties that went with their suits. Ties that didn't clip on. Ties, period. They eyed one another suspiciously across the red carpet which Bliss and Rachel walked down, arm in arm. At the end of the ceremony, when he stepped on the glass, one side, Rachel's, shouted *mazel tov* while the other side, his, startled by the sound of shattering glass, reached for their guns looking for the perp working the B & E. His dad retired from the cops the next year and moved to Florida. If Bliss had known, he would have waited to get married.

Bleecker Street ended at the Bowery, where he turned left

and headed up to St. Mark's Place. His father once threw him in the car and drove down here to look for a cousin, one of the old crowd from Brooklyn who didn't make it, who got caught in the net of the city and couldn't get out. They didn't find the cousin, but they did have a piece of gefilte fish the size of a softball at the Grand Dairy Restaurant, so it was worth the trip.

He turned right on St. Mark's, past what used to be the 5 Spot, where Monk and Coltrane played together and which later became the gay baths until they were shut because of AIDS. Now he wasn't sure what it was. He parked on Second Avenue and walked the last block.

The sign in front of the What Knot? Club was old, from the forties, and said simply "BAR." It was probably there from when it was just one of the local Polish watering holes. Seventh Street and First Avenue was the heart of what was once a thriving Polish neighborhood. But the only things left from the old days were a couple of bakeries, vacuum repair shops, a Polish employment service, and a few coffee shops catering to local Bohemian types who liked to eat breakfast late in the day because it was decadent and because eggs and French toast were cheap. Vintage clothing, bookstores, and independent jewelry and fashion designer emporiums were now scattered among the blocks of brownstones. The oddly clad and Technicolor-coiffed denizens of Alphabet City (the avenues farther east had letters instead of numbers) passed him on their way to the subway or shopped at the organic food stores. They were poor and angry and proud of it, their bodies a celebration of their disapproval of all social graces; chains hung from nostril to lobe, like Ghosts of Christmas Past; as many pierced noses as in Pamplona; enough rings on a single ear for a Jolly Roger full of pirates. A giant magnet could clear out the whole neighborhood.

The few blocks around Seventh Street were somewhat gentrified in the eighties, when young Wall Streeters, wanting a little danger in their lives, thought living in the East Village would supply them with the antidote to their boring Establishment lives. But they didn't realize that the more of them who moved into the area, the less exotic it became. Besides, once they married and had kids, they realized all the fancy private schools were uptown. So they dumped their pads and moved to Park Avenue.

Things hadn't quite gotten started at the What Knot? when Bliss arrived. Two sapphic types with short, bleached hair, black tank tops, and black miniskirts were setting up a microphone and amp on the tiny stage at the back of the club. One wore black paratrooper boots, the other red sequined tap shoes. Bliss scoped an accordion on the floor by the mike. Boots probably played the squeeze box while Tap Shoes did the tapping. It was just like any act in any amateur hour anywhere in America. That was what was so sad about these kids—they so desperately wanted to be normal—hall monitors, 4-H-ers, teacher's pets, but they didn't have the courage to be so uncool. These two girls were actually beautiful—even with their Lee Marvin haircuts. They had great bodies, thin, long legs, and from across the room he could see the paratrooper's nipples pushing out her tank top in an alluring little dimple. Bliss wondered what you had to do to sleep with one of them—hum a few Frankie Yankovic polka riffs and sport a tattoo of Nietzsche.

Bliss needed a drink. He walked to the bar. The stools were covered with pink patent leather. Elena Koroshevesky had sat in one of them. When she was still alive. When she still had dreams of crowns and fillings. She waited here. Checking her watch. Meeting someone? Picking something up—what? Red panties? Paying someone off—her pimp maybe? More likely. Sax player said she looked nervous—kept checking her watch. Because she's got a pocketbook full of cash she wants to get rid of. Then she disappears. Because he doesn't show, or because he does. They go outside. She gives him the envelope. He wants to buy her a drink. He wants a quick feel under the steps of a brownstone, where the street whores go. But she says no, because she's not a whore, she's a dentist. Two weeks later she's dead.

"It's Negroni Night," the bartender said to him by way of hello. "Two bucks each. You want one?"

"What's a Negroni?"

"I'll mix one for you," he said politely. "If you like it, keep it. If not, I'll make you something else."

The bartender looked out of place—a clean-cut kid, fraternity looks, maybe working his way through college. His parents probably owned the joint, maybe the whole building. He placed a red-colored drink in front of Bliss, which looked menacingly like a Shirley Temple. He took a sip.

"Campari?"

"With vodka and vermouth," said the bartender. "How is it?"

"I'll go with the flow," he said, then played his hunch. "Your folks own the bar?"

The bartender gave him a curious look.

"My uncle Wencel does."

"Couldn't make a go of it as a local?"

The kid nodded. "Two guys from Scarsdale, not much older than me, offered him a lot of money to take the place over. They left it pretty much the way it was, except they bring in these weird acts and play Hawaiian music the rest of the time."

"And the pink bar stools."

"No. Those were here before. My aunt re-covered them."

"Nice. You work here long?"

"All summer. And I'll be here until January. Then I go back to school."

Bliss showed the kid his badge. The kid stood up straight—actually showing respect, like people used to do.

"Is something wrong?" he asked. "Is my uncle in trouble or anything?"

"No. I'm investigating a murder. A young Russian woman, twenty-eight years old, but she looked about twenty-three. Black curly hair, shoulder length. Her name was Elena. Someone saw her here a few weeks back. A musician. Played sax with another guy who had a raccoon in an oil drum."

"Jesus, don't remind me!"

"The sax player said he saw her sitting at the bar."

"Russian?"

"Yeah."

"Oh. She have anything to drink?"

"I don't know." Bliss replayed what he could of his conversation with the sax player. She was waiting for someone—looking at her watch. Nothing about a drink. Bliss should have asked. But if she wanted to make a quick exit, she wouldn't have ordered anything. "Probably not. Maybe water." Rinse, please.

The kid thought for a few minutes, putting in a good effort, but Bliss knew he didn't remember her.

"I'm sorry," he said. "I don't remember much from that night except the raccoon."

"That's okay. You ever meet any other Russians here? Dangerous looking. Criminal types." Bliss wasn't sure what he was fishing for. The black pimps used to help him out. Wide-brimmed red beaver homburgs, floor-length fur, black leather coats with fur collars, sunglasses. Twenty years ago he could have asked the kid if he'd seen any pimps around and the kid would know what he meant. But a *Russian* pimp? What the hell did *he* look like?

"I don't remember any. Sorry. Really. You want another Negroni?"

"No thanks."

Bliss looked around the club. There were about a dozen more stools at the bar. Only a few were taken. There were ten tables against the opposite wall. A waitress with a bouffant hairdo, green sleeveless T-shirt, and pink stretch pants leaned over a table and placed two Negronis in front of a pair of stockbroker types. One smiled at her. She smiled back. Bliss wondered would she trade in her fifties drive-in waitress look for a three-bedroom colonial in Westchester. Maybe if there was a pool in the backyard. And plastic flamingos.

The bartender cleared his throat. "Say, Officer . . ."

"It's Detective."

"Excuse me. Detective. You may want to talk to Lew over there." He pointed to a fattish, balding guy with his shirt open and a bunch of chains around his neck.

"Who's Lew?"

"He's a small-time manager. Sort of like Broadway Danny Rose," the kid said. "You know, the Woody Allen movie. He's here a lot."

"What the hell," said Bliss. "I'll talk to Lew."

Bliss carried his drink across the room. The accordion-dance

duo seemed to have a busted plug. Tap Shoes was working on
the connection with what must have been a six-inch buck knife.
Bliss wondered where she carried it. He shook his head. It
would take a lot to get *that* one in the sack. Maybe if he shot
someone she'd be impressed.

Lew looked like Akim Tamiroff on a bad day. He was sweating
and he wiped his brow with a soiled hankie that probably hadn't
been washed since Harry Ritz and his brothers played the
Palace. Forty years of flop sweat clinging to a few emaciated
strands of cotton. He had a little notepad and pencil the size of
the ones you get at a miniature golf course. When Bliss sat down
across from him, Lew was in the process of gnawing his pencil a
new point.

"Can I help you?" Lew said, spitting out a small piece of wood.

"I'm Detective Bliss. Homicide." He flashed his badge and
Joe Friday-ed his words, a little drama for Lew. Bliss figured
he'd like it. "I'm investigating the murder of a beautiful Russian
woman." Bliss gave him the skinny on Elena.

Lew swallowed hard. "So how can I be of some help, Detective?"

Bliss wasn't sure. "I'm looking for anyone Russian, anyone
Russian who you've seen here."

"Seen here?"

"Yeah."

"Russian?"

"Yeah."

"You mean *born* in Russia, right?"

"Yeah."

"Born in Russia, born in Russia." He mulled this over. "I
know every comic in the city, but I don't know any from Russia.
You want Eastern Bloc? Does that count? Eastern Bloc?
Because there was this Hungarian guy doing comedy harmonica
for a while, but he was really from Yonkers. Wound up going into
the family tire business. I could get you a deal on some radials, if
you want."

Bliss let this slide.

"Then there was this chick from Prague. Did a whole bit on

Kafka, you know, the writer. Comedy Kafka. Not smart. But she was *genuine* Iron Curtain, but not what I call bookable, you know. No C.P.—that's commercial potential."

"You know my wife, Rachel Davis?"

"Rachel Davis? *The* Rachel Davis?"

"Yeah."

"That's your wife?"

"You know her?"

"Of course. She's fun-nee. *Very* fun-nee. So you're her husband."

"That's me."

"She could be big, if she wanted to. Big? Hah! *Colossal!* I *told* her. I practically discovered her. That night. Her first night. I was there. Lot of people *say* they were there, but I was *there*. Laughing and crying. That's how you *know* I was there. Because I was laughing *and* crying. I was *ready* to sign her. Right then. She only did ten minutes, but I was *ready*."

"So you really know every comic."

"Posilutely. Look, there are twelve comedy clubs in New York. I mean, there are more, but there are only twelve where the comics are actually *funny*. Each club has about eight regulars. Eight times twelve is . . . is what? Come on. Help me out here."

"Ninety-six."

"Really? That many. So. Anyway. Ninety-six. That's it. Think about it. You must know ninety-six of something. Baseball players? Cities? Birds? Flowers? You must have a hobby."

"Jazz."

"There you go. You definitely know ninety-six musicians, right? So, I know comics. Mostly ones you never heard of. Joey Springer. Bobby Richards. Little Arnie Roth. Tex Schwartz. Lester Jacobs—the *black* Lester Jacobs, *not* the Jewish one. Elaine Cohen—'and then I went on *another* blind date.' Elaine Birnbaum—'My menstrual cycle? Like a Harley DAVID-son.' Elaine Edwards—'Cute. Cute.' Carmine Dell—'Oh-HOHHHH.' See, if they're good, they have their little tags—something unique. Like Rodney Dangerfield—'I don't get no respect.' It's immediate recognition. And it doesn't have to be vocal. Henny Youngman had his violin. You need something. Like Jackie Marlin—'I gotta million of them.'"

"That was Jimmy Durante," Bliss said.

"What?"

"That's what Jimmy Durante always said. 'I gotta million of them. Hotchachacha.'"

"Oh." Lew scratched his head. "Shit. I knew Marlin was a dumb fuck. Anyway, take it from me, I know all the comics in town. So naturally I know your wife. I mean, you *are* her husband, right? I mean, you ain't shittin' me, right. Don't kid a kidder."

"Yeah, I'm her husband."

"She's fun-nee. Ve-reee funny. She could be bigger, but she gets into this whole thinking thing every once in a while. Like Paula Poundstone. I mean, we get a lot of people from *Jersey* here. And the Island. Anyway, tell her Lew says hi."

"Yeah." Bliss started to walk away. "Hey. Lew. You ever see any Russians in the audience here?"

"In the *audience*? I don't know. How do you tell if a Russian is in a comedy club? Hmmmm." Bliss watched him thinking this over, scratching the few hairs on his head, picking at his chin, thinking hard. Bliss expected smoke would soon be coming out of his ears. "How do you tell if a Russian . . . if a *Russian* . . . how do you *tell* . . ." His voice trailed off. He shook his head sadly. "You see? You see? That's why *I'm* sitting here and the comics, the *funny* ones, are up there. That was a perfect setup, the Russian in the comedy club line, the *perfect* setup. A comic would have jumped all over it. But with me, nothing happened. Nothing clicked in. That thing that clicks inside your head to make the joke. The *zing*. That's why they call them zingers, because of what's inside your head. The zing thing. Mine goes clunk. Mine goes pfffft. Mine goes shlub."

The zing thing. He was pretty sure his daughter Julia had it. That click that makes the joke. Bliss wondered what she would do with it.

"You're sure about the comedians?" he asked Lew.

"Russian ones? Yeah. Of course there's Yakov Smirnov. He's BIG. Not very funny, but BIG. He USED to come here. I mean, not *here* here, but other small clubs. I talked to him. I was *ready* to sign him. Places I used to work. Not anymore, though. He's BIG."

"No one else."

"There *was* a kid in here once. Amateur night. The audience thought he was strictly from hunger but I felt he had potential."

"He was Russian?"

"With a name like Johnny Tolstoy, where would you *think* he'd be from—China? No, wait." He closed his eyes tight, working hard. "With a name like Tolstoy, where *else* would he be from—Iowa? No. The Yucatan? Southern Yemen? You see? You see? I can't do it. I'm zingless."

"His name was Johnny Tolstoy?"

"Yeah. From Russia."

"You know how to get in touch with this guy?"

"Who? Tolstoy? No. I just saw him once."

"She was a dentist, Lew."

"Who?"

"The woman who was murdered. She was the mother of two kids. Girls probably. Young girls. What about Tolstoy?"

Lew calmed. "Just that one time. Honest. He was intense. Not funny. A little scary. Then he took this enormous bow. Then he walked out. Never seen him again."

"You think the manager might know something?"

"Who? The Scarsdale Twins? You can ask. But if I don't, no one does."

"And no other Russians?"

"That's it."

"Thanks, Lew. You've been a big help. Hey Lew, you hear about the murderer who always ate a bowl of Cheerios at his victim's house? He was a cereal killer."

"Hey! That's funny. Fun-nee. Cop humor, right? Like in the locker room after work. Right?"

"Yeah. See ya, Lew."

Shit, Bliss thought, walking out of the club. Now I've got two comedians in the family.

"So my husband the cop comes home after a long day and his shoes are filthy. He's out on Potter's Field, digging up graves of deceased John Does to make dental impressions. Or else he's finding dead bodies; in the garbage, in the park, in his soup, when it comes to floaters he's got a green thumb. So naturally the first thing I tell him when he walks in is to wipe the mud or blood or flecks of dried organs off his shoes.

" 'Honey,' he tells me, 'why do you have to be such a nag?'

"And I wonder, why *am* I such a nag? I mean, would Harriet have minded if Ozzie came home with blood splattered on his cardigan? I don't think so. She'd just take it in stride, get his sweater soaking in Woolite, and pour him a glass of milk. That's what Harriet would do, I'm sure. I guess I don't have that kind of fortitude. A blackjack is not my idea of a stocking stuffer. Lipstick and rouge taken from a murdered woman's medicine cabinet just doesn't cut it as a sorry-I'm-home-late kind of present.

" 'Isn't this evidence?' I ask, looking at the makeup my hubby's just handed me.

" 'C'mon, babe,' he says, getting all cuddly, 'would I *ever* give you *anything* that hasn't already been dusted for prints? I mean, hey, what kind of cop do you take me for?'

"I don't know. It isn't easy. I think he's married to his job.

"Sundays, when he finally has some time with the kids, instead of going to the museum or the movies or a ball game, we go to night court. My husband's father was a cop, and that's where they went, so, of course, that's where *we* have to go. I mean, after all, my husband wore the same bullet-proof vest to our wedding that his father was married in, so what do you expect?

"Anyway, my husband's a regular at night court, so we always get great seats. Right behind the dugout. The opposing team knows him well. The Rikers Island Regulars. I guess it makes him feel special.

" 'Look, Daddy,' our youngest daughter, Cori, will say, 'that man with the bandages is waving to you with his good arm.'

" 'That's Rocco, sweetie,' he says, bouncing her on his knee. 'He's a tough egg. I'd hate to see what happened to the other guy.'

" 'Oh, and Daddy, look, that lady is blowing you a kiss.'

" 'That's not a lady, honey. That's Carl. He just likes to dress up like a lady.'

" 'You mean like when I put Barbie's dress on Ken?'

" 'That's right, sweetie.'

" 'And look, Daddy, that man in the black T-shirt with the big tattoo, he's making a gun with his finger and he's pointing it at you.'

" 'Yeah, honey, that's Rafael. He calls himself the Cobra.'

" 'Daddy, he scares me.'

" 'You shouldn't worry about him, sweetheart. He should be going to jail for a long while. But hey! Enough of this talk. Any of you kids want a doughnut?'

"And I wonder why my kid is having a hard time paying attention in class, why she wakes up in the middle of the night crying because she thinks the Cobra has his hands wrapped around her neck. My kids have friends at their private school that never step outside. They go from the lobby to limo to lobby. That's the way to do it. That's the way to live in New York.

"Sometimes we all stay home together like a real family. But instead of sitting around the piano singing folksongs or show tunes, we play Crime Scene. My husband is in charge. After all, he's the detective.

" 'Okay, Julia,' he says, 'you be the body. Cori, you get the chalk. Now just trace right around your sister's legs, then right along her back. Julia, stop giggling! Stiffs don't giggle. They don't move. That's why we call them stiffs. I don't *care* if she's tickling you! If we're going to play Crime Scene then you've got to do it right! Ah, forget it. I don't want to play.'

" 'But Daddy.'

" 'No.' He's pouting now. 'I'm going to my room. You guys don't play right. You don't even eat the doughnuts. How can we play Crime Scene if you won't eat the doughnuts?' Then he sticks his thumb in his mouth and stomps off to his room.

"Thank you. You've been a wonderful audience. Thank you and good night."

"Good night," she said.

"No. Wait," Bliss said to his wife. "I wanted to talk."

"Is it important?"

"No. It's just . . . I mean . . . " His voice trailed off.

Rachel was almost asleep when he got back.

"I got tired of waiting up," she said.

"How'd the show go tonight?" he asked.

"Okay. I think I have to work on the Crime Scene bit. There's not enough payoff."

"There usually isn't."

He lay down next to her on top of the comforter, still in his clothes.

"Did you take off your gun?" she mumbled. "You know the rule—no guns in bed." She yawned.

"I was down in the Village tonight," Bliss said. "Passed some of our old haunts. I realized we haven't been down there for a while."

"Did you find the bad guy?"

"I got a name. That's all," he said. "Joe Henderson's at the Vanguard."

"Is that the name?"

"No. He's the saxophonist. I thought maybe we could go hear him one night."

She turned toward him, smiling a little.

"Like a date?"

"Yeah. I was thinking about those Italian pastries, too."

"The sfogliatelli."

"Yeah."

"Could you do that, Lenny?"

"I think so."

"But you might get a lead? What if the name you got tonight turns out to be *the* name? Then the name turns into a face and the face into a person to locate and apprehend?"

"I'll turn off my beeper."

"But Ward will find you anyway. Like one of those incredible dogs you hear about. The family leaves them in California by mistake—three weeks later they're scratching at the screen door in New Jersey. Ward's like that with you."

"I'll talk to him."

"Of course you'll talk to him." She wasn't smiling anymore. "Ward's the one you always talk to. I should call *him* in the morning to find out how you are."

She rolled away from him and curled up tightly. Through the blankets he could feel her body tensing, wound tight, like the inside of a golf ball.

"Hey, I'm trying here," he said. "I'm making a concerted effort. Be sure you put that in your next routine. That your husband the cop was trying to make some contact the other night. You can come up with any punch line you want, but make sure you mention that I tried."

He waited, but she didn't say anything. Then something clicked in his head. "What're you, a wife or an oil painting?" Something went zing. "I know you're out there. I can hear you breathing." She still didn't respond. "That's not fair," he said. And since he didn't know what else to say, he said it again. "That's just not fair."

She didn't speak, but slowly a hand slid out from underneath the covers.

"Hey, the sound of one hand clapping," he said. "Thank you very much, ladies and gentlemen." He looked at her beautiful and delicate fingers lying nestled in the soft, white cotton of the blanket. Floating there. Maybe if held on to them, they would keep him from sinking any further. So he did. He held on tight.

Johnny should have known something was wrong when he first walked in the door and Tatyana's father was smiling. He was sitting at the table as usual, drunk, unshaven, his eyes dead, looking like the gulag poster boy. But for some reason he was smiling—his black teeth peeking through his thin, cracked lips.

Why the fuck is he smiling, Johnny thought. He opened the door to Tatyana's room and when he saw Sascha, "the Bear," standing there, he knew.

The door slammed and the huge man standing behind it grabbed Johnny's arm and wrenched it up behind his back until a burning pain ran down the whole right side of his body. Johnny screamed. The guy relaxed his grip just a bit and with his other hand tried to grab on to Johnny's hair but came away empty as there wasn't enough to hold on to.

"Fucking cue ball," he said, and settled for looping one of his massive arms around Johnny's throat.

Tatyana was cowering on the floor in a corner of the room, whimpering and looking for pity. Sascha the Bear, a kingpin of the Russian Mafia, the one person Johnny most needed to avoid, leaned against the bureau, doing his nails with Tatyana's file. Sascha the Bear, who ran several hidden casinos and whorehouses scattered around Brighton Beach; who collected protection from the local liquor stores and those restaurants doing a lively tourist business from people wanting an *authentic* Russian experience; the same Sascha who owned the St. Petersburg, the largest and liveliest restaurant-nightclub in the area. The nightclub where Johnny had met Tatyana. Where she used to work.

"Sit down, Johnny," the Bear said, without looking up.

The man holding Johnny released him and flung him on the bed. Johnny righted himself and sat on the edge of the sagging mattress.

"Who in the fuck do you think you are?" the Bear asked him. "No, don't answer. Don't *try* even to answer. Instead, I tell *you!* I practice English and now I be telling you who in the fuck you are. You, Johnny, are blind, stupid child, wearing short pants, sitting down to piss. You are waiting for your mother to take you home from school, waiting for her to give you special treat. Aren't you, little boy? Your mother is promising you fucking *treat* and you are still waiting for it. So give him treat, Malcolm. Go ahead, give the little boy Johnny special treat."

Malcolm reached out with an arm as thick as Johnny's leg and grabbed him by the neck. He lifted Johnny a few inches off the floor and with his free arm hit him in the stomach.

"Thank you, Malcolm. This is just right. Not *too* hard. After all, this is only *little* treat. "

Johnny was doubled over on the bed, writhing as he held on to his stomach. He started retching, but nothing came out. He saw the Bear move away, fearing his Armani suit might get splattered with Johnny's lunch.

"Careful of clothes," the Bear said. "Now sit up."

Johnny did his best to right himself. Tatyana was crying more loudly.

"Tell bitch to be shutting up."

"Quiet, Tatyana. Please."

"Malcolm," growled the Bear. "Give the hat."

Malcolm shoved a brightly colored cap in Johnny's face. It had a propeller on top.

"This is little boy's hat," said the Bear. "Put it on."

Johnny did what he was told.

"Now you can be looking in mirror and seeing who in the fuck you are. So, little boy, you think because of something you learn in school that maybe the Bear is in hibernation. And so you can dance around with this fine young Russian beauty—keeping her for yourself. Putting in your pocket what belongs to me. Do you think that?" He reached down and flicked the propeller. "Do you, little boy? But you never take time to think that perhaps maybe *I*, the Bear, have same idea. That is *reason* she gets job, because manager Mikhail thinks the Bear might have use for her. Not *you.* Me!" The Bear threw the nail file at Johnny. "And when I show up at St. Petersburg restaurant, *my* restaurant, to introduce myself to fine young piece of Russian mink, I am finding she is not there! Mikhail telling me she is *quit!* That she is coming in to pick up paycheck and tells to him that she doesn't *need* job anymore—that she is not having to wait on drunk Russian assholes anymore—that she has gotten *better* job, making— what does she say to him?—making same money in twelve minutes as one week at restaurant." The Bear got in Johnny's face. "She call them 'Russian *assholes.*' My customers! My *people!* Two days ago she is lousy waitress and now she is calling other people names. And all because of *twelve minutes' work!* So I think to myself, what could ignorant bitch from Moscow *do* in twelve minutes to make herself hundred dollars?

"So, this is what I am think. I am think that Tatyana is whore and you are pimp. *And* because she have easy time finding the high-class john, turning first trick two days after she is meeting you, I am believing she is *not* first girl to work for you. Am I right?"

Johnny didn't answer.

"Am I RIGHT!?"

Johnny didn't look up.

"Hey, this not school," the Bear said. "There is not test next week. This is being life, Johnny Tolstoy. You get *hurt* here. The Bear working whole life not be low-life trash, not to be scraping coins off sidewalk. I start this when I am ten years old. Robbing to the drunks. Watching while truck is emptied out. Selling cigarettes and vodka my uncle is making with rubbing alcohol until I am under arrest. Then I spend time in Russian jail, which is like living in Russian housing project, only food is better. In prison I am learning things. I am learning there is two ways to think about people. There is Barbra Streisand way, people liking people, needing people, special people. And there is Joseph Stalin way, people being machines, only better. Because when machine is breaking down you have to fix, because machine cost money. When people breaking down, you are throwing away. Dig big pit in woods and throw them in. This is lesson Stalin teaches Russia. Work people, then throw them away. This what I am learning from friends in prison.

"But now I am in America. I come here so I can live like gentleman. Others you are hearing of, acting like they are in *Godfather* movies, *they* can be putting bullets in people's heads, throwing each other in front of subways, cutting off toes in front of wife and children. Bear not doing this anymore. This was old days. Shooting roomful of people to get one I am mad at. Sticking firecracker in ear of person I am angry with. But now I am moving past this. This is why the Bear does not like little boys coming into restaurant and stealing silverware. Taking what is mine. This is America. You cannot *take* what does not belong to you. Unless—unless you are IRS."

The Bear waited for a laugh. Johnny forced a weak smile, hoping to appease him. He didn't. The Bear turned to Malcolm, shouting "The IRS! THE IRS! Don't you get it?!"

"You want for me to . . . ?" Malcolm made a fist in Johnny's direction.

"No, not to hit him. I make joke. In English."

"Oh," Malcolm said. "Joke? Then I laugh. Hah. Hah. Hah."

"Thank you. So, Johnny Tolstoy, to make long story short one, you are owing me money. I am thinking Tatyana good for two throws each night. That is twelve throws every week. Give one night off to rest pussy, unless *you* want her."

"No."

"This your first wisdom. Anyway, two-fifty a pop, she is taking in five hundred each night—this is three thousand a week. My share forty percent or twelve hundred. Every week. I am quick with multiplying, no? This from Russian schools. Better than America. So from now on you are owing the Bear twelve hundred a week. Plus times before with other women, we say . . . what? . . . how does five thousand sound?"

"What can I say?"

"Well, little boy, you can say thank you."

"Thank you."

"This five thousand I am wanting right away. In one week. I want in cash, of course. *Dollars*, my little Johnny. No rubles.

Five thousand American Land-of-Free dollars. Five thousand
next week. Then twelve hundred each week after that. Or else,
tovarich, I will Stalinize you—I will make massive purge on
your head, I will *pogrom* your privates. My English not so good.
So I ask, do you understand me, Comrade?"

"Yes," Johnny said.

"Good. I go now." The Bear headed for the door, which Malcolm held open for him. Before leaving he turned back to
Johnny. "You feel need now to be hitting your woman, maybe
because perhaps you think she fuck up everything in your
mouse-and-man plans. But this is not wisdom. She can work
tonight. Men not liking to pay for girl with black eyes. Not even
Japanese. Be nice. Play with her patty-the-cake. Keep your
hands busy. Be nice, Johnny. The Bear has speak."

Tatyana was trying to pat Johnny's head with a cool washcloth,
but he kept brushing away her hand. It had been an hour since
the Bear left. He lay in Tatyana's bed. His arm still throbbed. His
stomach ached. His whole world was now upside down. The one
thing, the worst possible thing, the thing that he had secretly
dreaded in silence for the last two years had happened—the
Bear owned him. Now he was a Pimp. Now he had to work. His
days of freedom were over. He was no longer in America. He
had been transported back to Russia. Now he carried his own
Siberia with him—his debt to the Bear, a gulag around his neck.
He would never be on Letterman. Likewise, Leno didn't want
pimps on *The Tonight Show.*

> JAY: *So, Johnny, I heard you were doing stand-up for a while.*
> JOHNNY: *That's right, Jay.*
> JAY: *But I read somewhere you gave it up.*
> JOHNNY: *Yeah.*
> JAY: *So now you're doing . . . what?*
> JOHNNY: *[Inaudible]*
> JAY: *Sorry. I didn't hear you.*
> JOHNNY: *I'm a pimp, Jay.*
> JAY: *A pimp? No kidding! Is that a good gig?*

Yeah, it's a great gig, Jay. A great fucking gig. I get to sit around and wait for my girls to come back with the money. Wipe their tears. Buy them new underwear. Hair spray. Condoms. Make sure they douche regularly. Yeah, it's a great gig, Jay. My dream has come true. As long as I give 40 percent to the Russian mob, my dream has come true in America.

He could leave town. He had cousins in New Jersey. He could get a job with the moving company they all worked for. Loading and unloading. Eight dollars an hour plus whatever change you could find in the couches. He'd marry a Russian girl and watch her get fat—watch hair sprout from every pore on her face. Once in a while he could treat him*self* to a whore—two hours in a motel in Fort Lee. They would be cheap ones—twenty, thirty bucks, plus another twenty for the motel—the special Hourly Rate. He wouldn't be able to afford anything like Tatyana—thin, beautiful, blond, drug free.

Tatyana. She got him into this mess, she would be his ticket out.

The episode came to him in a flash.

"The plastic surgeon." He grabbed her wrist as she went to wipe his forehead and held it tight. "The one you saw a few days ago. In his office."

He was thinking of the *Kojak* episode. One of his favorites. The one with the pimp and the girl.

"I want you to give him a call. Make another appointment."

"When?"

"Now!"

"Johnny, I'm scared."

"There's nothing to be scared of. The Bear wants us to do well. He *wants* us to be happy. The happier we are, the more money we make for him. He's married, right?"

"The Bear?"

"No. The doctor."

"Married?"

"Did you see photos on his desk? A wife? Kids?"

"I don't remember."

"Did he have a ring? A wedding ring!?"

In the episode, the girl set the guys up. The pimp took the photographs while the men were screwing her.

"I-I didn't get . . . I think so."

"Did he or didn't he!?" Johnny tightened his grip.

"Yes. Oww!"

"Stop crying!"

Blackmail. All Tatyana had to do was get the shades open.

"Let go of my wrist," she said.

Once the guy saw the photos, once the pimp threatened to show them to his wife, he paid off. The guy paid right away. The trick was not asking for too much money. It was a great episode.

"I'm calling him now," Johnny said. "I'm setting up something for tomorrow. Or the next day. I'm going to tell him you've been thinking about him. That he was your first and you want to give him a special thank you. Because he was so gentle."

Ten grand sounded good. Maybe twenty. Plastic surgeons probably made that in an hour stuffing tits. The doctor certainly wouldn't want his wife to find out. A divorce would cost him a lot more.

"Where are you going?" she asked.

"I need to get a camera," he said.

Simple. Just like *Kojak*.

Bliss and Ward were at their desks waiting for something to happen. They had run out of bait and were hoping the fish were hungry for empty hooks. Bliss had the friend of Elena's to see later, but that was about it. Then the phone rang.

"I guess I have to be more careful about what I say to you."

It was Dumpsterman. Bliss flashed Ward the *Seahunt* signal to pick up line three.

"Why more careful?" Bliss asked, keeping it slow.

"Oh, well, let's just say the specificity with which I described the color of the car I saw . . ."

"The car you *drove*."

"There's no need to raise your voice."

"Sorry."

Bliss keyed on the background. Not silence this time. Plenty of noise. An amplified announcement. Subway, maybe. He'd listen for trains.

"The color I mentioned—meridian—seemed to lead you to make certain inquiries."

"How do you know?"

"I called the dealers as well. Said I was a policeman. A Detective. 'Yo,' I said, 'yous guys got any meridian?' I'm afraid I wasn't very convincing. They told me another cop had already called. I said, 'It's dat rookie Bliss. He's just wantin' to impress me.' "

"You're too kind," Bliss said. Weak comeback. No zing. He sounded stupid. He wished Ward wasn't listening in. "So what's your name?"

"What do you call me?"

"How do you mean?"

"What do you call me around the precinct? When you're talking to the guys about my case. 'Gee, I sure would like to get ahold of that good-for-nothing so-and-so. He makes me sooooo mad.' "

"I don't say 'Gee.'"

"So what do you call me?"

"Asshole."

"No. Really. I know you're more creative than that."

"Dumpsterman."

"Oh," he said. "That's it?"

"That's all we came up with."

He sighed deeply. "I was hoping for something with a little more pizzazz."

"Sorry. You're Dumpsterman. From now on."

"So if another body turns up, the papers will say 'Dumpsterman Strikes Again'?"

"What would you like us to call you?"

There was a pause. "Phil," he said, "as in I won't stop until I get my." Then the subway roared into the station, drowning him out. There was the screeching of brakes. Extreme commotion. Does he go on the train? Does Phil leave us hanging? Doors close. Train lurches away. He's still there. "I think I shall take my leave of you now."

"Got a train to catch?"

"Wouldn't you like to know."

That always means yes.

"Where are you?" Bliss shot back. "Let's have a drink together. Scotch. Single malt. You like Glenlivet?"

No response. That meant yes, too. Expensive tastes.

Bliss kept up the flow. "I'll tell you what I've figured out so far. About the case. You can tell me whether I'm right or wrong. Hey, I'm buying."

The guy seemed to think about this for a few seconds.

"That's very kind, Detective," he said. "Very kind indeed. Another time perhaps. But not today."

Bliss played his hunch.

"You didn't want it to happen, did you, sir?"

Bliss waited. If the guy hung up, he was gone for good. If he stayed, they would have his balls over pasta very soon.

"I know you didn't want it to happen," Bliss continued. "That you were just driving home with milk for breakfast and there she was, young, helpless, lost, a runaway maybe, with lovely blond hair, maybe not wearing a bra, and the next thing you know she was sitting next to you, rubbing your leg, and you didn't want it to happen. I know. But she was rubbing your leg, so what could you do. So you found a place in the woods and before the car was even stopped she was all over you and then . . . and then . . ." Bliss waited. "And then . . . ?" Bliss waited longer. "And then what happened, Phil?"

There was a moment of dead silence. Ward and Bliss both held their breath. Finally the man spoke.

"It wasn't milk, you prick. It was dry cleaning."

Then he hung up.

"If I hadn't been listening carefully," Ward said as he put down the receiver, "I would have sworn it was a different person."

"The guy's moving closer to the edge."

"He was careful this time."

"But he called us. He wants us to know he's still out there. You get the trace?"

"Yeah. A pay phone underneath Grand Central."

"Maybe he got off the subway. Maybe he's on his way upstairs. To take a commuter train."

"Possible. But he could be getting oysters at the Oyster Bar. Or taking the shuttle to Times Square to pick up a bus to Jersey. Or he could be switching to the seven Train and heading home to Queens."

"This guy ain't from Queens, Ward."

"True."

"But he's definitely looking to get caught. He's got too much pride to let it happen easily."

"Where'd you come up with the scenario?"

"It just came to me. I saw him with an opportunity—the girl winds up in his front seat and he caves. The demons took over. Hieronymus Bosch-ville, to the max. Now he can't live with it. He's asking for help. He wants the roller coaster ride to be over. He'll climb down the scaffolding if he has to."

"One would think," Ward said, "that with all that insight into the workings of the human soul, Lenny, you wouldn't have to shoot so many people. By the way, I was on the cusp of some very politically correct intercourse with Malikha last night when I remembered to ask her about the lingerie. I said, 'Please remove your panties, I want to see the label.' She thought I was being cute."

"So?"

"So, it's from a shop in Brighton Beach—Olga's Lingerie."

"Did you bring them?"

"What?"

"The panties."

"They're in the wash."

"I'll go down there tomorrow. Talk to Olga."

"Brighton Beach seems to be the direction this case is taking."

"Yeah. But now I have to see Elena."

"Lenny, I have some bad news for you. Elena's dead."

"Yeah. I know. I have to see Elena's *friend.*"

"Take it easy, Lenny," Ward said. "You're pushing too hard."

So maybe he was, pushing too hard. But what else was he going to do? Driving to Alexa's he passed right by Cori's school. If he had the courage, he could have picked her up. Call Alexa, tell her he'd talk to her later and then take his daughter to the movies. Have dinner. Ice cream. Buy her . . . what? Anything. It would be a day to remember, that was the important thing. The *memory.* In twenty years she'd be at Thanksgiving remembering the time Daddy suddenly appeared at the classroom door, took me out of school two hours early, and we went to the movies. Remember, Daddy? It was right there in front of him. For the taking. He was Jack with the seeds to a giant beanstalk of memory and he was throwing them in his glove compartment instead of planting them in the heart of his youngest daughter.

He drove past the school. He didn't stop. Why was he so afraid of his own kids? He'd become like so many of the other private school dads. Always too busy. He was growing apart from them. Cori, hardly talking to him. Julia, sarcastic all the time. He missed them, even when he was sitting right across the table from them at dinner. Well, at least he was *at* the table, unlike his own father, who ate at the bar by the precinct.

But still, he should have gone in and picked up Cori. All the kids asking the next day why she left, and Cori talking about the movie and the lunch they'd had at Primeburger and the huge sundaes he'd sprung for at Rumplemeyer's. But no Thanksgiving twenty years from now will be one memory short. At least. Bliss drove on.

It was an intensely hot day in the city. The air was thick and dead. The traffic was backed up on Central Park West, but Bliss didn't bother with his siren. He wanted to sit for a while. There was construction, as usual. It was like some M. C. Escher print. Crews dig holes to fix one thing, rupture something else, then seal up the hole and tell the next crew, who fix and rupture and then pass it on. Fixing with one hand, fucking up with the other. The zeitgeist of New York.

Car horns wailed. New Yorkers have the most complex horn vocabulary in the world, expressing a wide range of emotions—the Tap, when the light's changed and the first car in line doesn't see it—just a reminder. The Gentle Alert, to let the guy in front of you know that if he keeps moving into your lane he's going to cut you off. The Fore, like its counterpart in golf, to let pedestrians crossing against the light know you're coming and you're not slowing down. The Fuck You Motherfucker, when a taxi swerves in front of you and stops to pick up a fare. The Keen, longer and louder than any mother at an Irish wake ever wailed, saved for when someone has double-parked and blocked you in.

So that was fun, a little riff on car horns. That killed a few minutes, and now here he was, a whole block closer. He felt miserable. He needed something. He needed a foe. An enemy. The Cyclops and he, Bliss, would be playing Ulysses instead of Harry Hamlin. He wanted someone *there,* in the open, where he could see them! A Goliath, so Bliss could be David. *That's* what the story was about. Not Good versus Evil. Hebrew versus Philistine. Lefty reliever versus righty slugger. No! David and Goliath was about how easy it is to be a hero when the enemy is right in front of you—hugely there, where you can see him, see his weaknesses.

But Bliss had no visible foes. His enemies were nefarious.

They lurked in the dark. Like Dumpsterman, hidden in a crowd somewhere. Mowing his lawn. Pruning his shrubs. So ordinary they were invisible. And in Elena's case, he had only a pair of panties and the name of a wacked-out comic who could, for all he knew, be Elena's half-brother. The rest were hunches; meaning-less clues; "Did you happen to see . . . ?" "Where were you the night of . . . ?" "Do any of these faces look like the man who . . . ?" It was pathetic. Being a hero was a cinch with a Cyclops to fight. He had only corpses, which cried to him at night, begged vengeance on their bony knees, so loudly and persistently that his pillow was soaked in the morning. Maybe *that's* what his daugh-ter would remember at Thanksgiving. "How you used to wake up whimpering, Daddy, with your eyes red, flipping over your pillow so we wouldn't see where it was wet. Now finish up your pump-kin pie, Pop, because we have to get you back to the home."

He had been a hero once, if you call being a novelty a kind of hero. It was back in college, at Brown University. Word got around that his father was a policeman.

"Your dad's a cop?!" Their Ivy League eyes were as big as saucers. "Cool." For them, this was better than Am Civ, better than Comp Lit 101. "Wow!" They were thunderstruck.

A six-foot-four hulking son of a cop who read T. S. Eliot and lived right in their dorm, an unadvertised college bonus that wasn't in any of the brochures. He sat in the common room and told stories of visiting his dad's precinct, going to lockup, spend-ing an evening at night court, watching every variety of sleazeball in New York pass by in a steady parade. Though he was only a year older, the other frosh all seemed like little kids to him. Though they went to better schools and had seen the world, he felt so much wiser. Indeed, they'd been most everywhere, from Zanzibar to Berkeley Square. And though Bliss had only seen the sights a boy could see from Brooklyn Heights (née Yonkers), wow! what a crazy pair—his Patty to their collective Cathy. You could lose your mind.

Even the fact that he had to work his way through school, something he at first thought would be humiliating, only enhanced his mystique. Turning down invitations to parties because of his job made him more of a celebrity. To the prep school boys and girls, this "working thing" was strange and fascinating. They relished his stories, were willing to skip classes to tag along, see the locales he worked in, dangerous and exotic, dark streets and back alleys, doors with no handles, that required secret knocks.

Weekly he drove a truck of unmarked boxes from Smith Street, in the Italian section of Providence, up to the North End in Boston. Again, it was his father who made the connection for him, coming into town, getting on the blower, introducing him to guys in long leather coats, toothpicks dangling from their lips. He got paid in large bills, which he casually left on the dresser in his dorm, causing jaws to drop on the sons of millionaires who walked around campus with nothing but lint in their pockets. They wanted to go with him, ride shotgun, pump the gas into the truck, so desperate were they for real-life adventure.

They coveted a spot at the stool next to him in the bar, watching in wonder as he sat, shoulders hunched, solitary and silent, in tune with something larger than all of them. Bliss didn't drink like a college boy. Didn't down Jagermeisters to give his hands courage to forage under a coed's blouse. He drank like a man, like Bogart, they thought. Like Hemingway.

But what was allure in the eyes of the Brown freshmen was melancholy to Bliss. Ironic, he thought. The weight on his shoulders was the weight of his father, Monty the cop. Irrepressible, irreverent, unreachable. Bliss learned in class that Joyce wrote *Ulysses* in exile, but that the separation from Ireland only served to bring the details of his homeland into more vivid focus. The same was true for Bliss and his father. Now that he had moved away, the full scope of his father's grip on him emerged with terrible clarity, especially when he found the .22 snub-nosed revolver in his trunk as he unpacked his first day. A surprise gift from his dad. His roommate got an electric pencil sharpener from *his* folks. The gun, which he kept hidden under his mattress, was a constant reminder that he was different. That he would never exactly fit in.

Not that he didn't try. He sat in the circle with the others as the joint went around, while garbage music like Poco, Procol Harum, James Taylor, or, at best, Return to Forever played on the stereo. And when the weed came to him he took a hit like the others. But as the evening wore on, he began to look through them, to a future that held no surprises. Because he knew from the first day that he wasn't on the college bandwagon. That he was without rah-rah. *Sans* sis, *sans* boom, *sans* bah, *sans* everything. That class discussions were, at best, interesting, that rooting for the football team and eating pizza at four in the morning were cute diversions, but there was a gun under *his* mattress, bullets in a Band-Aid box in his top drawer. And those few minutes on Smith Street, eating his sandwich of sopressata and provolone while the chooches loaded the truck, then handed him the keys and the name of the guy he was to see at the end of the line, *that* was real to him. That was who he was.

Even getting laid. Even having the precious daughters of the rich and powerful proclaim their love for him had little meaning. They'd gaze into his forlorn eyes and stroke his already hard and callused hands as if they were seeing real life for the first time. It was dazzling, the Wizard of Oz turning from black and white to color. He wasn't like any of the guys they knew in high school. He was dangerous, enticing, D. H. Lawrence's stable boy come to life and living in their dorm.

It was a novelty at first, and he enjoyed their soft, perfect skin, the reckless abandon with which they made love, wanting to please him, to somehow prove in bed that *they* were real people, too. But serving as both camp counselor and hedonistic avatar wore him down. And he knew his novelty would soon wear off. Because they were at college for a different reason; to explore, to find themselves. But for Bliss, college only reinforced what he already knew, that his father's grip was too tight. That for Lenny, son of Monty, there was no exploration, no voyaging to new lands. His *Niñas* and *Pintas* were in permanent dry dock.

So he left school and came back to New York, to pursue a future in a world the college boys and girls would never know. What his father did. What Bliss would do. And what he learned in those two-plus years only succeeded in making his being a cop even more of a challenge. Because in college he read Melville's "Bartleby, the Scrivener." And some mornings he'd get up and say to himself, "I'd prefer not to. No dirty streets and housing projects today, dodging bullets and stares vindictive enough to crack marble." He'd think about the plush offices and sleek desks his former freshman classmates were headed to and how they didn't have gaping wounds on their agenda, no drive-by shootings penciled in their Filofaxes, no babies bleeding to death in their mother's arms over lunch, and he'd say again, "I'd prefer not to." But then he made sure his safety was on and headed out into the street.

Alexa Gurevich, Elena's friend when she was alive, lived on the third floor of a brownstone on West Eighty-fifth. Lenny double-parked in front of her building and put his police parking permit on the dash. He'd probably get a ticket anyway—the traffic patrol was crazy, living by their own rules like futuristic bounty hunters, blade runners.

He sat in the car for a minute. He was nervous, like he was going on a first date. He checked his face in the rearview mirror. He looked like shit, like it was three in the afternoon of a day full of paperwork, useless phone calls, false hopes, dead leads, and general futility. A la Dumpsterman—the good news: Volvo had a meridian blue. The bad news: it was their *only* shade of blue for the last three years. Result: at least 780 meridian blue Volvos sold in the Tri-State area in the past three years. Way too many to follow up on such a gimpy hunch.

And there were three other cases he was working on, all involving drug dealers, all equally tenuous. Homicide had to wait for Vice to arrest Drug Dealer A who, in order to lessen his sentence, gave information on the murder of Drug Dealer B. So then he and Ward could go after Dealer C, named by Dealer A, and arrest him for the murder of Dealer B. But Dealer C has information on the murder of Dealer D that *he* wants to trade to lessen *his* sentence. And around it goes, like musical chairs in reverse.

None of which explained why he was so nervous. Maybe it

was because he really wanted Elena the dentist to open the door. He wanted it undone, the investigation to go away. He wanted the blood for once to wash off his hands. The damn spots to come out, out. Bliss didn't want to have to look for murderers anymore. It gave him little satisfaction now when he found them. Because he knew, once they were sitting across the table from him in the interrogation room, that they would either seem so absolutely normal that it was terrifying, or so completely mad that it should have been obvious to everyone they were psychotic maniacs who should have been locked away long ago.

Bliss wanted Elena to be undead so he could talk to her. He wanted to hear about her life, about St. Petersburg, the fall of Communism. He had so many questions. He wanted to listen to her accent. Tell her that his grandfather came from Russia. That maybe they had some long-lost connection—their families making revolution together, fomenting, building Molotov cocktails, his side pouring the gas, hers stuffing in the rags. He wanted to go back to Russia with her—the new Wild West. They'd homestead in the Urals. He'd help her get her office started, install the reclining chair, the special dentist light. Be her dental assistant, hand her the tools, flip the X-ray switch ("Hold still"), reprimand the patients. "You're not flossing, Natasha." (He actually said this aloud.) Clean teeth for her, schedule appointments. "You have a cleaning next Thursday, Boris." (This too, for the world to hear.)

Why did he want this when he already had a family? Because it was easier to start over? Easier to break away to a breakaway republic, to hide in some no-man's-land than to dig himself out of the trench of silence he was in now? Easier to have someone else bring home the bacon while he stayed home and took care of the kids and peeled the beets? He could be more like an uncle to *her* kids. It was always easier being an uncle than a father. You didn't have to be constantly reminded of your faults and failures by seeing them reflected in your own kids' faces.

But Elena was not going to be opening the door. Because Elena was on her way to NYU med school to be used for dissection training and Bliss was alive and Bliss had to find her murderer.

"I don't want any more dead people in my life!" he shouted, banging his fist on the dash, losing it entirely now. "What are you looking at?!" he shouted at a concerned old woman staring at him through the passenger window. "I'm the police!" he yelled at her. He grabbed the emergency light from under his seat, put it on his head, and turned it on. "See!?" he shouted. "See!!?" The red light flashing spastically in her face. "I'm not the one you have to worry about!!"

A few minutes later, as he rang the bell on Alexa's front stoop, he noticed his hand was still shaking. After a short wait the buzzer sounded and he pushed open the door.

He walked the two flights to her apartment and knocked. The door was opened by the most beautiful woman he had ever seen. Almost as tall as Bliss, she had soft black hair that flowed to her bare shoulders. She wore a startlingly small dress she could have swiped from Shirley Temple and an incredible smile set off by her coffee-colored skin. It was a smile so radiant that he felt certain she had never smiled until that very moment when she first saw him. O brave new world.

"Hi. I'm Shamika. Alexa will be done in a second," she said.

He was stunned into silence. Drug dealers he was prepared for. Fifteen-year-old girls holding screaming babies while their primary suspect boyfriends climbed out the window, *that* he was ready for. A mother grieving because her daughter caught a stray bullet in the head while doing her homework in the living room, *that* he could deal with. *That* pain and ugliness he was accustomed to, inured to. But to encounter such beauty made him feel weak and vulnerable. He wanted a hug.

"You shouldn't open the door without looking through the peephole and asking who it is," he said, but his voice lacked conviction.

"Alexa knew it was you," Shamika said.

"I never identified myself."

She became more soothing, comforting—a young nurse at the front, easing water down parched soldiers' throats, bandaging stumps while shells exploded outside.

"It's okay," she said. "Really." She reached out and gently touched Bliss's arm. "Alexa *knew*." She led him down the hall into a kind of foyer. Soft sound cushioned the apartment. Soft waves, lake water lapping. "Please forgive Alexa for not being ready," Shamika said. "It's my fault. I called at the last minute. I have a superimportant audition and I needed to feel . . . I needed . . ." She paused for a moment, closing her eyes as a glow spread across her face. "Alexa's magic hands." Bliss felt if he was exposed to any more rapture, he would sink down and melt into the floor like the Wicked Witch of the West and all that would remain would be a pile of his smoking clothes.

Then Alexa appeared, holding a stack of clean sheets, the smell of which instantly made him think of his mother folding laundry, smiling down at him as he sat cross-legged on the floor watching her. He made a sound in his throat like a bottle of beer being opened.

"Hello, Mr. Bliss," Alexa said. "I apologize for not being ready."

Alexa was also beautiful, with pale, porcelain skin. She carried two small but distinct scars, both starting near her right eye and curling like rivulets, to the top of her cheek. Rivulets that he sensed led to deeper waters. He could get lost in those scars. Her smile was soft and open but showed a faint hint of pain, turning down slightly at the corners of her mouth, like in the movies when a woman goes to the door to tell the cops everything's all right but really there's a man hiding inside pointing a gun to her belly.

"Come in," Alexa said.

Bliss looked from one woman to the other. The statuesque Goddess; the scarred, beneficent Mother. They smiled in unison for all womankind. They reached out and touched him.

"It's Detective . . ." he said. Then he passed out.

In the dream he was supposed to do something about it.

He was running because he had to be somewhere, *had* to be somewhere to do something about it, but he couldn't. He was supposed to have what she needed, what Elena needed. But he was a fool because he didn't have them, because they weren't in the . . . weren't where they were supposed to be. *Candles!* Yes!

He was supposed to have candles, to bring the light, to shed some light on the situation because how could Elena *see* to extract a tooth without light? But wait, now Elena is in the chair and now the doctor is there, the bad doctor in the meridian blue coat. Bad Doctor Dumpsterman is hurting Elena and she is crying out to Bliss to help, and he reaches down and now it is his daughter Julia in the chair, and she's afraid because the doctor is not a doctor and the knife he holds in his blue hand is not for healing. But Bliss can't move, he can't move to save her. And he, Bliss, he needs to shoot, needs to shoot the doctor *now*, silly, before he eats, silly, before the doctor cuts out Julia's heart and throws her in the Dumpster. But now there are hundreds of doctors in the room, all in blue, a sea of meridian, and he needs to see the doctor's face to shoot him but the doctor is wearing a mask and they're all wearing masks and they all look the same and the bad guy has disappeared because they all look the same and Bliss the Fool is helpless, sitting on the floor and then the doctors throw their blue coats in the air and they float down slowly, billowing over him, covering Bliss, until he almost drowns.

Some dream.

He woke up on a table in the middle of the living room. The model was gone. Alexa stood above him, looking down with concern.

"Are you all right?" she asked.

"It's me," he said. "I spoke to you on the phone. I'm the Fool."

"The Fool is a noble card," she said, patting his forehead with a cool towel. "The Fool sees what others don't. He's not afraid to climb the mountain to pursue his vision."

"Did I pass out?"

"Yes. Shamika helped me lift you to the table."

"My partner says I'm working too hard."

"I think so."

"I miss Elena."

"Did you know her long?"

"No."

"Did you sleep with her?"

"I never met her," Bliss said.

She looked puzzled.

"I only saw her dead. She was twenty-eight. She had two children. She was a dentist."

"Sit up," she said.

"She was a goddamn dentist," he said.

She pressed a finger to his lips to quiet him, then helped him up. She loosened his tie and unbuttoned his shirt.

"You must be a trusting person," she said. "To let a stranger do this to you."

"Yes," Bliss said. He had never once thought of himself as a trusting person. "I'm the Fool. The trusting Fool."

He took off his shirt.

"Turn over," she said.

He turned over.

"Move to the front of the table."

He inched himself forward until his face was nestled in a kind of cushioned headrest like a catcher's mask without the bars.

"For most people," she said, rubbing oil on his back—oil that smelled of . . . what? Some kind of flower, woods maybe. "For most people their only physical contact with another person is through sex." She was working the oil into his back. "But physical contact is a basic need. Holding someone close. Snuggling. Stroking someone's cheek. We need this on a regular basis." Her hands were divining rods, finding the muscles, the vortices of tension, each with a name and a date and a corpse associated with it, a map of Bliss's cases for the last few years. Just below the right shoulder blade was the dense knot of Estelle Dixon, shot by her estranged husband, left to die, sacrificed beneath the altar of her ironing board; under the other shoulder blade, the huge knot of a Chinese kid who crawled to the precinct in time to collapse on the steps from a knife wound, his last words, perhaps his killer's name, urgently repeated, only they were in Mandarin— case unsolved; just below that was a triple knot for the triple murder of husband and wife crack dealers and their three-year-old daughter—case unsolved.

"I sometimes have to wrestle someone to the ground," Bliss said. "I sometimes have to kick them in the belly, to quiet them down. That's physical contact, isn't it?" It was hard to speak. The words were losing their meaning. "I have to subdue a perp. Perp, perp, perp, perp." He was sounding like a canary. "Once they're subdued, I have to cuff them. Cuff, cuff, cuff." He laughed. "And my kids."

"You have children."

"Two. My daughters. They . . . they, well, my youngest still . . . she still grabs my leg and wants me to walk . . . to carry her around the room while she holds on." He thought for a moment. "But otherwise, no. You're right. No physical contact except sex." And how little of that, he didn't care to say.

"Don't talk for a while."

"Okay. Me no talk."

"I'll tell you about my cousin Elena."

"Thank you."

"She was born in St. Petersburg twenty-eight years ago. Her mother and my mother were sisters. Her mother was the perfect Soviet woman—a doctor who worked hard for little money, who made a home for her family in the three rooms they were allocated. Her father was an engineer, designing roads and bridges. He was Jewish, but Russian first. So, unfortunately, he drank a great deal. My father, too. Our families spent vacations together—two weeks in the summer. We shared a cabin by a small lake. Our fathers drank and fished. One summer my father stood up in the boat to make a speech to the trees and birds about what a fool Kosygin was—'An empty-headed fool!' he shouted. To the trees and birds. Then he lost his balance and fell overboard. He couldn't swim. Elena's father went in after him. He couldn't swim either. But he was so drunk he probably forgot. They both drowned."

"I'm sorry," Bliss said softly.

Alexa was quiet for a while. Her hands kept moving, however. Bliss sank into the table. He could feel himself relaxing, his tension softening. Alexa was working on the charred remains of a ten-year-old black kid found under the Manhattan Bridge. The muscles, loosening, breaking apart, the memory, crumbling, burnt flesh, blackened bones—disappearing. Perhaps forever. Hopefully forever.

"Elena was always the smartest in the class. She was best in science and literature and history. We all looked up to her. We all wanted her to be a cosmonaut. We wanted her to be the first person to stand on the moon. She could have done it, too. But . . ."

"But what?"

"Her mother got married again. To a poet, this time. He was famous in St. Petersburg and wanted Elena to be a writer, too. She was taken with all the attention and tried hard to please him, tried to feel and see the world as he would. She kept a journal. Her work in school suffered. Math, he said, was for government workers, fools. Poetry, he told her, was for great minds, like his and Elena's. Instead of school, she was always with him. Up at six, they spent the day observing. Sitting on benches, standing on busy street corners. For hours. Studying the tourists, government officials, street sweepers, KGB agents, everyone who passed by. He wanted her to see people as they really were. Communism. Capitalism. Buddhism. None of it mattered, he told her. The choices in life are simple. In grade school, one kid sticks a sign on another kid's back that says 'Kick Me.' Each one then chooses: to be the one to write the sign; to be the one to stick on the sign; to bear the sign and get your ass kicked; to be the one who does the kicking; or to rip the sign off your back and bravely face the consequences. 'That's all there is,' he told her.

"One night Elena's mother had to work late at the hospital. A month later, Elena announced she was pregnant. She told her mother it was an American tourist she met at a nightclub. They went back to his hotel. His name was Ed. The next day she woke up and he was gone. The baby changed Elena. She returned to her studies and excelled in school. Her bond with her stepfather became less consuming. She started studying to be a dentist. Just before her graduation she announced she was pregnant again. About that time her mother found a poem her husband had written about the joys of fatherhood. The next night, St. Petersburg was minus one living poet. Poisoned. Elena's mother was arrested. Elena stayed in the apartment until she had her baby. Then the State took it back and she came to live with my mother. I had already come here. One morning she was gone. To

America, the note said. My mother is still taking care of her kids. The rest you know."

But Bliss knew nothing of the rest.

"I need to hear about her life in New York," he said. "What she did. Where she worked. Who came to her apartment."

"She didn't talk about it."

"She ever mention a Johnny Tolstoy?"

Alexa laughed. "No Johnny Tolstoy. No Tommy Turgenev."

"Then give me something, Alexa. I have no leads, nothing to go on. *Bobkes.* I need a name, hair color, accent. I need height, weight, ethnic origin. I need distinguishing characteristics up the kazoo, tattoos, missing teeth, glass eyes, a gimpy leg, a stump for a left hand, six fingers on the right. I need a trail of bread crumbs, footprints on the floor like an Arthur Murray dance lesson."

Alexa lifted her hands from his back and moved to his scalp, gently raking her nails through his hair, leaving tingling tracks of pleasure.

"Bliss," she said. "Elena was not proud of what she was doing. She could live with it. Close her eyes and lie there, making sounds of pleasure, thinking about how she was building a future for herself and the children. For her, that was ecstasy. But she would not say any more about it. Not even to me."

He turned and faced her. "Do you think she was going back soon?"

"I did a reading for her last week," she said. "I told her the cards said it was time to be with those who love her most."

"She trusted the cards."

"She trusted me. The *cards* actually said she should stay where she was. That it was a bad time to travel."

"So you lied."

"I told her what she wanted to hear."

"But it wasn't in the cards."

"There is nothing in the cards," she said, expressing the first bit of anything like anger Bliss had heard from her. "I could fill a box with kitchen utensils and tell you your life's story. You close your eyes and pick out the spatula. I look at it and from the spatula I can tell you are someone who wants to look at both sides of things, who likes to see underneath. Do you do this?"

"Yes."

"This could be your new sign. The sign of Spatula. But say you pick the whisk. I say you like to make more of something than was there before. You take a small problem and make it bigger. Do you do this, too?"

"Yes."

"So, your moon is in Whisk. And if you grabbed the strainer? This means you can only grasp the obvious things in life, the ones that stick out. These you make a big deal about. But the more subtle parts of your life, having to do with love, with tenderness, with caring, this you let slip right through. Your wife complains to you about this?"

"All the time."

"And now do you think I have a gift?"

"You do."

"Perhaps."

"You told Elena to go back because . . ."

"Because she was desperate to go back. To see her children and get her life started again. Was this a lie? Who can say?"

She was working on his toes, rubbing spots on the soles of his feet that sent currents of energy careening through his body. He tried to think of the last time anyone had touched his feet. Bliss's *feet*. Their aroma was legendary. It was as if all fetid fluids ran in an intricate series of tiny rivulets just under his skin to finally collect in a pungent vortex in his socks. But there she was, running her fingers between his toes. Rubbing them with oil. He was starting to reek of exotic scents. If Rachel tried to embrace him tonight, he'd slip through her arms like a wet bar of soap, like a greased pig. How would he explain that? How would he explain that for once his feet smelled like a field of lavender? Bliss lay there trying to relax, but the pathetic feeling that his case was nowhere kept creeping in. He smelled better, but he was still no closer, still had no clues.

"What should I do?" he asked her, like he was asking for milk and cookies. "How can I . . . what can . . . I . . ."

"Just put yourself in my hands," she said. "And everything will work out just fine."

And that was the last thing he heard before he fell into a deep, long overdue sleep.

CHAPTER 12

While Johnny waited on the corner of Park Avenue and Eighty-fourth Street for the doctor to show up, he opened the manila envelope to look at the photograph just once more. It was perfect. He loved that zoom on the camera. You just press a button and the lens gets longer. The photo was just like the one he sent the doctor. Tatyana was sitting on his dick. She had her shirt off and she was arched back, her breasts pointing to the ceiling, her hands resting on the doctor's ankles. The doctor had his white coat on, but his pants were down by his feet. He was on his back, propped up on his elbows, his eyes closed, but his mouth was wide open, like he was waiting for someone to throw something in there. Like Johnny's mother used to do with him when he was young. With a bunch of grapes. She'd sit across from him on the sofa and close her eyes and open her mouth wide and Johnny would throw his grapes into her open mouth.

He told the guy at the photo shop he needed to take a picture through a window of two people fucking. The guy sold him this camera with the super zoom and some fast 1,000 ASA film. He said the picture would be grainy, but you'd be able to tell what was going on. The guy had been right. You could definitely tell what was going on.

Which reminded Johnny that in a few of the shots you could see Tatyana kissing the doctor on the lips. *Kissing.* Jesus Christ, he thought he explained to her very clearly that you don't kiss the clients. But Tatyana was so eager to make men happy, there was no controlling her. Soon she'd be inviting them home for dinner.

I couldn't believe it, Jay. I mean, next thing I know, after she sleeps with them, she's inviting them over. Doorbell rings. She opens the door. Guy standing there with flowers. "Hi, Marty," she says, "you're just in time." She kisses him on the cheek. "Johnny, this is

Marty. Marty, this is Johnny. I guess you two have never actually met. And this is my mother and my father. Isn't this special?"

Things had happened fast since his visit with the Bear. Johnny got right on the phone and yes, the doctor said he was very eager to make another appointment with Tatyana, that tomorrow afternoon was fine. Johnny then spent the evening practicing with his camera. He took lots of pictures of Tatyana in all kinds of different positions. She was very funny when she posed. "It's the Miss U.S.S.R. Contest," she said. "And here's Miss Siberia," she said, holding an ice cube over her head. "And here's Miss Moscow." She pretended to stand on line—looked at her watch—take a tiny step forward—looked at her watch again. "And here's Miss St. Petersburg." She took some imaginary money from an imaginary man and knelt down and gave him an imaginary blow job.

It was good material. Johnny thought maybe he could use her in his act. "Russian Women—Past and Present." Now that he'd solved his problem with the Bear, he was excited about performing again. He would do some open mike nights soon. The What Knot? Club, Dixon Place, maybe even the Comedy Cellar. A flood of memories of his mother was coming back to him; late at night, she is sitting in the kitchen sewing up rips in their clothes, shortening his pants so they could fit his younger brother, while the beans soaked for the next day's dinner, while the laundry boiled in a pot on the stove. A hundred elves couldn't do the work of his mother. Now Johnny would share her story with the world. As soon as he got another wig. He thought he might take up the clerk's offer at the wig store and return it for a different shade. This one was too tight as well.

JAY LENO: So, I hear you're back doing stand-up.
JOHNNY TOLSTOY: Yeah. Lately it's really been clicking.
JAY: And that other thing.
JOHNNY: You mean being a pimp, Jay?
JAY: Yeah. I guess . . .

Then Johnny saw the plastic surgeon walking toward him.

JOHNNY: Yeah. I'm still in the pimp business. I'm actually think-
    ing of expanding. Opening a franchise. With drive-through.
    This is America, after all.

The doctor was wearing expensive sunglasses and a fancy cream-colored suit. That wasn't how doctors dressed in Russia when Johnny was growing up. Of course, they didn't have plastic surgeon doctors in Russia. If they did, then they should have made it mandatory for most of the women, like going to the dentist. Johnny saw the doctor was carrying the manila envelope. Good, now we're getting somewhere.

The doctor stopped and looked Johnny over.

"Who *are* you?" he asked.

"Never mind," said Johnny. "All you need to know is that I'm the guy with the negatives to these photos."

"Fine," the doctor said. "I'll give you five hundred bucks for them."

Johnny laughed.

"Try twenty thousand."

"You're kidding."

"Twenty thousand in small bills. And that's dollars, not *rubles,* or else I'll send these to your wife."

"What wife?" the doctor said.

This was to be expected, that the guy would try to weasel out of it.

"Don't play games with me, asshole." Johnny was pretty sure this was a line from *Kojak,* except for the "asshole" part.

"I'm not playing games. I don't have a wife. Now I'll give you *four* hundred."

"Yeah, what about the photos on your desk? I can see them in the one I took."

"Those are before-and-after shots, nose profiles, chin choices. For my *patients* to look at."

"You got a ring. Tatyana said you had a ring."

The doctor looked surprised.

"That really *is* her name. Tatyana. It sounded *too* Russian, if you know what I mean. I thought she was making it up."

"She told you her name?"

"Yeah. Kissed me, too. I think she kind of liked me."

"What about the ring?"

"Pinkie." He held it up. "I paid a grand for it. I don't know what they'd give you in a pawn shop. You're better off with the four hundred."

"Don't fuck with me."

"I'm not fucking with you. You screwed up. It was a nice idea, but I guess you didn't do your homework. Listen, Tatyana's quite a number. Must be nice to have her around. Take the four hundred and go away. You can keep the photographs. When can I see Tatyana again? Can she come to my house? How much if she stays the night?"

Kissing him. Telling him her *name!* What is *wrong* with her!? What kind of whore *is* she?!

He was walking like a maniac down Park Avenue, crossing against the lights, not caring that the cars had to jam their breaks, not caring if the cars hit him.

"And then to not *see* what was on his *desk!*" he said to himself in Russian. "To not be able to tell the *difference* between a bunch of noses and chins and a bunch of kids."

"Chins and noses!" he shouted. "Chins and noses! Chins and fucking noses!"

He stopped and surveyed the elegant buildings with their huge lobbies lining Park Avenue, buildings that smelled of wealth and power; a man charged down the sidewalk holding the leashes of a dozen dogs—the rich people's dog-walking service; a black nanny was pushing a white baby in a fancy stroller—the baby-walking service; a maid in uniform carried bags of groceries, probably back to the cook who was preparing dinner; a fancy lady got into a waiting limousine to take her . . . where? probably to the plastic surgeon, to get a new nose and chin.

Johnny crossed to the grassy median dividing the avenue and, standing there, screamed at the rich people. "In Russia we may not have much, but at least we died with the noses God gave us!! All our moles! All our scars! And we were proud of them!! My mother's tits sagged from the weight of a thousand years of Russian pain! And she was proud of that, too!!"

He lay down on the grass. Traffic roared past him—one side heading uptown, one side downtown. Underneath, the trains rumbled through the tunnel leading from Grand Central—people with destinations, jobs, homes, plans. Johnny lay there and had nothing. No, that wasn't true. He had a necklace with a five-thousand-dollar chunk of Siberian ice hanging around his neck, given to him by the Bear.

He used to have Elena. Elena was a gift. They were a team. She was the one who made it work. She got things organized. She kept track of the appointments and all the expenses. Maybe she actually *was* a dentist. All Johnny had to do was take down the numbers on the answering machine, distinguishing between those who were potential clients and the school kids who spent their afternoons calling escorts in the back of *New York* magazine. "Hi," she said in her deepest, sexiest voice, heavy on the Russian accent. "I can't come to phone right now, but I'd really like to get to know you better, so leave your number and I'll call you back."

It only took a month for them to become regulars, so captivating was she. Elena saw them every week—size 40-short cigar-smoking garment center types who met her in hotel rooms during lunch hour; accountants who sent their secretaries home early so they could have the office to themselves; and, the most regular of all, men in town for conventions. Elena found a hotel on the Upper West Side run by another émigré who rented her a room for the day. It was just an eight-minute cab ride from the Javits Center. When the boat show was in town, they could have started a ferry service. For the auto show, they could have arranged car pools. Her johns were devoted to her. They'd call the machine weeks before they arrived, making sure she had their usual time reserved. They'd bring her presents, samples they picked up at the convention. During the fancy-food show they filled the hotel room with expensive chocolates and exotic dried fruits. Elena made all the arrangements. She didn't even let him walk her home. Most of the time Johnny felt like her nephew, not her pimp.

He was surprised when she gave him his cut every week. But he knew in his heart she wasn't going to give him the thousand dollars he demanded before she split for Russia.

So now what was he going to do?

Fuck the Kojak plan.

He still had eight hundred dollars of Elena's money. He could buy a ticket back to Russia himself. His brothers were there. Two still lived in the apartment where he was born. They could make room for him in the bed. One with a family—wife and two daughters. Johnny's nieces. Couple of years he could put them to work. His brother wouldn't mind. Maybe then he could move to a bigger place.

But nothing as big as these apartments on Park Avenue— three, four bedrooms, living rooms, dining rooms, fireplaces. He'd heard about them from his girls when they did out-calls. Lawyers, doctors, bankers staying at home in the summer while their wives and kids were vacationing. How they did it in living rooms on Oriental carpets in the shadow of grand pianos; on bunk beds in the kids' rooms on the second floor, or the *third* floor. Johnny tried to imagine an apartment with three floors; or the bathtubs they screwed in, as big as swimming pools. How the girls would dress up in the maid's uniform and do it in the maid's room, itself bigger than the apartment he grew up in. Or they'd wear a pleated skirt, letter sweaters, and knee socks, just like the daughters wore to high school, and do it on her bed while Brad Pitt looked on from a poster on the wall. These Park Avenue places could hold six Moscow apartments. Twenty-five, thirty people. They had penthouses with patios that had more trees than his entire block.

Penthouses.

Why didn't he think of it before? The Fat Man. The Fat Man in the penthouse! The one Elena refused to service because he liked apparatus, quirks that she shied away from. Because he wanted to be sat on. But of course Elena, the *doctor* who wanted to *heal* people, make them *better*, well, *she* would have nothing to do with the Fat Man. She was adamant, though he didn't understand how anyone who wanted to stick their hands in people's mouths, put their nose close to the foul breath of a country full of pickled herring eaters would have a problem, but she did. Because it was Elena, he didn't push it, even though the Fat Man paid two grand for a night of anus and heels and any kind of improvised punishment a woman in black lace and leather schlong harness was willing to deliver. You know, just run with it, go with the flow, riff on the whip.

It would be good for Tatyana. Toughen her up. No kissing here. No passion. No twelve quick minutes of boffing and then back on the F train heading for Brighton Beach. The Fat Man was serious. The Fat Man was Dostoevsky—long, slow, exacting, with great attention to detail. But Tatyana had no choice. She opened her mouth, now she had to open her cheeks. Two sessions with the Fat Man, after which Johnny would reward her with another night with the plastic surgeon. Charge the flesh sculptor a thousand bucks. After that, she could move in with him, for all Johnny cared. Kiss, fondle, get herself wider lips, a new chin. Whatever. As long as she got Johnny the four thousand from the Fat Man and another thousand from the plastic surgeon. That would be enough to satisfy the Bear.

His plan set, he got up from the grass and walked to the crosswalk. He waited for the light before he crossed to a pay phone on the corner. Then, as the world of the wealthy passed him by, the liposuctioned and hair implanted, the well leashed and well nannied, the daily tanned and radicchio-ed, the faux people living their trompe l'oeil lives, he searched through Elena's trick book, looking for the Russian word for *fat*.

Bliss was back with Kevin and Neal, the two men who lived under Elena. They were sitting around the Mission coffee table going over the phone report—all their local calls in the last three months. More than four hundred.

"So how do you propose we do this?" Neal asked.

"Look them over," Bliss said. "Cross out the ones you know—friends, relatives, Chinese take-out. The rest you just dial and see who answers. Hopefully it won't be anyone you owe money to."

"That could be a couple of hundred calls," Kevin said.

"Then you better get started."

They each took a few sheets and got to work.

"Nine-eight-three-four-five-eight-one," Neal said. "Who's that?"

"Nine-eight what?"

"Nine-eight-*three!*" Neal said emphatically.

"That's Celia, isn't it?"

"No. Celia's nine-eight-*six.*"

"Then I don't know," said Neal.

After twenty minutes they traded sheets.

"You sure called your parents a lot," Kevin said.

"It was my dad's birthday. He was sixty-five."

"Yeah, but his birthday was in July and you called them . . . let's see . . ." Kevin studied the sheet. "Once, twice, three times on the eighteenth of *August.* How do you explain that?"

"I have to explain? I called my parents because I, at least, am still speaking to my parents."

"Fine."

They glanced at Bliss and resumed their silent perusal of the numbers.

Watching them, Bliss thought about how he and Rachel would handle the same situation, with some dispassionate cop was sitting in their living room, leering at their furnishings, waiting to see what secrets emerged. On their phone list, Rachel would have been responsible for most of the calls. The ones that documented their lives. Doctors' appointments, plumbing emergencies, letting the school know the kids were sick, arranging play dates. Bliss did none of this. On school conference day, the teachers were always strangers. He didn't know who the kids' pediatrician was. He hardly knew any of their friends. And Julia would be going on dates soon. Pimply boys with green hair and skateboards would be ringing the front bell. He'd wear his dress blues and carry his gun to the door. Pat them down before they entered the house. Maybe then they would call him "sir." But he'd have to be around to find out.

And there were the calls Rachel made to her parents. Calls for help, maybe. Calls that admitted they were right. That in settling for someone so far beneath their expectations maybe she really had made a mistake.

Bliss's calls were mostly to Ward. Sometimes he would phone even when he knew Ward wasn't home, just to talk to his partner's machine, to go over his thoughts about a case, hunches, potential leads.

And then, sometimes he'd hold the receiver to his ear, wanting to call his dad, to tell how well things were going.

Hey, Dad, it's Lenny, your son. Well, Pop, you should be proud of me. I just got through another day where I only saw my kids for five minutes. Applaud me. Toast your boy with your next beer. I got home just in time for the beddy-bye kiss and that was it. Didn't have to answer any questions about boys or help with their homework. Just a quick peck and I was out of there. Easy on, easy off. No waiting. Missed dinner, too. Missed the piano duets earlier in the evening, missed bath, missed story time. Not bad, huh? I guess I inherited your sense of timing. I hope someone's making a video of all this so I can watch it sometime. When I'm down in Florida, like you, sitting alone in *my* BarcaLounger with my teeth soaking in a cereal bowl. I can watch on TV the family I once had while I clip coupons. Maybe we can time it out—I retire and you have a fatal stroke on the same day. I'll be down there before the chair gets cold, before the milk spoils. Let's synchronize our watches, Pop.

He would have called to speak to his mother, but Rachel did that for him. Ran interference with his old man. Softened up the enemy with an air strike before handing the phone to Bliss with his mother on the other end.

So he didn't call. He just listened to the dial tone until the recording came on saying the phone was off the hook. Then he hung up.

Most of the numbers Kevin and Neal knew from memory. To identify the others, they started dialing. Kevin took the first batch.

"Dry cleaners," he reported after the first number. "When you complained about that spot on your jacket."

Neal crossed it off.

Kevin continued.

"Ray's Pizza," he announced.

"Too cheesy."

"The pharmacy."

"Your dandruff shampoo."

"Tell the world, why don't you."

"I use coal tar," Bliss said cheerfully. He realized too late he sounded like he was talking to first graders.

They looked at him with disdain. Kevin dialed again, listened, then quickly hung up.

"That was your aunt. Why'd you call them?" he asked Neal.

"My uncle was sick."

"The devil never gets sick, unless maybe one of his horns is infected or his tail got caught in the door of his pickup." Kevin turned to Bliss. "Neal's uncle told this story last Thanksgiving. A guy walks into a bar with an alligator . . ." he said.

"Cut it out," Neal said.

"With an *alligator*," Kevin continued. "And he says to the bartender, 'Two beers.'"

"Kevin."

Kevin turned to face his significant other. "You didn't *have* to call him. It was only a forty-five-minute procedure," he said to

Neal. "He didn't even stay in the hospital." He turned back to Bliss. "So the bartender says to the man, 'Hey pal, we don't serve alligators in here.' So the man asks, 'Do you serve faggots? I repeat, do you serve FAGGOTS?' "

"My mother *asked* me to call."

"It was an operation for his *fistula!*" Kevin said. "He *deserved* a leaking fistula. He deserved Jockeys full of bile and pus." Then back to Bliss. "So the bartender says, 'Yeah, we serve faggots.' So the guy says, 'Okay, a beer for me and a faggot for my alligator.' This was at Thanksgiving dinner, Detective."

Bliss nodded. "I usually hear it told with *schvartzers* instead of faggots," he said. "If that's any consolation."

"Oh yes, Detective," Kevin said. "That makes it all right. Absolutely."

Neal grabbed the phone. "I'll try some," he said.

He got two hair salons, Barneys, Tower Records, and three different take-out Japanese.

Then he dialed another number, listened in silence, then slowly returned the handset to its cradle.

"Who was that?" Neal asked.

Kevin looked to his lover.

"That," he said, "was Lester's machine."

Neal sucked in a loud, short breath.

"Our Lester."

"Yes. I guess his family hasn't disconnected it yet."

"Yeah."

"His message said he wasn't at home right now."

"No. He's not."

"That he would get right back to us."

They sat in silence for a minute. Bliss felt incredibly uncomfortable. He was wondering if this was all worth it. He gently cleared his throat.

"Did he . . . ?"

"What?" Kevin was getting angry again, like he did the first time they met, after Elena was killed. " 'Did he . . .' what?"

Bliss wanted to drop it, but he couldn't. Maybe he needed to punish himself, do a big Yom Kippur right there, a hyper-atonement for all the faggots and *schwartzes* and stupid wop motherfuckers and drunken Irish assholes and rat-bastard Chinks that, despite his best intentions, had left his mouth and piled up around his shiny black police shoes over the past eighteen years. Let Kevin and Neal blow the shofar and clean up his cop sins with one deafening blast.

"Did he die?" Bliss asked.

"Let me help you, Detective. Did he die from AIDS? Yes. Did he get AIDS through intercourse with another man? Yes. Did he take a long time to die? Yes. Was it hard for his relatives, his close friends, everyone that knew him? Yes. Did his mother have a stroke two days after Lester died? Yes. Did his father forgive him? Yes. Do we forgive him? Yes. Was he thirty years old? No. He was twenty-seven."

"Kevin," Neal said calmly, "he's trying to find Elena's killer."

"Yeah," Kevin said, going back to the phone. "I almost forgot."

Neal made some more calls, Kevin crossed them off, and Bliss drifted, feeling humiliated but slightly cleaner. And it was certainly cheaper than tickets to shul during the High Holidays, even if he sat in the back row.

What else? What else would be on the Bliss family phone bill besides the kids' appointments and take-out food and Rachel's calls to her parents? What *else* would be revealed about the Bliss family? What secrets would *he* discover? His daughter calling the sex lines advertised on cable? Special ones for kids. 555-CACA. Or there could be a phone number revealing an affair his wife was having. It wouldn't surprise him. Frequent calls to some handsome fan. Maybe a doctor, a *specialist,* a *brain* surgeon—from London, probably—tall, rich, dashing, Oxford graduate, in New York for the brain surgeon convention. He goes to the Comic Strip for a lark and falls madly in love. He buys her champagne. They talk long past the last set. She calls him the next day at the Plaza. He says to her "Darling, you're so terribly funny and so terribly, *terribly* beautiful. Come back with me to Kensington. Live in my flat. Have tea. Eat crumpets. Drive on the left. Pee in my loo. Darling, leave your dreadful beast of a husband before he shoots you or himself."

Or maybe it would be some young bartender at a club, or some mook from Jersey in whom Rachel would find a certain uncircumcised kitschiness, the silver pepperrino around his neck dangling against her breasts as he pumped on top of her in the back seat of his car. Any of *those* scenarios he would understand, maybe almost expect. Because he knew he'd let her down—that he'd become something else, some*one* else since they'd met and gotten married. Not just the usual paltry caresses, lack of hand-holding, petty petting, but something deeper.

What happened to the Sunday mornings when they went to Chinatown for dim sum? Or ate pizza in bed, all four of them, and watched a movie on the VCR? All that fun? Why had he lost the desire? Why were there were no more Hallmark Moments left in his life?

Maybe it had something to do with seeing his first stiff, an actual dead body. Like everyone else he'd seen hundreds in the movies, guts flung across the room from a sawed-off shotgun, arrows in the back ("Those are Comanche feathers, Captain Parker"), knives in the belly, but then it was there, in front of him, finally, a live dead body—granted, it was a common one of the fifteen-year-old black kid variety, strictly run of the mill, lying on his kitchen floor. Tyrone Robinson was his name, the mother sobbing in the living room, cops walking over him and around him like he was a passed-out drunk in a Penn Station toilet or just a stain on the rug. Bliss felt the need to comfort her somehow, what his mother would have wanted him to do, but the other cops, everyone on the scene just ignored her, so Bliss stared at the kid and forced himself to make the body insignificant, so he could walk away, so he wouldn't need to care, turning the boy into a spill, tomato sauce that had fallen off the shelf. "Breakage in aisle 6" and Bliss was just there to mop it up. Rachel had married Bliss pre-Tyrone—Bliss the Younger. Now he was post-Tyrone—Bliss the Elder. Bliss the Bitter. Bliss the Terrible. Bliss the Entirely Fucked Up.

He'd say they should all take a vacation together, get away to a beach somewhere and frolic in the sun, but every time a cop said that in the movies, something bad happened. Though something bad was happening now. Just slowly, one cell at a time.

•   •   •

After another forty-five minutes of calling, Neal and Kevin had almost finished up the list. They had found three numbers where no one answered and two that were disconnected. But there was no one with a Russian accent. No possible johns. Elena had made two calls for sure. One was to a travel agency, about booking a ticket, one-way to Moscow. The other to a courier service, also inquiring about taking something to Moscow.

"She was about to go home," Kevin said.

"It seems that way," Bliss replied. They were sitting around the coffee table, sipping some cognac. "She probably had some cash saved up. Whoever killed her must've known."

Then Kevin blew reveille. He was holding the phone at arm's length, making a face like he'd gulped some bad milk. "What's the What Knot? Club?" Kevin asked. "You ever go there?"

"What did you say?"

Kevin hung up and dialed again, handed the phone to Bliss. He listened to a recorded message, a deafening sound, like screeching tires or a raccoon in an oil drum, then a voice doing bad Bela Lugosi giving the hours when the What Knot? was open and the names of that night's acts. Bliss hung up.

"That meant something, didn't it?" Neal said.

"Yes. It means something. I'm just not sure what."

"So this . . . tonight . . . this calling, do you think it will help?"

"Yeah. I think so. I'll try these others myself," Bliss said. "The phone company can tell me tomorrow who belonged to the disconnected numbers."

"On *Sixty Minutes* once they had this police detective who said most murders needed to be solved in forty-eight hours, otherwise it becomes quite difficult. Is that true?"

"Yeah," Bliss said. "It's true."

They sat for a while in silence. Bliss was pretty sure he would never have to come back there, never have to see these men again. So he told them about his wife's cousin who was HIV positive, about how Bliss hated him at first because he couldn't deal with it, but now, when he has the chance, Bliss picks him up some chicken soup from Zabar's and a half pound of chopped liver and a challah bread and maybe some lox or a smoked white-fish.

"What I would want to eat," he told them, "if I were, you know, not feeling well. That's what I do," he said.

"It's nice of you," Kevin said.

"Thanks," Bliss said. "I'll let you know if anything comes of the other numbers. By the way, it was a big help what you did tonight. It really was."

Then he got up and left before he got all stupid and weepy.

Johnny was in his aunt's apartment, on the phone with a hyster-
ical Tatyana. She was screaming in his ear.

"He was disgusting! He was like a . . . he wanted me to . . .
to . . ."

She was crying.

"Stupid cow," he said with his hand over the receiver, so she
couldn't hear. So, now he had to worry about what he said to her.
To not hurt her *feelings!* This ignorant Russian pig of a woman,
closer to a beet than a human being, last week she was licking his
armpits clean like a cat, but now, because he owes the Bear five
thousand dollars, he has to console her, he has to worry about
her *feelings!*

"I'm sorry," Johnny said. "I didn't know."

Johnny heard murmuring in the background. Someone talking to Tatyana. A man. Where was she?

"No. I wasn't going to," she shouted. "I wasn't going to but I
will tell you. Everything!"

"It's best if you just forget . . ."

"I won't! I won't forget." Pause, more murmuring. Like she
was being coached. By who?

"Tatyana, are you with someone? Where are . . ."

"Everything he did! So no one has to go back there. He can
find one from the street."

"Tatyana . . ."

"First he made me drink water . . . glasses and glasses of bot-
tled water . . . a hundred-dollar bill for each glass and then I had
to take my pants off . . . not my shirt . . . just my . . . and he had
these shoes, with long heels in every size, he had a whole closet
full of them, and he made me put on ones that were really tight,
so tight they wouldn't come off, and he lay down on his stomach
on the floor naked and pink and hairy and pimply and I had

to step . . . I had to step in . . . he made me smear Vaseline so it would go in . . . so the heel would go in and I had to step down . . . in and out with my heel and then he rolled on his back and I had to stand over him and he was staring up at me and he said I had to make all over him . . . that I had to pee on him and he said not to worry that he would just throw out the rug and get a new one and he laughed and closed his eyes and opened his mouth and waited for the pee but I couldn't . . . I . . . he hit me with his fist in my . . . he hit me and shouted that I should piss piss piss but I couldn't so he pulled me down and made me sit on him . . . not like . . . but with my . . . pulling my cheeks apart and his nose going up and then he gripped me tight by where my bladder . . . he gripped me with his fat fingers and pushed and pushed and I couldn't hold it then I started and he just lifted me up . . . with his huge arms he lifted me up over his head like I was a little baby so I sprinkled down all over him."

The money, Johnny thought. What about the money?

"Tatyana, did he . . ?"

"Then he wanted me to kiss him . . . down there . . . he wanted me to but I couldn't . . . it wasn't . . . I couldn't find it because his belly was . . . because it was buried underneath his belly and he held me behind my neck and shoved my head down and I had to . . . I had to push against the wall . . . I had to lean my shoulder into his stomach and push against the wall so I could find his . . . so I could kiss his tiny . . . it was so tiny and he did it in seconds and it dribbled out and it was like a little boy's."

She was sobbing now.

"He had a belly like a whale but his dick was like a little boy's."

Someone was comforting her. He could hear it. Who? The Bear? Did she track down the Bear? Who else did she know? She finally caught her breath.

"Did he give you any money?" Johnny asked.

No reply.

"Tatyana, did he give you any money?"

He heard whispering.

"Yes. Yes, Johnny. He gave me . . ." More whispering. "Yes, Johnny, are you there?"

"Yeah."

"Yes, he gave me one thousand dollars."

She was lying. Shit.

"He told me two thousand."

"I know, but he said I didn't . . . he said he wasn't happy with the . . . with the heel . . . with the heel job that I . . . and that he could only give me one thousand."

"What about the hundreds for drinking the water?"

"Ummm . . . well, I thought that was like a tip, you know?"

"Yeah."

Someone was putting her up to this. Who did she know who would possibly have her best interest at heart?

"Johnny?"

"Yeah?"

"I have to go now."

"NO! Wait! You don't go! You don't just walk away from this, Tatyana. You need to give me the money."

"How much?"

"How *much!?* How *MUCH?!!* Who do you think you are? You owe me two thousand bucks."

"But he didn't pay me what you said."

"How do I know? How do I know what he paid you? Two thousand bucks is what he told *me* he was paying you, so that's what you owe me. You should've drank more water. You should have let him stick his tongue in further. That's not my problem. Two thousand bucks or I take your father's vodka bottle and stick it in his mouth and hammer it down his throat until it comes out the back of his neck. Then I'll go into your mother's bed and tuck her in while she's sleeping—one straight, hard tuck with her knitting needle, right through her nightie."

More whispering. Who did she *know?*

"Johnny, I'll have to call you back."

"You'll call me back?! You'll fucking call *me* back!!??"

Then she hung up.

His plans were unraveling. What else? What was the next thing to backfire?

Johnny heard a sharp crack, wood splintering, and then his

aunt's front door swung open and Malcolm walked in, followed
by the Bear. Behind them was a jittery man with close-cropped
gray hair and wire-rimmed glasses who proceeded directly to a
chair in the corner of the room and sat down with his legs
together. He held tightly to a little black bag that sat in his lap,
like he was playing the doctor in a cheap production of a Chekov
play. The Bear gave Johnny's aunt a crisp ten-dollar bill and
asked her to get what she needed to make stuffed cabbage.

"Johnny will need comforting meal tonight," he told her as she
headed out the door, her rusting shopping cart in tow, wheels
squeaking like a small animal in pain. "Something to be remind-
ing little Johnny of the Old Country, of simpler times and softer
currency. Because here in America, money is hard. Very hard."

The Bear closed the door behind her and turned to Johnny.

"I'm still on Moscow time," he said. "There it's a day earlier.
That makes here a day later."

"Meaning what?"

"Meaning today is tomorrow. Meaning it is already payday. So
I am thinking maybe you could be giving me some of what you
are owing me. Now. A thousand dollars or two, perhaps. Pocket
change. Blintz money."

"I'll have it all tomorrow," Johnny said.

"But it is already tomorrow. So I am wanting some of it today,
and *rest* of it day after tomorrow. Meaning day after today."

"I don't have it now."

"Oh."

There was silence in the room. Malcolm softly whistled a
nursery rhyme Johnny remembered his mother singing to him
as a kid in Russia. The doctor fidgeted nervously with his bag.

"You are new to game, Johnny," the Bear said, stretching his
huge feet on the coffee table. "So let me be giving you the clue-
in. Basically what we are having here in Brighton Beach, in our
tight-knit little émigré community, is anarchy—anarchy which I
run. Now you may ask, if someone is *running* the anarchy, how
can it *be* anarchy? Right? But actually, the only time the anarchy
works is when you have leader keeping everyone on anarchist
toes. You ever hear of Makhno?"

"Who?"

"Nestor Makhno. Great Russian anarchist. You heard of Kropotkin?"

"Yes."

"Of Bakunin."

"Yes."

"Makhno was the greatest of all. Because he didn't just *theorize*—he *did*. Makhno lives in Ukraine during Revolution. When he is twenty years old he is arrested and put in prison. There he is learning political theory from cellmates. Marxism does not interest him. Anarchism did. You learned none of this in school. I am right?"

"Yes."

"Fucking-A right. It wasn't until I leave Russia that I discover true heroes. In Ukraine during Revolution, Red Army is fighting White Army. Red Army also fighting German governor who is running Ukraine. Red Army also fighting Ukrainian nationalists, who want Ukraine for Ukrainians. Red Army fighting everybody in Ukraine. Into chaos is coming Makhno. He talks to peasants who are not happy with Reds, Whites, Germans, or Ukrainian nationalists. So Makhno gets peasants to make army of their own. They fight everybody, hiding machine guns under hay and blankets in *troikas*—this before Vietcong doing the same thing. Makhno is first guerrilla army. When Makhno wins battle and takes prisoners, he is right away killing all the enemy officers— in one town he ties them to horses on merry-go-round and is shooting them as they circle by. But enemy soldiers he sets free. Some switch sides and stay with him, fighting with peasants. Makhno sets up anarchist town in Ukraine. No one is ruling. No one is owning anything. Makhno's spirit is holding everything together.

"But when war ends, Trotsky is having no patience for radicals like Makhno. So Trotsky puts price on Makhno's head and he has to flee. Everything falls apart. The anarchy becomes anarchy. Makhno dies years later in Paris. His last job was as taxi driver. But for a while, Makhno succeeds. And now I, Sascha the Bear, will create new perfect society. Soon everything here will

run smoothly—no one being afraid. No one needing punishment. And you can be part of it, Johnny. You can have place of
honor. Just give me money you owe me."

"I can't."

"You *can't?* This is all you can say after wonderfully inspiring
speech I am just making?"

"I can't."

"Well, this really is problem, Johnny," the Bear said. "I'm
afraid we're going to have to Shylock you. A pound of flesh and
all this jazz." He glanced at his henchman. "Malcolm," he said,
as casually as one ordered coffee and danish.

Malcolm quickly maneuvered Johnny's arms behind his back
and deftly pinned them there. Johnny felt no need to struggle.
The doctor rose from his chair and set the bag down at Johnny's
feet. He opened it up and removed a scalpel and deftly made a
slit down the front of Johnny's shirt. He pulled the fabric aside,
exposing Johnny's left breast. Then, without any hesitation, he
cut off Johnny's nipple.

The shock made Johnny gasp, but there was no pain. The doctor reached back into his bag and brought out some ointment
and a curved needle from which a foot of suture dangled down.
He dabbed the bleeding wound with the ointment, then deftly
stitched it shut. He held some gauze over the wound until the
bleeding stopped, and then covered what used to be Johnny's
nipple with a Band-Aid. Then he closed his bag and returned to
his seat, legs together, bag at his side. The whole operation took
about ninety seconds.

Johnny stood motionless. He looked at his nipple. A tiny bit of
blood leaked out from the Band-Aid and trickled down Johnny's
chest about three inches before it stopped.

"Tsk, tsk, tsk," the Bear said. "You're getting sloppy, Doc."
The doctor hung his head in shame.

"Doc used to work for Soviet hockey team. Sew up cuts and
get players on ice for next shift." The Bear wiped away the blood
with his handkerchief. "It won't grow back, I'm afraid," he said.

Johnny watched the doctor pull a Wet-Nap out of his pocket
and clean off the scalpel before putting it back in his bag. Then

he had a flash—it was the plastic surgeon. That's where Tatyana was.

It was the voice of the plastic surgeon urging her on, leading her on to defy him. He was probably showing her the photos on his desk—laughing at her thinking they were his wife. Laughing at *him*. Before and after. He'd show *them* before and after. The plastic surgeon would take her back to his apartment, wouldn't he? Get her some fancy clothes. Shoes. Champagne. "Let's go to Acapulco with the two thousand dollars," he'd say. "You earned it. Not that pimp. Not Johnny, the fool." He'd kill them. He would. He'd kill them both.

Ward had his hand over the receiver and mouthed the word.

Dump-ster-man.

Bliss picked up his phone.

"Hey, pal, we were just thinking about you."

Crowd noise. Clinking of glasses. Jazz in the background. Roy Eldridge. Dead ten years. Must be a tape.

"Detective Bliss."

"Dumpsterman."

"Please."

"Sorry. *Mr.* Dumpsterman."

Restaurant? Bar? Club? No. 8:30. Maybe the first set was starting.

"I'm feeling a little lonely tonight, Detective."

"Why don't you come on down and have a beer? We'll watch the Knicks."

Ward was notifying the switchboard. In less than a minute he'd have the number the guy was calling from. Then he simply had to look the number up in the computer for an address. Given Ward's ineptitude at the keyboard, Bliss had two, three minutes tops.

"Nothing personal, Detective, but I'm feeling the need for some female company. Some softness. Some sweet nothings. Sweet, sweet, very sweet . . . then nothing."

"Got your Dumpster picked out?"

"Oh, Detective. You think I'm so cold and calculating. I'm really so much more impulsive. Improvisational. I'll leave the Dumpster to chance. They really are quite abundant in the city, after all. And then, of course, I can always improvise in New Jersey. The Land of Dumpsters."

"Cute."

Wait. Drums. A sax tuning up. That was *live.* Hang on! Hang on, Dumpsterman! Out of the corner of his eye, Bliss caught Ward writing down the number. Then he started typing it into his computer to get the address. He typed like a three-year-old—like a not very bright three-year-old. Bliss still had time.

"Who's writing your material?" Bliss asked him. Dumpsterman chortled. "Wait, did you just chortle?" Bliss heard the bass. The tune was starting. Keep him talking.

"Pardon me?"

"I asked if you just chortled. Or was that a snicker?" Ward poked the keys like he was killing roaches. Bliss strung Dumpsterman along. "I mean, it started off like a chortle, but then it had a strong snickerlike finish."

"I think you're in need of a respite, Detective."

"That's what everyone keeps telling me." Drums now. Brushes. Medium tempo. Still, he couldn't tell who was playing. Could be anybody.

"But in answer to your question, I write my own material. It may not make you laugh, but certain young ladies find me absolutely irresistible. But I feel I've disappointed you."

Piano comping. The tune starting. "I'll Remember April."

"That I haven't done my share. That I've been lax, lazy. A tease."

The melody was coming around. Two, three more bars. Just keep talking.

"I'll satisfy you tonight, Detective. I'll give you something to talk about to your buddies in the locker room."

Then he hung up. But not before Bliss heard the saxophonist—only two bars, but he knew the tone and phrasing immediately. Illinois Jacquet. And where was Jacquet making his rare quartet appearance that week? Bliss knew. He whipped his chair around. Ward was just copying something from the screen.

"The Blue Note," Bliss shouted. "By Sixth Avenue and Fourth Street. Who needs the fucking computer. Let's get him!"

Bliss stood in the entrance to the club, tapping his foot to a medium-tempo blues. At almost eighty years old, Jacquet still probably had the best tone of any swing tenor player alive, and he was making the most of it—bending the notes like Ben Webster, then finding the unexpected dissonance like Paul Gonsalves. And man, could he swing! Bliss almost forgot that he was looking for a murderer. He scanned the crowd.

Of the hundred or so people having dinner and drinks that night, at least forty were Japanese businessmen. Bliss ruled them out. One table was a group of six young women—officemates celebrating perhaps? Maybe the birthday girl liked jazz. Two Wall Street types were eyeing the women from the bar. They seemed harmless. Bliss counted six tables with middle-aged couples. He ruled out one with a Michelin Guide on the table, but he couldn't dismiss the other five. Hell, the guy was just sick enough to send his wife home afterwards in a taxi and then go out looking for his prey. Ward was riding around the nearby blocks, looking for a meridian blue Volvo. He would also check the two garages nearby the club, then join Bliss.

Bliss counted eight men sitting by themselves at the bar. Perhaps the bartender saw one of them use the phone—maybe he even asked for change. That would be too much to ask for. He'd talk to the manager—get him to quiz the bartender. Meanwhile, Bliss scoped the rest of the club.

Two sultry young women sat near the bandstand—probably dates of the band. Wives perhaps. Bliss made that mistake in college, buying drinks for sharp women like these, only to watch them walk off with the rhythm section at the end of the last set. An older woman sat alone at another table near the stand—a martini glass in front of her, her eyes closed, tapping a finger to the beat, lost in some memory of happening nights in the Village long ago. Maybe she knew Kerouac.

The remaining five tables each had a group of four men. They reeked of conventioneers, but Bliss couldn't be sure. He wished Ward was with him. He had a knack for figuring out people's jobs. He could tell the shoe salesmen from the pharmacists from the guys who dealt in paneling and drywall. Without Ward, he had to keep these gin-and-tonic guzzlers on his possibles list. There were twenty of them, plus the four husbands, and the three at the bar. Normally, Bliss would also include anyone working at the club, but unless Dumpsterman was enraged about not getting an acting job or a green card, that ruled out the waiters and busboys.

Not seeing the manager, he sauntered over to the hostess, a tall, winsome redhead in a black spaghetti strap dress, and flashed his badge.

"Where is your pay phone?"

She was unimpressed, to say the least.

"You can use the phone by the bar if you desire to make a call, Officer."

"It's Detective. And I don't desire to make a call. I desire to *see* where the pay phone is. If I desire to make a call or anything else, I'll ask."

She was pouting.

"Stop pouting, please. A suspected murderer just called our precinct from your pay phone. Where is it?"

"Just inside the alcove," she said, pointing across the room.

"Did you see anyone using it in the last ten minutes?"

"No. You can stand on the far side of the phone and be pretty much hidden." She bit her bottom lip.

"Look, I'm sorry I was mean to you," Bliss said.

"How sorry?"

"This sorry," he said, spreading out his arms. He felt like he was talking to one of his kids. Except his kids knew when he was full of shit. "Now please tell the bartender to come over here. Pretty please. I need to talk to him."

She was smiling. Bliss should have seen it coming.

"Hey John," she called to the bartender. "There's a policeman over here who wants to talk to you. Something about a murder." Then she pointed directly at Bliss.

Great. Now everyone at the bar knows what's going on. The music picked up. The band was cooking through the finale of "Flying Home." Jacquet's signature number. How many times had he played it in fifty years? Bliss could see the bartender was annoyed. He was throwing up his hands and seemed to be telling the redhead he couldn't leave. He gestured to the customers.

Bliss walked over to the bar. He flashed his badge at a thin, gray-haired guy in his forties, sitting on the first stool drinking Scotch and tapping his finger to the music.

"Let me see some ID," Bliss said.

"For what?" he asked.

"That Scotch?" Bliss said. "You gotta be twenty-one to drink liquor in New York. Let's see some fucking ID."

The man stared at Bliss for a second, saw he was serious, and started fishing out his wallet. The bartender finally began to get the picture and came from behind the bar.

"Please, Officer. This is Oren. He's in here almost every night."

Bliss checked Oren's license.

"What kind of car you drive, Oren?"

Bliss kept his eye on the rest of the bar, making sure no one was trying to slip away.

"A Volvo. Station wagon."

"What color?"

"Beige."

"Yeah? You make a phone call in the last ten minutes?"

"I was here all through the opening number. Jacquet was in his Lester Young bag. You can ask him."

"I believe you, Oren. You see anyone get up to make a call?"

A lady at one of the rear tables turned around and shushed them.

"Please, Officer," the redhead said. "Is there anywhere else you could do this? In the office, perhaps?"

"Excuse me, man, but I happened to see someone at the phone."

It was a guy at the next stool. Horn-rimmed glasses. Corduroy jacket. Jeans. Paperback book stuck in his pocket. College professor written all over him.

"When?"

"Like just before the set started. I copped a glance at him when I was coming out of the bathroom."

"What's your name, professor?"

"Abbot. How'd you . . . ?"

"Come with me."

Bliss gestured to the professor to follow him and they went outside.

"Tell me about him," Bliss said.

"The guy was toking those thin cigars. Like Tiparillos, man. Remember the commercial?"

"Cigar? cigarette? Tiparillo?"

"I didn't think they made them anymore."

"Do you see him now?"

Professor Bop scanned the room through the window.

"No."

"What was he wearing?"

"Oh. Yeah. That's the other reason I noticed him. He had on a kelly green sport jacket, blue pants. Like he was on his way to the country club. He kinda stuck out. Not what you'd call a typical jazz fan."

"Did you see his face?"

"Ix-nay. The man was like dancing with the wall. Cheek to cheek."

"Hair color? Was he bald? Stoop-shouldered? Fat?"

"The man was flush, you could tell just by looking at him. Everything neat and pressed."

"How old?"

"Fifty. Sixty. I couldn't tell."

Bliss rushed back into the club, grabbed the redhead by the arm, and marched her to the reservation desk.

"Who was he? The green blazer. Where was he sitting?"

"Table six, I think."

Bliss was feeling it now. Feeling the rush.

"He make a reservation? I need a name. Check the book!"

"Ssshhhhh!" someone said.

"Here." She pointed a scarlet nail at a name written in faint pencil. "Bliss—party of two. Is that him? The murderer? Is it?" she asked, aglow now. Something exciting to tell her parents in Des Moines after so many disappointing auditions. "Mr. Bliss? Is he the one?"

"Yeah, he's the one. We've been on his trail for years."

Ward showed up, out of breath.

"Any luck?" he asked.

"The big K."

"Strike out?"

"Yeah. But he was here. Made a reservation. So now we're wise to his moniker."

"Which is?"

"Last name, Bliss."

"Cute."

They took a seat at the bar. Bliss ordered two iced teas.

"Anyone see him?" Ward asked.

Bliss didn't answer. He was lost again in the music. A slow ballad. Jacquet could play them like no one else. Forlorn. Wistful. Angry. A story that could only be told in jazz. The desperate, elegant truth from someone who's been there and just barely made it back. Even the salesmen shut up. This was a Johnny Mercer special. "Mandy Is Two." About a little girl. "You should see her eyes of cornflower blue." About a little girl excited about life, who brings joy to everyone around her. "Now Miss Amanda's proud as can be. Cuz she's a big girl now."

Probably no one in the club that night except Bliss listened to Illinois's sultry playing and thought about Mandy's cornflower blue eyes winding up dead in a Dumpster somewhere. No one else had that burden. He wondered if that's what happened to his father, if contact with so much evil drove him away from his family, from his son. Monty the cop thinking, "I'd better not get too close to my boy, not love my Lenny too much because one of the crazy evil bastards lurking in the city is going to take him away from me. And so if I don't get too close, then the pain of losing him won't be as great." Bliss wondered if this was why he kept his distance from his own kids. That no matter how hard he tried, he couldn't protect them. When Cori had asked if they were safe, he should have answered her truthfully. That you're only safe from what you don't know about.

Bliss looked for Ward but he was gone. He flipped a ten spot on the bar. It probably wasn't enough, but the bartender would slip it in his pocket anyway. Cab fare home. On the way out, Bliss gave the redhead his card.

"If he comes in here again, Mr. Kelly Green Jacket, give me a call right away, okay, sweetie?"

"Sure, Detective."

This was one of the biggest nights of her life. A real live New York detective. Just like the movies. Just like TV. He knew he'd hear from her again. That she wasn't sure, but there's a guy here at the club who looks just like the guy who . . . oh, my God, he's going to the pay phone! He's . . . he's . . . dialing! You have to come quick! Please, officer! Detective! He's coming up the stairs! He's in my room!! You have to . . . Aghhhhhhh! Aghhhh-hhh!

Sorry, wrong number.

"I want to talk to the ladies out there for a moment. The men can play with their gimp for a while. Ladies, do your husbands ever have engine trouble? You ever want to take an early morning ride and they won't start, they just won't turn over? No spark? Battery dead? Well, bring the old fart down for service at Ms. Goodwench. Our team of expert mechanics will put him up on the rack and give him a diagnostic he won't forget. We'll investigate, lubricate, and calculate exactly what's not working. Nine times out of ten it's something simple, like his battery needs charging or his tailpipe requires stimulation. Our mechanics know just what buttons to press, to get him started but leave him wanting more. Unfortunately, once in a while the men don't want to leave the shop, they just want to be repaired, over and over. But usually they go home and immediately start working at peak performance level for at least a week and a half, which is probably all you want to get out of them anyway.

"My husband the cop gets like that. Disinterested. He tells me it's because of the kids, but I don't buy it. He tells me it's because of work, but I don't buy it. He tells me it's the specific anxieties of being a cop, the stress, the fear, the danger. All right, maybe. But personally, I used to think he was getting some on the side—from hookers he busted giving it to him for free in the back of the squad car so he wouldn't arrest them. So I asked him if that was it and he looked at me with his puppy dog eyes and said, 'Honey, I'm Homicide. I don't bust hookers. That's Vice.'

"But maybe a little vice is exactly what we need. Maybe we should go through the bottom drawers of some vice cop's desks and see what's been confiscated over the years. Take a few of those toys home, eat some oysters, and settle down for something seriously NC-Seventeen. That's the way things used to be with us. But now we're both lost in the woods. Lost in the forest of moodiness. And ladies, there's nothing you can do for moodiness. There's no cure. It's worse even than the Big C—Cheating. When they cheat you actually get more sex, at least that's what my girlfriends tell me. Because the husband feels so guilty he wants to make it up to you.

"But with moodiness you got nothing. You're left empty-handed. No caresses, no fondling, no hugs, no pats on the back. Nada. It's like sitting in the bathtub after all the water's drained out—clammy, cold, and your skin starts to quiver and there's nothing you can do but pull your knees up close to your chest and hold them tight and gently rock back and forth and wonder what happened to the young couple who used to dance in ecstasy with the satyrs in the moonlight. I'm sorry. I wasn't very funny tonight. Thank you. I'm sorry."

"Rachel DA-vis, ladies and gentlemen. Rachel DA-vis."

It took a few nights of waiting, but finally the plastic surgeon ordered dinner delivered to his Park Avenue apartment. Pizza. With grilled vegetables. Johnny had lurked just down the block, speaking to the delivery boys as they rode up on their bikes or scooters.

"Is that mine?" he'd ask. "Eighteen C?" Then mention the plastic surgeon's name. "I was just going out for beer. I can take it now."

The first night, nothing but blank looks. Some of the delivery boys he spoke to twice, several hours apart. They didn't remember. Or didn't care. Two bucks an hour salary to a Mexican or Chinese kid living six to a room doesn't buy a lot of fealty. Besides, Johnny thought, in the short time they'd been in New York, these guys had probably seen everything.

The kid delivering the pizza was happy to take care of business out on the street, saving him a trip on the elevator. And the generous five-dollar tip Johnny gave him induced hearty and effusive thanks in Spanish.

Johnny quickly tied the apron he'd brought with him around his waist, put on the thick black eyeglasses, and slipped the paper soda-jerk hat on his head. He was glad it was pizza and not sushi. It would have been tough to pass for Japanese. Chinese would also have been tricky. He had dyed his hair jet black just in case. The doormen didn't look too closely anyway. Just another in the steady stream of disheveled immigrants delivering a shopping bag full of dinner for the rich people upstairs who were too busy to cook. He took out a packet of ketchup and smeared some on the apron so it wouldn't appear too new. That was the other good thing about the pizza, any blood that splattered would look like sauce. He walked in the lobby of the surgeon's building. The doorman rang upstairs.

"Pizza delivery," the doorman said into the house phone with a heavy Irish accent, and then waved Johnny through. If it had been one of the buildings with an elevator man who waited while the deliveries took place, the scheme wouldn't have worked. But the doctor's building settled for video cameras in the elevator, which wouldn't help the surgeon much once he opened his apartment door.

On the way up he went over the plan. Kill the doctor first with the ice pick held under the pizza.

"Check-a to see-a if this-a is-a yours-a," he'd say, in his best *Godfather* accent, which, if the surgeon was smart, would be a dead giveaway that something wasn't right, seeing as all the pizza guys were Mexican now. No self-respecting New York Italian kid would settle for two dollars an hour when they can make five hundred a day working the *zeppole* booths at the San Gennaro Feast. "I think-a they make-a mistake-a in the kitchen-a." And as the surgeon bent over to check for the grilled vegetables, Johnny would grab the back of his head with one hand and shove him toward the pick, which he held tight in the hand supporting the pizza and it would go through his eye and into his brain and no fucking plastic surgery could straighten him out after that. You ordered toppings? How about pupils instead of olives? How about brains instead of extra cheese? Then he'd go after Tatyana, scare her into giving up the money in exchange for her life, then kill her anyway.

It was a good plan. The only snag was if Tatyana answered the door. Then he'd have to start the operation with her and play the doctor by ear.

The phone rang as he knew it would. It was Ward.

"Better get here soon, Pal," Ward said. "We got a twofer. Buy one, get one free."

"Shit."

He knew the phone would ring because the morning was going too well. Letting Rachel sleep, he'd tiptoed with the kids into the kitchen and was making them pancakes. Little ones with funny shapes. They had to guess what they were. Cori sat with her stuffed giraffe, Julia with her book, but for once she wasn't reading. She was eating and laughing. "This one sort of looks like Florida," she said. "See, Cori?" Cori nodded in agreement. "And this one looks like a frog after it was stepped on by an elephant. See, here are its legs." Cori giggled. Bliss stood at the stove and laughed. And then something clicked, went zing, and Bliss was overwhelmed with a desperate need to not have his kids hate him when they grew up. He didn't want them holding on to the receiver like it was something foul, something putrid and decayed, unable to dial the phone because the anger of the call would ruin the rest of their day. He wanted them to remember this breakfast, the fun they were having that minute.

"Who wants more?" he asked. "Cori? Julia? Seconds?"

"Me!"

"Me!"

Then the phone. Corpses calling to him from the electric mist, their dead voices drowning out the fragile laughter of his children.

"Is it bad?" Bliss asked.

"It's a Peckinpah, pal," Ward said, giving him the address on Park Avenue. "And do yourself a favor, don't have any tomato juice on the way over."

He got back to the frying pan in time to discover that the second batch of pancakes had burned.

Bliss joined Ward, who was leaning against the door frame of the surgeon's apartment. The surgeon lay on the white marble floor in the foyer in a pool of blood like a large red halo. Ward always liked a good blood pool, and he was relishing this one. It was damn near perfect, he said.

"Because of the marble. It cools and clots the blood quicker, maintaining the integrity of the pool. Carpets, however, are the worst. Like sponges. They blot. Wood, too. Soaks it right up. Then you're just looking at a big patch of red. A patch doesn't compare to a pool." They moved aside to let the photographer in. "In those situations the best thing is to go to the floor below and check the ceiling, see if it leaked through. Nothing like a good scarlet stain on a white ceiling. When I was just a rookie I used to just stare at those ceiling stains the way kids stare at clouds. Looking for witches, dinosaurs, magical figures. Do you think that warped my sensibility? Whattaya say, Officer Krupke?"

"Ward, I think your sensibility would have shown up warped in your mother's ultrasound."

Ward gave him one of his Mr. Spock single eyebrow lifts and continued with his reverie.

"Linoleum's not bad, but marble's the best. One day maybe we'll have a tong war in the lobby of the Metropolitan Museum. You could go up to the balcony and look down. It would be like a poppy field, with the dead tongs for stems and the blood pools for blossoms. Majestic. You'll call me if you hear about anything like that, won't you, pal? Even if I'm retired down in the Keys, you'll call me?"

"Yeah. Sure."

"Thanks."

Ward took a deep drag on his cigarette and flicked the butt into the blood, where it sizzled and stuck standing straight up.

"Thicker than water," Ward said. "Okay, let's see what we got." He pulled out his notebook, flipped it open, and started reading. "Spoke to the evening doorman on the phone. He recalls the doc getting a pizza delivery at about six-forty-five last night. He'll go down to the precinct to help Marlene put a composite together. Says he didn't get a good look at him, though. He was wearing one of those paper hats and kept his head turned away."

"He have an accent?"

"Yeah. Italian."

"Not Mexican?"

"That's what I said. No Italians making pizza in New York anymore except John's and Patsy's."

"And they don't deliver."

"Tell me about it," Ward said. "Anyway, turns out this ain't the delivery guy the pizza place sends over. The real one *was* Mexican and *he* says he sold the pizza to some guy on the street who claimed he was the doc—that he was just on his way back from buying beer and he would take the pizza up himself."

"You've been a busy boy."

"I like to do all the Commissioner Gordon stuff so when Batman gets here he can go right after the criminals."

"So right now we have one dead doc lying in the front hall with a pizza on his face."

"Mr. Pizza Head," Ward said. "With pepperoni for his eyes, a mushroom for his nose, and a big slice of green pepper for his mouth."

Bliss saw the photographer's flash coming from one of the back rooms. There was also a trail of blood where someone's heel had caught the edge of the doc's lurid halo and tracked spots of his holiness into the apartment.

"Those the perp's footprints?" Bliss asked.

"Nope. No perp perpetrated these prints. They belong to the super, Mr. Galoot, who, judging from his extensive tour of the apartment, walked away with a few of the doc's trinkets before calling the local constabulary."

"Us."

"You and me, partner."

"So why the Weegee?"

"I told you there were two."

"Right. The other one bad?"

"Yeah."

"*Straw Dogs?*"

"Not quite, but . . ."

Bliss gripped Ward's arm and froze.

"No kids. Please." While thinking, Bliss had brought his fingers to his lips and was startled by the taste of maple syrup. "No kids, Ward. Not today." His voice was a whisper, starting to crack. "Don't show me any little girls. Okay? Not this morning?"

Ward tenderly stroked the back of his partner's head.

"No kids, pal. In fact, let's pass on the room. Maybe one corpse before cornflakes is enough for one day."

Bliss took a deep breath, got things under control.

"The wife back there?" he asked.

"Doc lived solo," Ward said. "It's a woman in back, though. Young. Pretty. Great tits. But den dat Ol' Man Rigor makes 'em all stand up straight. Anyway, nothing back there you haven't seen already. No purse. No prints. No ID. But I did find you a little present. Better than the Smokey Robinson CD I got you for your birthday. Hard to believe I found the time, what with all the investigating and phone calling and lab boys dusting for prints and a quick necro poke . . ."

"Partner, you didn't."

"Just joshing. Like I say, it ain't the meat, it's the motion, and you *know* I stay away from any meat that ain't moving. Remember what happened to Detective Sully. Stiff's snatch went stiff on him, rigorously mortised his pecker in place. Had to lie there till the coroner came. Needed the Jaws of Life to pry him out. His circulation cut off so the tip of his prick turned blue. I saw it once in the locker room. Looked like a safety match. Totally fucked up the DNA test, too. Literally. Took the lab boys a week to separate the semen."

"What about my present?"

Ward showed him a clothing label.

"From her panties," he said. "The rest of her was straight Gap. But her panties sported a label from Sylvie's Lingerie."

"Sylvie's!!? Oh, goodie! Now my collection is complete."

"Hey, putz. I made a few calls. Sylvie's happens to be located in Brighton Beach."

Bliss shut up.

"You're kidding."

"That's my little gift to you. What better way to start off the morning, I say, than with a bit of evidence that links one case with another. It's as if the doorbell rang and there was Godot."

"I owe you."

"Good. Payback starts immediamente. I have a little errand to run. Right in this neighborhood. You'll come, too."

They drove in Ward's car. Six blocks up Park, past the old armory to Ninety-fourth Street. Ward pulled around the corner and parked in front of the nearest hydrant.

It was a little before 8:00 in the morning. Park Avenue was bustling. Kids were walking to school in small groups, knapsacks for book bags slung over the shoulders of their school jackets— Spence, Dalton, Collegiate. Ward pointed to one cluster of six Daltonians waiting at the corner to cross the street.

"Probably a hundred million in assets right there," he said.

Bliss knew it well. Those were the kinds of kids Julia and Cori went to school with. Having birthday parties in fancy restaurants the parents owned or renting vans to take the kids to huge country houses in Connecticut with pools and three-hole golf courses in the backyard. Rachel would probably just be getting on the crosstown bus with their kids, on their way to school. Bliss had woken her up before he left. She wasn't happy, so he didn't bother telling her about how much fun they'd had with the pancakes. Maybe the kids would. Or maybe, in the wake of being abandoned once again, they'd already forgotten.

Rachel's parents lived a few blocks away. He hoped he wouldn't run into her father, rushing into the private car waiting to take him to the office, her mother strolling out for cappuccino and croissants with one of her friends. Her father still hadn't called to say how he felt about Rachel's performance. She took that as a form of chastisement. On the other hand, they hadn't gotten a call from his lawyer telling them the will was changed.

"Come on," Ward said. "We've got to hurry."

Ward led them into a posh lobby and gave his name to the doorman, who directed them to the rear elevator. They got in.

"When was the last time you were scared?" Ward asked him as they rode up.

"I can't remember."

"Try. I need a little performance from you. Some Method acting. Think about the older brother with the shotgun."

They'd been investigating the murder of a twelve-year-old boy. Someone was after his older brother but they'd shot the kid instead. He was lying on the living room couch in his pajamas, the remote control on the floor by his outstretched hand. Bliss and Ward were looking around when they heard behind them the distinctive sound of a shotgun being racked. The older brother had come in through the fire escape, saw the two cops, saw his dead brother, and figured they'd done it. Ward talked him out of it, convinced the guy that someone else shot his brother, at which point the guy sprinted past them and out the door. Later that day they were investigating a double shotgun murder and had an APB out for the older brother. But when he'd heard that shotgun sound behind him, Bliss had definitely been scared.

They got out of the elevator. Ward knocked on a door.

"First look tough," Ward whispered. "Then when I say 'back off,' act scared. Okay?"

Before Bliss could ask what was going down, a kid answered the door. Twelve-, thirteen-year-old boy. Prep school shirt and tie.

"Go get your pa, sonny," Ward barked. It sounded like a line from *Shane*. The kid turned pale.

"Who is it, Byron?" called a voice from inside the apartment.

Ward snarled. "Get him! Quick!"

"Dad!" the kid shouted. Panicked.

The old man came rushing out. Pinstripe suit. Power tie. Still in his socks. He walked right up to Ward.

"Hey!" he shouted. "Who in the heck do you think you are, coming to my house?!!" Spittle speckling Ward's cheek.

Bliss cringed, waiting for a patented Ward right cross to turn the guy's nose into a bloody spigot.

"We just want to negotiate," Ward said

"Negotiate?! You want to negotiate?" The guy working himself up, his voice getting higher. Into falsetto land. In a second
he'd need a falsetto teeth. "You want to negotiate with me, you
can . . . can . . ." He seemed to lose the flow for a second, like he'd
forgotten his lines. "You can . . . call me in my office! That's it.
You don't come to my home! Where I live! Where my family
lives."

Bliss could see the wife and daughter peeking from behind
the kitchen door.

Ward put up his hands. "Okay, man. Back off."

But the guy kept coming, picking up steam.

"You want me to back the heck off!?"

"Yeah. Please. Back off." Bliss had never heard his partner say
"please" before. Then he felt an elbow in his side. "Back *off*,
man," Ward said, pointedly.

Shit. His cue.

Bliss cleared his throat. "Yeah. Please, man. Be cool." It was
dumb, but sounded right. Bliss wondered what was going on.

"I'll be cool!" the guy shouted, "as soon as you get your butts
out in the street where you belong!!"

He slammed the door.

"What the . . .?"

Ward hushed him. "Wait till we get outside," he said.

The rode down in silence. Once outside, Ward burst out
laughing.

"Academy Award time, partner. Shit."

"You mind filling me in?"

"That's Byron Senior. My cousin's wife's brother-in-law. I met
him last month at Buddy's wedding."

"The one on the boat."

"Yeah," Ward said. "Anyway, he finds out I'm a cop, he makes
me this proposition. He doesn't want Byron Junior thinking he's
some kind of wimp, you know, because he's just an accountant.
So he says he'll give me two hundred bucks to show up at his
door and let him yell at me."

"To look tough in front of his kids."

"Yeah. Almost a day's pay. In cash. So whattaya say to some blintzes for breakfast? I know a nice place down in Brighton Beach."

There used to be a sign on the Brooklyn Bridge Bliss remembered as a kid. "Welcome to Brooklyn" it said. "America's Fourth Largest City." It took a couple of explanations from his father before Bliss finally understood that the Borough of Brooklyn, by itself, was bigger than every city except Chicago and the rest of New York. But now the sign was gone and most of Brooklyn's luster was gone with it.

The new Brooklyn was a great mystery to Bliss. And one corner of that mystery was Brighton Beach, the Russian section, sometimes called Little Odessa. Bliss used to have an aunt who lived there when it was primarily a Jewish neighborhood. She walked along the boardwalk in a crazy pink rubber hat and floppy white rubber sandals. He was pretty sure he'd seen some girl dressed the same way the other day in the East Village. Or maybe it was a boy. Now most of the older Jews were gone and Brighton Beach was a lively, sometimes volatile, Russian community. He'd heard some talk around the precinct about the lawlessness, how the Russian mob, or several factions of it, were vying for power.

It was a long ride, past Bush terminals, so crucial to sending supplies overseas in WWII, past the Verrazano Bridge, past Coney Island, home of Nathan's, where his father used to take Bliss and his mom for hot dogs and corn on the cob. He closed his eyes as Ward drove and thought about the dead plastic surgeon and the girl, wondering if there were any similarities between their murders and Elena's. The girl didn't have any cuts on her like Elena, yet it was very possible that she was also Russian. Ward pointed out that she had the vaccination mark, and the trail of panties seemed to be leading to the same place. Maybe something would develop. It would help if they could ID the girl. So far, there were no missing persons reports fitting her description.

He tried to think about the case, about Elena, but he kept

going back to the accountant putting on the show of toughness for his kids. Because his father had done the same kind of thing for him many years ago. Only when Monty the cop put on the show, it was for real.

It was a guy named Henry. Bliss knew because Henry's wife or girlfriend called his name repeatedly, to come away when Monty got out of the car. Just walk away, Henry, she said. He's crazy. This guy (Bliss's father) is crazy. I have a right to walk here! Henry shouted. It's a free street! His father didn't say anything. Henry's girlfriend continued to pull on Henry's sleeve, sensing trouble. Henry, please, she said. Lenny heard it all from the car, which his father had to stop suddenly and unexpectedly in the middle of the block because Henry felt he needed to cross the street right there. His dad blew his horn. Henry flashed the finger. His dad got out of the car, not talking. Lenny knew he had a gun under his Yankees jacket. Another in his ankle holster. He wasn't sure what was going to happen. C'mon, Henry, the woman said. He's nuts.

Fuck you, Henry says to his dad.

His father hit Henry first in the belly. There was no big windup like in the movies. It was more like he was reaching in quickly to pull out a plug from Henry's stomach, but the force was so extreme, Henry immediately doubled over and began retching. The woman started screaming. I told you, Henry! You fuckin' idiot! I told you! His father hit him again directly in the nose, which lifted Henry's head up. Through the windshield Lenny could see the nose mashed to one side like it was made of clay. His father then grabbed Henry by the hair, led him off the street, and threw him into a chain-link fence the same way Lenny had seen him throw garbage bags to the curb on pickup day.

The woman was now screaming at his father. I'll get you, you fuck! You crazy bastard! I've got your license! His father looked at her with such deep contempt, a look that until that point Lenny thought his father reserved only for his mother, that the woman shut up. His father got back into the car, put it in gear, and drove off. He'd never said anything. He wasn't even breathing hard.

This happened when he was about thirteen years old. Looking back on it, Bliss figured this little show was what he got instead of a bar mitzvah. His dad's way of letting him know it was time for Lenny to be a man. And while his friends were putting their savings bonds in a safe place and writing thank-you notes for the staplers and the Webster's dictionaries, Bliss was lying awake long into the night, seeing Henry's broken nose, hearing the woman scream her obscenities, watching his father over and over again, as if it was a movie projected on his ceiling, his hand dug into Henry's scalp, holding him at arm's length because, Lenny realized after replaying the scene for the twentieth time, his father didn't want to get his clothes dirty by having them splattered with Henry's blood. His father, holding another person like you would a leaking cup or a soiled diaper.

And maybe that was his initiation, his being bar mitzvahed not into the synagogue, but into a more exclusive community: the cops. For he knew he looked at the world differently after that incident. Saw the mean in people, the violence. In his dad. In himself. And although this moment had profoundly shaped his life, he had never told Rachel about it. He'd kept it to himself, feeling somehow his dad wanted him to keep it secret, just between them. But now he was thinking maybe it was better to tell someone, spill the beans before he started putting on shows like that for his own kids.

The BQE started slowing down as usual before the Verrazano. They still had a half hour, so Bliss leaned his head against the window and tried to sleep.

Johnny finished his eggs and kasha and downed the last of his coffee. He laid two grubby dollars on the counter. His last two singles. The three grand he had in his pocket was all in hundreds. He also had the plastic surgeon's pinkie ring and Rolex, which, he hoped, would make up the balance of what he owed the Bear. He also wanted the doctor who took his nipple off to check the stitches. They were starting to itch.

Malcolm opened the door and led Johnny into the main room of the St. Petersburg. Chairs were stacked on all the tables except one up front near the dance floor where the Bear sat alone, having breakfast. Johnny took a chair across from him. Malcolm stood to the side. The little doctor was nowhere to be seen. Probably making a house call.

The Bear had a napkin tucked under his chin, eating blueberry blintzes and savoring each bite.

"These are fresh blueberries. From New Zealand. None of that canned crap." He sipped his glass of tea. "So, Johnny, what are you having for me?"

Johnny took out the wad of hundreds and placed them on the table.

"Nice," the Bear said.

Johnny took out the ring and watch.

"This I don't care for," the Bear said. "Watches, rings usually coming with limbs attached."

"I found them in the back of a cab," Johnny said. He was feeling a little more brazen, sensing maybe the Bear was starting to like him.

"What am I, pawn shop?"

"I thought you needed a watch."

"I got a watch," the Bear said.

"Yours is set to Moscow time. This one tells time in America."

Malcolm started to laugh, then thought better of it. The Bear glared at his "muscle," then his face softened.

"How much cash is there?" the Bear asked.

"Three thousand," Johnny said.

"Malcolm, you need a watch to be telling time in America?"

Malcolm raised his sleeve.

"I got one," he said.

"Johnny Tolstoy," the Bear said, "you have cousin could maybe use nice watch?"

"Sure," Johnny said, trying not to smile, trying to be cool while being accepted by the man who owned him.

"How about ring?" the Bear asked

"I wanted to give it to the doctor," Johnny said. "Thank him for the nice job he did sewing me up."

This time the Bear laughed and Malcolm joined in.

Johnny smiled. Then he noticed the cash was no longer on the table.

"So I guess we are being even now, Johnny. Even Steven, like they are saying in America. Paid in the full. This means now you can be working for me. Like you are supposed to be doing in first place."

"It would be an honor," Johnny said.

"Kid is learning fast, eh, Malcolm? How about some tea?" He shouted to the kitchen. "Irina! Bring tea and make another pan blintzes!" He turned back to Johnny. "Irina is fabulous cook. I get entire family out of Russia. Six Jews. Not so easy. So she works for me while her children driving cabs and learning English. When they are getting ten grand together they can buy her back and move to Israel. Meanwhile, Irina gets to cook with fresh blueberries and have Friday dinner with her family."

The Bear was offering him blintzes. Johnny felt good.

"So, I am wishing to put you to work for me, Johnny. You like this idea?"

"Yeah."

" 'Yeah,' he says. Like an American. Johnny, I hear you like to tell jokes. Maybe once a week you come to the club. Tell funny jokes."

"They're the best kind."

"But not Russian jokes, about lines for food and how KGB has microscope up everybody's assholes. Tell jokes about America. Where we live *now*. Tell jokes with the three guys. You know, three guy jokes—the Polack, the Italian, and the Jew. The Negro, the Catholic, and the Jew. The Indian, the WASP, and the Jew. The priest, the minister, and the rabbi. Real American jokes. With 'yeah' in them. Say it now."

"Yeah."

"Again."

"Yeah!"

"I like that! Now, Johnny, I am wanting you should meet someone. This is Iris." She was sitting so quietly in the chair by the wall Johnny hadn't noticed her. "Iris not her real name, but I am giving her this name because she is delicate, like a flower."

Her head was bowed. Johnny got up and stood over her. He put his finger under her chin and tilted her face toward him. She was delicate, all right. She also seemed intelligent. Like Elena. Maybe she could get things running smoothly again. Johnny could take a few ads out, like he used to—*New York* magazine, maybe *The Village Voice*, too. "Russian Princess will make you feel like a Czar." Take his share and give his percentage to the Bear. Then maybe things wouldn't be so complicated. They might even be easier. Less worries. He could get back to his performing. Start writing the material for his old woman act.

"Say hello Iris," the Bear said. "Say hello to Johnny Tolstoy."

"Hello, Johnny," she said

"Johnny is funny guy," the Bear said. "He is taking care of you from now on. He taking good care of all his girls."

She reached out her hand and Johnny shook it. Her grip made him wince. Her hands were like rocks. She had two curious scars, one by her cheek, one by her eye. But instead of turning him off, they made her very attractive. Very alluring.

She smiled at Johnny, and suddenly he felt a great sense of relief. That everything was going to be all right. That everything was actually going to be all right.

Bliss and Ward were each biting into one of Avram's knishes—
"Best in Brighton Beach." Ward had the cherry-cheese, Bliss the
blueberry.

"Of course it's fresh blueberries," Avram said, hand over his heart.

"Avram," Ward said, "no offense, but the only fresh blueberries around now are from New Zealand and they cost per
blueberry what you charge for a knish."

"I do it for my customers! I love them! I lose money on every
sale," Avram shouted.

"Then how do you stay in business?" Bliss asked, picking up
his cue.

"Volume!" Avram said.

Post-blintzes, they walked together under the elevated
tracks. The train thundered overhead. The road was a patch-
work of sunlight bleeding through the tracks.

"For two detectives investigating one of the crimes of the
decade," Bliss said, "we don't seem in much of a rush."

"No one cares about the crimes anymore, it's the *trials* everyone remembers."

"Still, the *Post* and the *News* are going to go apeshit with this
thing tomorrow," Bliss said. "It'll be interesting to see how they
play the girl."

"Make her out to be a paid whore, and the neighbors breathe
a little easier. 'It wouldn't happen to *our* family. My husband
doesn't go to prostitutes. At least, he doesn't bring them home.' "

"They play it up as a simple robbery, then all the Park Avenue
socialites panic."

"The safe deposit box vaults will be hoppin' tomorrow," Ward
said. "Everyone storing their valuables."

"Then they'll put signs on their front doors like the 'No Radio'
signs in their car windows. Only these will say 'No Jewelry.' "

"'No Liquid Assets.'"

"'Nothing of Value, But You Can Take Our Children for a Week So We Can Go to Italy By Ourselves.'" His kid Julia used to tell him and Rachel how glad she was they didn't go on long trips and leave her behind like her friends' parents did. Now she'd probably be happy if they sailed off in a hot air balloon for eighty days. Or at least if *he* took off.

"They ID the girl yet?" Bliss asked his partner.

"Nope. The tag on her toe is still blank."

"So let's see what Sylvie has to say about all of this."

They walked another block until they came to Sylvie's Lingerie. A little bell over the door announced their entrance. Sylvie was a frail, hunched woman in her seventies. She wore a bright red wig and even brighter lipstick, which defined the general vicinity of her mouth. She moved toward them like Gretsky toward an open net.

"You vant I should show you something in an extra-large?"

Bliss looked at his partner, who for once had nothing to say.

"Don't be shy with Sylvie," Sylvie said. "All the boys come by me. I have the exclusive clientele. Doctors. Lawyers. Firemen. Professional tennis stars. You needn't be embarrassed. So, tell me, vich of you vears the panties in the family?"

Ward gently slipped his hand into Bliss's and gave a quick, sly nod in his direction. Sylvie looked Bliss over and gave him a maternal smile.

"So, vat are you, honey, a forty-two long?"

Bliss snatched his hand away.

"We're police officers," he said.

"Oh. You're police," said Sylvie. "You know Detective Sullivan? He's a regular."

Ward burst out laughing. Bliss put his arm around Sylvie's shoulder.

"Sylvie, darling, we're here because we found a young woman murdered this morning who was wearing a pair of underwear that had your label in it."

"Vat style ver they?"

"I don't know."

"Ver they the Raleigh? If they ver cut high, then they ver Raleighs."

"You're the expert," Bliss said to Ward. "Were they cut high?"

"Pretty high."

"By the crotch, vas their lace or vas there cotton?" Sylvie said.

"Lace."

"If there vas lace, then they ver Fountainbleaus." But if they had a lower cut, then they ver Diplomats. That's my three styles."

"I think they were Fountainbleaus."

"Vat color?"

"Black."

"So vat did she look like? Vas she a shiksa? You know from shiksas?"

"Her hair was blond," Ward said. "But I don't think it was natural."

"Then she vas Russian. How old?"

"Twenty-two, maybe."

"Did she have any tattoos?"

"No."

"No tattoos. Mmmmmm. She wore black Fountainbleaus and no tattoos. Doesn't ring a bell."

Bliss had a flash.

"Sylvie, have you sold any of these to any men who said they were buying them for someone else—a girlfriend, maybe?"

"Vel, a lot of them *say* they are buy them for their girlfriends, but Sylvie knows better. But there was a fella came in here. Strange. A little *meshuga.*"

"Crazy how?"

"Nervous," she said. "Like Barney Fife. You know, on *Andy Griffith Show.*"

"What did he look like, the guy who came in here?" Bliss asked.

"Short hair. Like you see on a soldier."

"What color?"

"Black. I think he put shoe polish in it. Like Reagan."

"Was he short? Tall?"

"Medium."

"He buy anything else?" Ward asked.

"Matching brassieres."

"What size?"

"Vat size? Tventy bras I sell a day. I should remember vat size?"

"It's important," Ward said.

She looked through a shoe box full of papers. All tossed together. She put on a pair of glasses taped together at the bridge and rummaged inside.

"Maybe this," she said, holding a receipt. "Three pairs Fountainbleaus. Three matching bras. All size thirty-four B."

"He pay by cash?"

"Everyone does."

"Where's Olga's?" Bliss asked.

Sylvie's eyes flashed. "Vat do you need by Olga's?"

"We have to talk to her."

"I have everything Olga has, only better quality. Olga sells seconds. Discontinued items. X-ed out. She can't fit correctly. Get a bra at Olga's, your cup runneth over. Okay, if you vant leopard panties? Olga has the spots. But after an hour doing the shimmy, they fall apart. So go. Go buy from Olga. You'll see. One vash, the lace frays. The vaistbands don't stretch. Her silk is really Dacron. I know. She changes the tags."

At Olga's they got the same general description of the man— early twenties, wiry, nervous.

"A little *geshpenkt*," Olga said. "Like *meshuga,* only beyond."

Olga knew him with short red hair.

"Where does he live?" Bliss asked.

"Near here," said Olga. "But I don't know where."

"He ever have anything delivered?"

"Like I can afford a delivery boy?"

"Okay. He ever buy anything else?"

"No. Just panties and bras. Skimpy. He knew just what he wanted."

"What size?" Ward asked.

"Thirty-six B."

"Not thirty-four?"

"Definitely not."

"You know for sure?"

"Unlike some people in this business, whose name I won't mention, I remember what my customers buy. Unlike some people, whose cheap wig I likewise won't mention, I don't say nasty things about other people. And unlike Sylvie, whose name I hate to mention, I don't wear the panties for a few days myself, then put the tags back and stick them back on the shelf."

"Sylvie does that?"

"I'm not saying yes. I'm not saying no."

"If you see that man again, you'll call. It's very important." Bliss handed her his card.

"Anything to help, Officer."

"It's Detective."

"What do you make of it?" Bliss asked Ward between sips of borscht. They were sitting in a dingy luncheonette. An old woman with a babushka was at the stove, stirring six pots at once. She looked like she'd been there for five hundred years. The counterman, about sixteen years old, her son probably, with a heavy Russian accent, had taken their order. He wore an iridescent paisley shirt and looked like he was a permanent extra on *Dance Fever*.

"Like borscht, eh?" Then he cracked into a demented grin. Bliss thought how he could have sorted a week's paperwork using the spaces between the guy's teeth. Elena could have fixed him up with some braces, but she was dead.

"Yeah, two bowls of borscht," said Ward. "With potato and sour cream both. And a couple of bialys." Ward leaned his elbows on the counter and propped his head in his hands. "The guy's buying underwear," he said. "Uniforms?"

"Could be. One set for Elena, one for the dead girl with the plastic surgeon."

"I spoke to his secretary. She doesn't remember anyone with a Russian accent calling. By the way, you know how much it is for a nose job?"

"No."

"Try five grand."

"That for both nostrils?"

"Isn't one comedian in your household enough?"

"This Johnny Tolstoy. There's gotta be a way to find him," Bliss said.

They sipped their borscht.

"Better than doughnuts," Ward said.

"If he's a pimp, why can't we just talk to the right guy? Get an address. Trade something."

"We can't because these Russian Mafia characters are fucking crazy," Ward said. "It's not like Cosa Nostra, with the codes of honor and respect, all that shit. It's savage. They do whatever they want. They don't make deals. In Russia, they run the whole economy. You want to sell something, the mob distributes it for you, takes their cut, gives you your percentage. It's their version of an MBA. Cut off a few fingers and shoot someone in the head."

"How do you know all this?"

"I get around," Ward said. "You know who Proust was?"

"Proust? The writer?"

"Yeah. Frenchie writer stayed in bed all day in a cork-lined room. Did you know that?"

"What?"

"That his room had cork wallpaper to keep the sound out."

"Yeah. How'd *you* know?"

"Malikha told me."

"Yeah? What else did she say?"

"That I could have majored in semiotics if I'd gone to college."

"You know what semiotics is?"

"Yeah. It's like how Beethoven and Liberace and *The Man From U.N.C.L.E.* theme song are all the same."

"Anything else she tell you?"

"Yeah. That she won't sleep with me again until I find Dumpsterman and the psycho who killed the Russian girl. She's holding me personally responsible. Can you imagine that?"

"Ladies, do you worry about whether your husband is working too hard? I do. I really worry. My husband, the cop, he's been under a lot of pressure lately. Murders and robberies up the wazoo. It seems like every three minutes he's getting beeped about something. If I didn't know better I'd think all the lowlifes are conspiring against me. Then again, maybe they are. They probably have some kind of meeting, like they're planning a church bazaar or something. But instead of deciding who organizes the white elephant sale and who grills the hot dogs, they work out plans to ruin my husband's life. Plans like this:

"'Okay, our inside sources tell us Monday he and his wife made dinner plans. They even have a sitter lined up. Juan, at four-forty-five you hold up a Korean deli at gunpoint. That should keep him busy through dinner. Wife'll have to stay home, order Chinese take-out. Hopefully they'll still have to pay the sitter.

"'Tuesday, his oldest daughter's got a piano recital. Bernard, it's up to you. I want a B & E right in his own building. Not only does he miss the recital, but he worries about his kids every time he leaves the house.

"'Wednesday he has lunch with his father-in-law. The old guy's telling him how to invest his meager cop savings. That should be a humiliation enough, so everybody take Wednesday off.

"'Thursday, let's make him feel old, vulnerable. We can leave that to the Murphy brothers, the Terrible Triplets. I want simultaneous purse snatches. Synchronized and choreographed. Like a ballet. Three identical descriptions. Make him do some running around, get him out of breath. And Murphy boys, make sure one old woman is on the sidewalk with a broken hip. I want him to see his *mother* down there on the pavement. I want him to see *her* down there crying about a lost Social Security check and stolen photos of her grandchildren.

" 'Friday he was planning to go to the country with his wife. They're leaving the kids with the grandparents and going to a quiet little inn. Just the two of them. Paid in advance. Nonrefundable. So let's give him another dead girl in a Dumpster. Young and blond. Just like his daughter. So he works through the weekend. So he's up long into the night, checking his kids' beds every ten minutes, so he drives his wife mad with worry.'

"Thank you very much. You've been a wonderful audience. I could be paying someone a hundred dollars an hour to listen to this. Instead, you people pay me. Isn't America a great country? Good night."

"Rachel DA-vis, ladies and gentlemen. Rachel DA-vis!"

It was all happening too fast. After the Bear introduced him to Iris, he told Johnny he had another surprise. Malcolm handed him a box, and when Johnny opened it up, there it was—a purple tuxedo! (A tux! Like Dean! Like Sammy!) with matching bow tie and cummerbund, a white ruffled shirt (Tom Jones!), and shiny white patent leather shoes. The Bear wanted Johnny to start that afternoon. Being the greeter. Making the customers feel happy. "Like they've been invited to my home," the Bear told him.

And up until a few minutes ago that's exactly what he had been doing—greeting the guests, coursing through the crowd of the St. Petersburg like some huge and exotic tropical fish, so magnificent in its shimmering purple iridescence that all the other fish had to take notice. That's how he felt.

Because finally Johnny had a job in Show Business.

He met the customers at the door of the St. Petersburg restaurant and greeted them and made them feel special as only Johnny could. A little quip. Nothing personal. Nothing too cutting. Just a snappy remark to get their evening off to a jolly start and to take their minds off the fact that at the end of the night there would be several dozen drinks on their bill that they didn't order. The Bear thought they should give it a try. Like in the Catskills. The Bear had picked out the suit, the shoes, the ruffled shirt personally. And Johnny's life had turned around in one afternoon.

But what the Bear giveth, the Bear also taketh away. Suddenly, after only an hour on the job, poof, it was gone, like one of those dreams Daffy Duck has in the cartoon, it just disappears. And instead of shaking the men's hands, giving the women a peck on the cheek, Malcolm had him by the arm and was leading him through the kitchen down the stairs to the basement.

"Who were they, cops?" Johnny asked Malcolm about the two guys he saw talking to the Bear. Johnny noticed them just before Malcolm grabbed him by the arm, knowing they were cops because they looked more like cops than any cops he'd ever seen. And then some secret signal must have passed between the Bear and Malcolm. For even though there were a thousand reasons the cops could have been there that night, the Bear somehow knew it concerned Johnny, and that the fledgling greeter had to be whisked away.

"Cops is not problem," Malcolm said as they arrived in the basement. "But two of these cops Sascha not knowing. *That* is problem. The not knowing. It is nothing good when you are not knowing cops." He led Johnny through the long row of steel shelves that held the restaurant's supplies—huge sacks of onions and flour and potatoes (a million latkes), giant boxes of foil and plastic wrap, plastic jugs of red dye (for the borscht? They *dyed* the borscht?), large jars of Manischevitz schav (they didn't even *make* the schav?). "It is meaning cops are not from here," Malcolm said. "Maybe from Manhattan." It was the most talking Johnny had heard from him.

At the end of the aisle was a heavy wooden door. Malcolm opened it.

"Getting in," he said, pointing.

Johnny suddenly got a sharp pain where he had been denippled. A premonition pain. A bad feeling pain. But he walked into the room, and Malcolm closed the door behind him. Then he realized it was cold and that the room was really a huge refrigerator. He heard metal against metal outside the door and figured Malcolm was securing some kind of lock.

So there he was. Two minutes ago he was made in the shade, now he's in the deep freeze, banished to Siberia. He couldn't believe it. The Bear actually exiled him to Siberia. You see, you can take the boy out of Russia, but you can't take Russia out of the boy.

At least there was plenty to eat in this gulag. He picked up a five-foot salami, took out his stiletto, and cut himself a hunk. It was cold. Everything was cold. He pulled his collar up and held it tight around his neck. Tuxes didn't provide much warmth. He saw a few cans of beer wedged behind a large piece of meat that was just sitting on the floor (flanken for a hundred). The beers were probably hidden there by one of the dishwashers, stolen from the bar earlier in the evening. He popped one open. It was cold. What he really wanted was some hot tea. He wanted to be lying in bed with his brothers, rubbing up against his sister, warm and cozy, falling asleep with her tit in his mouth.

This was bad. Ushering Johnny away so quickly meant somehow the Bear knew—about Elena and Tatyana. Which meant that the Bear owned him, and any time the Bear was feeling pressure from the cops he could always give Johnny up. And provide witnesses, too, if the police needed them. Someone prepared to swear in court Johnny bragged to them that he killed Elena, Tatyana, the plastic surgeon. And the Bear would *shtup* somebody who knew somebody who could get a copy of the police report, so the "witnesses" would be primed with information that only someone at the scene would know—about the cuts on the body, about how he'd stabbed the doc through the pizza box, added proof that Johnny had been spilling the beans as only the killer could.

It could be happening right now. The cops could be putting the squeeze to the Bear. "Look, Sascha. We'll overlook the twenty thousand gallons of gas you passed through six dummy companies to avoid the sales tax. Just give us the guy who gave the plastic surgeon the nose job." And then Malcolm would open the refrigerator door and shove an apple in Johnny's mouth and lay him on a giant platter with parsley all around him, and carry him upstairs and place him at the feet of the cops. Then the Bear would say, "Here you are, fellows. Now can I get you something to wash this down with?"

Johnny stabbed a pickle out of a barrel, took a bite, threw it back. He had to make a plan. This whole mess happened because he hadn't been able to make a plan.

So he planned. It had to be simple and it had to be now. His hands were shoved under his armpits. His toes were numb. First, get out of the walk-in. Then, go to Iris's apartment. Get her in with the Fat Man. Afterward, take the money, buy a ticket under his real name, which no one knew, not even the Bear, and fly to L.A., where he would start over again. Become an extra in the movies. Sinister backup to some bad guy. Uzi carrier. Switchblade producer. Hey, he could bring his own. Whip it out during the audition. Bring some reality to the part. He'd have to wait a while to be famous. Until things died down. Until his face on the cover of *People* wouldn't attract Kojak's attention.

Now he felt better. Now he had a course of action. He also had to take a piss. He looked around. He saw a pot marked "Chicken Soup." Right color. He pulled off the plastic wrap, stepped back, and let go. Steam emanated from the pot as his piss hit the layer of fat on top of the soup, melting a hole like someone would use for ice fishing. As he finished up, he thought how he was doing the Bear a favor. They'd get an extra bowl out of that pot tonight, and the crowd of drunken Russians eating there would never know the difference. He zipped up his fly and replaced the plastic wrap. They'd probably think it tasted better.

Then the door opened and a Mexican dishwasher charged in, his direct path to his stashed beers blocked by a purple-tuxed demon.

"Madre de Dios!" the guy said, eyes popping out of his head. "Holy shit."

"Table for one," Johnny said. Then he shoved the guy out of the way and started looking for a back door.

On the way over to the St. Petersburg restaurant, Bliss and Ward were getting the lowdown on the Russian mob from Mickey Sheehan, one of the detectives who worked out of Brighton Beach.

"You got a little of everything here," Sheehan said. "You know, we all grew up thinking Russia was one big happy Commie theme park, but really they got all these different regions and ethnic groups that have hated each other for centuries, and the thing that kept them all in line was fear of Stalin and poverty."

"That's pretty intelligent, Sheehan," Bliss said. "You been reading a book this year, or what?"

"They had some chick from Brooklyn College over at the precinct to talk to us. Sensitivity training. She was Indian or Pakistani or something. Wore one of those colored robes and had a red dot in the middle of her forehead. I didn't figure her for no Russian expert."

"So do you feel more sensitive now?" Ward said.

"Fuck no. These Russians are all crazy. The men all think they're John Travolta and wear these psychedelic polyester shirts with huge collars which stink after five minutes in the summer and you can't walk within ten feet of them. And the women all wanna be Jayne Mansfield, so they die their hair blond and sport these push-up bras and tight shirts."

"And the mobsters?"

"Craziest you ever run across. Some are ex-KGB. Some are just plain criminally insane. And some are Jews. They're the craziest of all. It's like they're single-handedly trying to undo the wimpy Jewish intellectual rap."

"What about Bar Kokhba?" Bliss said.

"Huh?"

"He was a great Jewish warrior."

"What he do?" Sheehan said. "Singlehandedly defend the Hamptons from the Philistines?"

"Yeah, Mickey, something like that. Anyway, this guy we're going to see now, he's like the John Gotti of Brighton Beach."

"No. You see, it doesn't work that way. The whole gentleman, Dapper Don, Mafia code thing, none of that goes on down here."

"The Don don't flow quietly through Brighton Beach?" Bliss said.

"Huh?"

"Never mind."

"Anyway, Bliss, like I'm trying to tell you, it's random. No one's really in charge. One guy gets a block for himself and holds on to it, his whole world revolves around those streets. They're not really upwardly mobile. It's more horizontal. And there's none of that respect thing, either. You see, Russia, the whole country, was really run by the KGB. Then, when Pere-tricycle comes in, the government falls apart."

"*Perestroika.*"

"Yeah. Whatever. Anyway, these crazy KGB guys are used to having absolute power, so they just kind of take over. And without the Commies watching over them, they're not really accountable to anyone anymore. From what I understand, they took over the whole Russian economy."

"I heard that, too," Bliss said.

"They shoot people out here?" Ward asked.

"Sometimes," Sheehan said. "But out here it's more like they trim people up to keep them in line. A little bit at a time. Like the pig with the wooden leg. You know that story, Bliss?"

"No."

"Oh, that's right. Your wife only tells jokes about fucked-up cops."

"Lay off."

"Yeah. Sure. Anyway. This farmer has this pig with a wooden leg. Keeps it in a special pen. A reporter visiting the farm asks him about it. 'That pig is very special,' the farmer says. 'Saved my life more than once.'

" 'Whattaya mean?' the guy says.

" 'Well,' the farmer says, 'once the tractor turned over and pinned me down. Well sir, that pig of mine grabbed my overalls in his teeth and pulled me out. And another time the house caught fire in the middle of the night and me and the missus would've burned up sure, but that pig came in and woke us up.'

" 'That's quite a pig,' the reporter says. 'But how did he get the wooden leg?'

" 'Well,' says the farmer thoughtfully, 'a pig like that you don't eat all at once.' "

Sheehan laughed and snorted and his face turned bright pink.

"Hey, Mickey," Ward said, "how come they got a Mick like you working down here with all these Russians?"

Mickey looked at Ward incredulously, then spread his arms out to his sides like he was measuring a huge fish.

"Who else they gonna get?" he said.

Once he and Ward met Sascha the Bear, Bliss could see right away what Sheehan was talking about, the difference between the Russians and the Italians. The Bear was big and soft and, in keeping with his nickname, exuded more of the feeling of a stuffed animal than anything ferocious. His smile was huge, like he wanted to sell you something that was going to make you really happy. A swell toaster, for instance. Or the Lord. He didn't have that chest thing the Italians did, puffing it out like pigeons, marking their territory like they were in some kind of *National Geographic* special, intimidating any other males not of the genus *Mafianus*.

"Bliss!" the Bear shouted, after Sheehan introduced him. "I never before hear of such a name for cop." He pronounced it "Blees." "In Russian we say *radost*. It is meaning 'great joy.' Tell me, Blees, you find much great joy on the job?"

"Oh there's plenty around, if you know where to look."

"I stand outside Catholic girls' school. At three-fifteen they appear in their skirts. Best in winter. Skin on legs is pink from cold."

"I knew you looked familiar," Bliss said.

The Bear's laugh roared over the din of the restaurant. He grabbed Bliss's hand, which practically disappeared inside the Bear's huge paw as he shook it. "Bliss is maybe short from Blitzstein?"

"Yeah," said Bliss. "They did it to my grandfather at Ellis Island."

"I land at Kennedy. They leave my name alone. Then I take bus to subway, then subway to here." Again the big laugh, the kind you heard from a favorite uncle at Thanksgiving. But there was something unsettling about it. "So, Bliss, shortened from Blitzstein, you have only German blood in you?"

"My mother's father was from Minsk."

"Ahh. This is good. Minsk blood is good blood. Brave. Close to Ukraine, so you get strength, but not *too* close, so you don't get stupidity."

"That's Lenny in a nutshell," said Sheehan.

"What does it mean, this 'nutshell'?" the Bear asked.

"It means," replied Sheehan, "that you could put it on his tombstone—Brave and Not Too Stupid."

Again the Bear laughed, and Bliss figured out what was bugging him. His eyes didn't crinkle. The mouth opened, turned up at the corners the way it was supposed to, and the noise came out, but the eyes were somewhere else, were focused on something of extreme seriousness. A mission: the relief pitcher protecting a one-run lead; the heart surgeon, in whose hands someone would live or die. Bliss had dealt with men like this before. Men who felt they could determine other people's fates, that they could decide between life and death. These were dangerous men. A pig like that you *do* eat all at once, get the chops in the frying pan, the butt in the oven, the hocks cooking in some pea soup, because if you leave him only crippled, give him any kind of a second chance, he'll creep into the farmhouse and cut your heart out.

"So, Bliss, what do you think of my restaurant?" the Bear asked. "Not bad, eh? It being quiet tonight, but on weekend, six hundred people come here. Mostly from Russia. They are singing and dancing, like they are at wedding, only it is better because there are no in-laws."

The band was blaring from the stand, wild up-tempo Russian dance music. Organ, accordion, and balalaika, a weird combo. But it was a weird place. Long tables filled with vodka bottles and smoldering cigarettes. Ashtrays overflowing. And the smell of sweat and alcohol was heavy. Bliss couldn't imagine Elena here, vodka in one hand, cigarette in the other, like most of the Russian women. She'd be home instead. Reading to her kids. Combing their hair. Besides, why would she want to see these people when she'd been in their mouths all day, cleaning cigarette stains dark as India ink, pulling teeth from gums soft as putty.

"Many here are laughing for first time," the Bear said. "Everyone together. Not like home. Here, come people from across Soviet Union—From Moscow, Leningrad, the Volga, the Caucasus, Black Sea, even Vladivostok. Everyone together. Even the Jews. No one in their lifetime thinking this is possible. But in America, anything can happen. In America, a Russian can sing and dance to Russian music. Wonderful, no?"

"Yeah. It's great," Bliss said. He gave Sheehan a look. No more chatter. Time to get things going.

Sheehan cleared his throat. "So listen, Sascha," he said, "Bliss works Homicide in Manhattan. Recently he found two Russian girls."

"Were they lost?"

"Can the herring. They were murdered and they were turning."

"Mickey, dear, excusing me, but if they are murdered, how can they be turning?"

"Tricks! Turning tricks. They were pros. Hookers."

"If they are turning pro hooker tricks, Mickey, why should I know anything about it?"

"Cut the shit, Sascha. We know you're working most of the girls in Brighton Beach. And we also know that if anybody else tries to do the same thing, they wind up losing weight the quick way. So maybe if you can help us out on this, I'm willing to look the other way around here for a while. Keep those cute Russian girls employed, if they can't find jobs as nannies for rich Upper East Side assholes."

"You forgot to say 'Jewish' assholes, Mickey," Bliss said.

"Fuck you, Bliss. Look, I got shit to do. I introduced you to two Russian princes, now work it out yourselves. Maybe you'll find out you're related. Then you can get drunk and roll down the street arm in arm puking and singing Russian songs and then I'll arrest the both of you."

With that Sheehan split. Ward wandered over to the bar, started talking to the bartender.

"This is a small man," the Bear said to Bliss, shaking his head. "Very fearful and simpleminded. He would have been good KGB."

"Except he hates vodka."

"So did KGB. For them, only Johnny Walker Black." And again the volcanic laugh. "So, there were some girls murdered."

"One strangled. The other with her throat cut. "

The Bear mulled this over. Bliss watched. Most people don't have a place to put this kind of information. But the Bear seemed to have a cubby for each, with room for more.

"There were *two* girls," he said.

He seemed surprised. By what? The act itself? Not this man. By the number, maybe. As if it was something he should have known about. He shook his head.

"The problem is they expect too much coming here. They think to just show up to America and money and happiness land in lap."

"Yeah. And when it doesn't, they let something else in their lap."

"This could be. But Detective, what Sheehan is saying about me, this prostitution, it is not so the truth. This"—he gestured expansively to the restaurant—"this is everything to me. Italians they have for front, restaurant, to laundry their money. But for me, restaurant is *life*. Is *people!* True, it make me rich man, rich like small town in Russia. I can buy Minsk, but who wants Minsk? Who wants poor, dead Russian city when you have every night here dancing and music and laughing and people eating and smoking cigars? Russian people dead for century. They come here and wake up."

"Look, Sascha," Bliss said, "we think the same person killed these two girls and one plastic surgeon. The papers will be playing this up big. The plastic surgeon had his nose cut off. The headlines will be 'Plastic Surgeon Gets Nose Job!' That means the mayor and the commissioner are going to get involved, which means everyone's going to get the screws put to them. If you know something, anything at all, I'd start talking. I'm sure if the IRS thought there was enough in it for them, they'd bring someone down here who spoke Russian. And it'd be a shame if all this laughter came to a sudden stop."

"IRS worse than KGB," the Bear said. "After IRS through with you, they *don't* kill you."

"So you get the picture."

"Well, I will ask people who maybe know something about these girls."

"It'd be a good idea." Bliss noticed a huge individual trying to catch the Bear's eye. The guy had "muscle" written all over him. Bliss could read that, even if it was in Russian.

"I think your maître d' is trying to get your attention."

"Oh, he will wait. Wants me to unlock liquor. I only one with key." He laughed again, though now it was somewhat forced. "You want drink perhaps? Or soup? We have great chicken soup. Best in America."

"You know a kid named Johnny Tolstoy?"

"*Johnny* Tolstoy? You mean *Leo* Tolstoy."

Oh, he was good, Bliss had to hand it to him. He was *very* good, having it sprung on him and covering like that. Bliss had new respect for the Bear. He could see now why he had the kind of control he did.

"What?" he said, a flash of concern over Bliss's silence. "He is important, this Johnny Tolstoy?"

"I don't know. He may not even exist."

"Only Tolstoy I know is famous writer."

"Yeah. Well, *dasvadanya*, Sascha. Keep in touch." He left Winnie the Poohski with one of his cards and, he hoped, a lot to think about. Somehow, he doubted it.

Bliss and Ward were again stuck in traffic on the BQE just like the two thousand other people too cheap to shell out the three bucks for the Battery Tunnel, but Bliss didn't care.

"We should've gone through Brooklyn. Stopped on Atlantic Avenue for some olives at Sahadi's."

"He knew something. Did you feel it?"

"I felt it," said Ward. "Bartender said there was a guy there about a week ago sporting the Johnny Tolstoy look."

"The Bear knows him," Bliss said. "He was good. He didn't flinch. But behind his eyes, he knew."

Yes, the Bear knew something, but it would take extreme measures to get the fat blintz to talk. He was probably a veteran of at least one KGB interrogation. He knew how to keep secrets.

"That Sheehan's a piece of work," Ward said.

Bliss nodded. "He's probably on the front line keeping the gays from marching in the St. Paddie's Day parade."

"The Bear didn't seem too impressed with Mickey's offer."

"No tit for tat."

"That's because the Bear wants the tit *and* the tat."

"We need a way to get to the Bear," Bliss said. "Squeeze him a little. Get him to give up Tolstoy."

"Who do we know?"

"Nobody right now. But maybe something will come along."

"Some kind of Tchaikovsky," Ward said. "Crack that fat Russian's nuts for him."

"Yeah. A nutcracker," Bliss said. "Sweet."

Johnny was very pleased with the first step in this, his new plan. He was in Iris's apartment, and he was beginning to feel like he did with Elena. Cozy and safe. Iris, the girl the Bear introduced to him—*gave* to him, wanted to take care of everything. That's what she said. All she needed from Johnny is to be there in case of trouble and to square things with the Bear. She had told him this as they were leaving the Bear's restaurant. She had also given him a key to her apartment, saying she had a futon in the closet and he could stay there anytime, as long as she wasn't, you know, entertaining. He had no idea what a futon was, but he was definitely starting to feel like his luck was changing.

Iris's apartment was even nicer than Elena's. More stuff, like she planned on staying for a while. That was a good sign. He plopped himself down in a white canvas sling chair and kicked off his shoes. He felt like a free man. Because he had his plan. All he had to do was keep a low profile for the next couple of days, keep Iris working steady, and then he was out of here. Off to L.A. Watch where Iris kept her cash and take that, too. Split on the Bear. Fuck what he owed that fat son of a bitch. In a year he would probably be dead anyway, some young mobster even crazier than the Bear deciding *he* wanted to be head of the pimp politburo. By that time Johnny would just be making his name in Tinsel Town.

"You want me to call you Iris?" Johnny asked her when he first walked in. "Or Alexa?"

She looked a little startled. "Why Alexa?" she asked.

"The Bear said your name was Iris. But I noticed on your mailbox it said Alexa."

"Oh. Right. You want some herbal tea?" She smiled sweetly at him.

"Maybe later," he said. "So Iris is your working name. That right?"

"Yes. I need to think of myself as Iris. If that's okay."

"Yeah. Sure."

The only thing that bothered Johnny was that it didn't quite make sense. Any of it. The nice apartment, plush rugs, everything clean and white. It didn't seem like the home of someone who wanted to shut her eyes and think of faraway places while strange men rammed fingers and thick tongues and scrotums of unknown size and history into places that should have been private, sacred.

"You sure you don't want some herbal tea, Johnny?" And again that smile. Like an activities instructor in an old-age home. Maybe that was her secret. After a half hour with her the johns are weaving pot holders, crocheting doilies. Sunday afternoon they all come over the house for bingo. "I have some iced. It's very soothing."

"No. That's okay. I'm plenty soothed." And why is she looking at me like I'm some kind of lost puppy? Jesus, she'll be giving me a hug soon.

"Where'd you get those scars?" he asked.

That stopped her. Keep the hugs at bay.

"I've had them since I was a kid."

"Mmmm-hmmm." He knew she was lying. What else? What else was she lying about?

"How'd you hook up with the Bear?" he asked her.

"It wasn't too hard," she said. "He's an easy man to find. Actually, I've been wanting to meet him for a while."

So she wanders into the St. Petersburg restaurant, asks for the Bear, says she wants to go to work, she needs money fast, and she doesn't mean as a waitress. It could happen. Wanting to cash in while she was still pretty. Still, he'd look around. Check a few closets, lift the mattress, open a few drawers. Figure out what was going on around here. Probably nothing. After all, what could this bitch have to do with me?

"Maybe I will have some of that herbal tea," he said. "And how about fixing me up a couple of eggs?"

"Ummm. I don't eat eggs. How about a tofu scrambler? You'll love it. Really. It's just like scrambled eggs. Yellow and everything."

"Whatever." She scurried off into the kitchen, seemingly happy to be taking care of him. Was she going to feel the same way when some Japanese businessman wanted to kamikaze his dick into her mouth? Maybe Mr. Sony would go for that tofu. He wished he could call the Bear, ask him what her story was, where she came from, but that was out of the question. In the meantime, he'd poke around.

He went through her bedroom into the bathroom and turned on the water in the tub. "I think I'll take a quick shower," he shouted. While the water was running, he started going through her dresser. He wasn't sure what he was looking for. Letters, maybe. A diary. Also, just for the hell of it, he might see if she had anything like jewelry or a stereo he could pawn on his way to the airport. Instead what he found were clothes folded with frightening neatness. He checked underneath each pile. Nothing hidden there.

A jewelry box held only long strands of beads, all of which looked pretty cheap. On the walls were pictures of Indian guys sitting with their legs crossed. Take away the weird designs in the background and stick a coffee cup in their hands and they could be sitting on Broadway begging for quarters. He took off his shirt, stuck his head under the shower for a second, then turned off the water.

"How's it coming?" he shouted.

"It's almost ready," she called back.

"Yeah. I'll be out in a minute."

He grabbed a towel and started drying his hair. Everywhere white. Even one of those furry toilet seat covers. Thick towels. Fancy soaps. She didn't seem to be hurting. Why suddenly does she want to be a working girl? Back in her room he checked the bookcase packed with books. Zen shit. Meditation. *I Ching*. He'd have to go through them later, fan the pages, see if anything fell out. But for now he'd give the tofu a try. Then maybe he'd see what Iris was made of, give her the nipple test, see how much she was willing to take. The key was whether he could get two sessions with the Fat Man out of Iris/Alexa, to speed up his departure. Maybe she liked it, the rough stuff. Maybe that's what this was all about.

A picture next to the door caught his attention. Actually, not the picture itself, which was a diagram of the "Properly Aligned Spine." No, what was curious about the picture was the inch-wide strip of wall around the frame that was a little bit whiter than the rest. It suggested to Johnny that another picture, slightly larger than the spine diagram, had hung there before. New York soot darkens your walls in a hurry, especially in the summer with the windows open. So she has taken down one of her pictures recently, Johnny thought. Now at least he knew what to look for. A picture, probably with glass, so she probably had it hidden somewhere safe.

When Iris opened the door with his food on a platter, he was just examining the photograph he had found in the back of the closet.

"So you knew Elena," he said.

She dropped the tray, further scrambling the scrambler and staining the white rug a rich, bright yellow.

Johnny looked at his late-night snack lying on the floor, then glanced up at Iris. "Well, that's too bad," he said. "I guess I'll just have to wait for another time to get my first taste of tofu." Then he slapped her across the face as hard as he could, just to get her attention.

"Blintzes, borscht, blinis, and babka," Julia said. "Does all Russian food begin with the letter B?"

The Bliss family was having dinner together—pizza from Garlic Bob's, half plain, half mushrooms and pepperoni. Julia was particularly interested in his day at Brighton Beach.

"And bialys, too," Bliss said. "Another B food."

"Why do they come here?" Cori asked. "What's wrong with Russia?"

"There aren't many jobs in Russia," Bliss said.

"So they come here to America to be furniture movers and taxi drivers," his wife said. "But in Brighton Beach, at least they live by the ocean. At least they can walk along the boardwalk."

"I want to go there," Julia said. "Will you take us for B food one night, Dad?"

"Sure." Bliss looked at his wife. "Did they tell you about the pancakes this morning?"

"Yes. They said they had fun."

"It was."

It seemed like a lifetime ago, pancake fun. Between his meals at this table, between breakfast and dinner, he had stood with his toes resting on the shore of a blood red lake, staring at a dead plastic surgeon, his nose now a divot in his face; he had walked the exotic streets of Brighton Beach, talking underwear and brassieres; he had dealt with Sheehan, backward Paleolithic prick of a cop who made Bliss's insides churn; and he had shaken hands with the Bear, a man with a chunk of solid evil tucked deep inside his soft body.

Then he and Ward had driven back home with the sullen realization that the case depended not so much on their will and cleverness but on the whim of this mad Russian who thought himself a colossus, and that those around him, including the police, needed to walk under his huge legs and peep about, looking for some crumb he might drop from his majestic height—a crumb like Johnny Tolstoy, for instance. And then the killer of Elena and the surgeon and the pretty young girl would be brought to trial. Some detective. Bliss was more a scavenger, a beggar, holding his hat on the sidewalk, waiting for the whim and generosity of a sociopath to help him do his job.

He looked up to see his children staring at him with great concern. Julia, her slice frozen halfway to her mouth, had a deep crease above her eyes. Her Daddy crease. He should autograph it for her one day. Cori was whimpering quietly. And Rachel, Rachel was reaching her hand toward his and covering it and gently stroking his fingers.

"You okay, Lenny?" she asked.

"Umm, yeah. I was just, you know, thinking about the pancakes. About breakfast."

He was also thinking that he had to go soon, to meet Ward at the Blue Note, to look through the charge receipts, because Dumpsterman needed to be caught. But he was afraid his family wouldn't let him go, that Julia would wrap herself around his leg, that Cori would grab hold of his hand. He shook the image loose from his head.

"Who wants Haägen-Dasz?" he asked.

He'd go after ice cream. Leaving was easier after ice cream. Something his father never knew about. It was at least a step in the right direction, away from Monty, toward he wasn't sure what. But it was definitely a step, even if it was just a small one.

Ward was waiting for him at the Blue Note. He introduced him to Malikha, who was sitting at the bar, an extremely beautiful black woman with very elegant round eyeglasses. Her picture alone on the book jacket would sell a lot of copies.

She and Ward had spent the last few hours going through the club's receipts looking for a Phil or Philip, the name Dumpsterman leaked to them. It was a long shot, but the man was reaching out to be caught, so they had to follow the lead. Not surprisingly, there were almost thirty Phils in the past two months.

"It wasn't hard finding them," Ward said. "Once you separated the Japanese names, there were only about a thousand we
had to go through. You know, it's expensive to hear jazz."

Half of the thirty Phils were ruled out for being large checks,
those generous Phils picking up the tab for the rest of the table.
They were almost certain their man would have been on his
own. Of the fifteen remaining, four were from out of town. Ward
had faxes of the drivers' license photos of the other eleven.

"A fistful of Philips," said Ward.

"A phalanx of Philips," said Bliss.

"A fillip of Philips," said Malikha, "as in something that
arouses or stimulates."

Bliss liked Malikha, and he hadn't even seen her in lingerie.

Ward had shown the bartender the faxes. A few were recognized as regulars, none of whom would sport a kelly green
blazer. They were waiting for the hostess to show up to see if she
recognized any of them as the man she saw on the phone. They
pulled up some stools at the bar and ordered cranberry juice.

"I don't think he's in here," Bliss said, looking over the faces
of the eleven Philips. "He wants to tease us, but he's not going to
make it too easy. Let's go over the receipts again. This time look
for a middle initial P."

They came up with ten. The bartender knew one, a longtime
fan now in his late seventies. The hostess, who arrived with just-
manicured hands and held her fingers stiffly posed like she was
casting a spell on the carpet, ruled out two more. That left seven.
Bliss asked to see the schedule for the last eight weeks and proceeded to nix three more who came to hear Joe Zawinul.

"A great player, but not Dumpsterman's bag."

"Dumpsterman?" Malikha asked incredulously.

"That's what Bliss dubbed him when he called. It seemed to
get him riled."

"He called?"

"Yeah. Once to the precinct. Once to my house."

"No shit. What'd he say?"

"He said basically 'Hi, I had nothing to do the other night so I
got a sandwich and went to the movies and killed a young girl

and stuffed her in a Dumpster and got a coffee and danish and then went home and got in my flannel jammies and went to bed. Oh, and by the way, please come catch me soon, because it's happening again, that bad thing inside me is waking up, turning over, stretching, wiping its eyes, throwing off the blankets. So come soon, come find me quick.' Something like that." Bliss realized he was showing off for Malikha the way he had for Rachel, when they were first together. It felt good.

After thinking hard for several minutes, scrunching up her face, and intermittently nibbling on two of her newly polished nails, the hostess drew a blank on the last three names.

"The three P's left in the pod," Malikha said.

"We can contact the DMV. Get the photos by tomorrow," Ward said.

"Or," Bliss said, "we can call Robin back in the Bat Cave."

He grabbed the phone and called his house.

"Julia, it's Daddy." Bliss ignored the snickering and continued. "We need some help to crack this case. Rev up the Mac and open up the big phone book on the CD-ROM."

In a few minutes Julia had numbers for all three.

"Thanks, kid. I'll be home in a little while." Bliss hung up. He was beaming. He expected Ward to say something, but perhaps tempered by Malikha, nothing came. "One lives in Greenwich, Connecticut," he said.

"Which?"

"Spencer P. Van Deusen."

"Save him for last," Malikha said.

The first two drew blanks. One had an English accent. The other had a resonant baritone and sounded like a late-night dee-jay.

That left Van Deusen.

Bliss took a breath, dialed, and recognized the voice as soon as he answered the phone. The lilt. The affected nasal languor. He threw his hand over the mouthpiece and mouthed "Dump-sterman." They were all frozen for a split second, then Malikha grabbed the phone.

"Yo, Corrine . . . What!!? . . . Well, is Corrine *there?!* . . . Yo, like don't be getting all hostile wit me . . . I know . . . I know, sir, but it's not like I *intentionally* called you. I don't *want* to talk wichoo. I *want* to talk with Corrine . . . Now watchoo have to go and say that . . . Well, fuck you too."

She slammed down the receiver. The hardness slowly drained away from her face.

"That's him, huh," Malikha said.

"It's the guy who made the phone calls, anyway."

"He wanted to be caught, right? I mean, that's why he gave you those clues."

"Yeah," said Bliss. "We did a good job, but we wouldn't have located him so quickly unless he wanted to be found."

Bliss could see the novelist at work, sorting this all out. Trying to wrap her mind around the act of murder. One man stuffing girls in a Dumpster. Another killing her friend Elena. What caused it, the crazy quilt of human desires that would lead someone to commit such a vile act and then compel him to want to be caught? Bliss watched as she tried to get into their heads, as he had tried to do many times before. Thinking there must be something in him, in each of us, some common pulse that could be tapped for an answer if you dug down deep enough, if you searched long enough. Answers to questions like, What started it? How does he live with himself? What does he feel when it's time? Hatred? Desire? Or something more? And then you realize that no matter how hard you try, you won't find it. Because the answer involves something none of us has even come close to. A tornado compared to the soft breeze blowing most of us through our lives. An orgasm of such blinding white self-loathing and pain that all he can do is . . . is what? Bliss saw a shudder pulse through Malikha's body and knew where she had gotten to. And suddenly the strong young writer looked helpless and pitiful, on the verge of tears. Just like a detective, he thought.

Johnny was mashing the tofu into the floor as he paced across Iris's room, more confused than ever. He looked at her, sitting cross-legged on the bed like one of the guru guys on the wall, holding a plastic bag filled with ice up to her cheek. She wasn't a happy camper.

"Who's going to want me now?" she asked him.

Maybe it was true, what she said. That she and Elena knew each other. That they'd lost touch and she had no idea Elena had been in New York.

"Really?!! In New York??! Elena??!"

Her surprise seemed genuine.

"Is she here now?"

"Not anymore," he added. "She's back in Russia, but not St. Petersburg. She went to a small village, a few hundred kilometers outside of Moscow. She's the only dentist and she's really happy. And I think she's even met somebody, you know, a man, a farmer, she was filling his cavity and well, you know."

Iris/Alexa or whoever she was started asking more questions and Johnny had to hold down his anger. He hated needing her. He hated relying on women. But he put on a good show, thinking that no matter what the true story was, if this one could give him two sessions with the Fat Man he'd have enough to leave town. He smiled.

"Well, at least Elena's happy," she said. "Working as a dentist. At least things worked out for *her*."

Which put an end to it. But Johnny couldn't help wondering why she took down the photo. That was the problem. Everything else seemed to fit. But the photo bugged him. Why take it down? Why hide it?

"I hadn't seen her for years," she said. "And I needed to put up that chart, for my massage patients, I mean, when I *had* any patients. And the chart just fit there, so I took the photo down and put it in the back of the closet. I didn't hide it. If I had hidden it, you wouldn't have found it, would you?"

Which he guessed made sense. But why didn't she ask him why he'd slapped her?

"I figured it was part of the job." She was in the kitchen area, lighting a match, setting a thin stick on fire. Incense. The room filled with a rich, exotic smell. "I mean," she said, "I didn't think it was like being a receptionist."

Then she did something really weird. She came behind him while he was sitting in the chair, walking very softly, and placed her hands on his shoulders and began massaging his upper back, running her fingers along his spine. He was desperate to believe her. Because if he did, then he could continue with his plan, which is what he wanted more than anything. Because he wasn't sure he could think of a new one. He was too tired. This one had to work out. So he'd watch her closely, proceed step by step, until he was on his way to the West Coast and Iris was . . . well, he wasn't sure yet where Iris would be. It depended on how things played out.

She was working on a knot just below his left shoulder, rubbing around it, over it, her fingers trying to ease out the tightness. He closed his eyes and, concentrating deeply, sent waves of condensed tension to the spot, to fight off her fingers, to double-knot the knot, triple it, make it impermeable to her efforts. He could sense her working harder now, frustrated, perhaps for the first time. He squeezed his eyes tight until he could see the muscle, feel the bulge grow, filling out under her hands, about to pop through the skin. She stopped, her arms falling to her sides. He smiled and spoke to her without turning around.

"Put some rouge on your cheek and get ready to go to work."

Johnny figured at that moment in New York there were at least a hundred thousand men who would pay to get laid. He just had to get in touch with five of them in the next two days. Meanwhile, he would get on the phone to the Fat Man, his ace in the hole, so to speak, and see if a double session was in order. The Fat Man wouldn't mind if Iris was a little bruised. He seemed to enjoy finding the girl's weak spot and insinuating himself into it.

As he dialed, he was thinking how if he had to hit Iris again, he'd rest the Yellow Pages on her head and then bang it with a hammer. A friend who had the shit kicked out of him by the KGB told him that's the routine they used—didn't leave any marks and generated a dull pain in the center of the brain that was extremely debilitating. Of course you could just pull the telephone book away and have done with it, but he was still two thousand dollars away from that proposition.

The Fat Man was very pleased to hear from him. Johnny could practically hear the guy drooling over the phone. Apparently Tatyana, for all her whining, had made a strong impression on him.

"She tinkled quaintly," he said.

Yeah, Johnny thought, and she was one of the first girls to even *find* your dick under all that flab, never mind do anything with it. When Johnny assured him this new one was an even more demure tinkler, he was positively giddy with excitement. Johnny set something up for that afternoon.

"This afternoon would be stupendous," the Fat Man said. "I'll have the deli send up some Evian right away." Then the Fat Man made his usual request. Johnny put his hand over the receiver and called across the room.

"Hey Iris, what size shoes do you wear?"

Bliss and Ward met Connecticut Trooper Drew Wilson at the Wilton Police Station. Trooper Drew looked like he might have been a high school football hero, with his crew cut and protruding muscles. The sleeves of his regulation short sleeve uniform looked like they were cutting off the circulation on his arms. He probably liked it. The local Boy Scouts' mouths dropping open whenever Trooper Drew came in the five-and-dime for some gum and a pack of Necco wafers. Trooper Drew was going to lead them out to the Van Deusen house, keep the city boys from getting lost on the narrow roads that wound through some of the most expensive real estate in the country.

Before they left, Trooper Drew took a few minutes to show them a new shotgun they just acquired, taking it out of the locked case and letting them feel the polished wood of the stock. Ward and Bliss politely took a turn putting it up to their shoulder.

"Nice weight," Bliss said.

"Great barrels," Ward said.

"We had to special order it. Been waiting six months. It's a beauty."

"Sure is," Bliss said. "Guys'll be lining up to get their asses shot off with this. You'll have to hand out numbers. Like at Zabar's on Sunday morning when everyone's getting their lox."

"Lox?" Trooper Drew looked quizzically at Bliss, then proceeded to carefully secure the rifle. Then he took a few more minutes to brag about some dates he'd had with Stacey, the oldest Van Deusen daughter, when they were in high school.

"This was in tenth grade," Drew said, puffing up his already massive chest. "Before she went to Miss Porter's School."

"Did you say tenth grade?" Ward asked him.

"Yeah."

"You still think about shit you did in tenth grade?"

"Hey, I guess I just started early," he said proudly, flashing a big, toothy grin. The kid obviously worked out, but strong as he was, he wouldn't last ten minutes working the streets in New York. After his first shift, he'd just stay in the car. Lock the doors. Eat at the drive-through McDonald's. Like Frederick Forest in *Apocalypse Now*—never get out of the boat, or you find yourself staring into the eyes of a mad, hungry tiger. So, never, never get out of the fucking boat.

"Stacey sure was some nice piece," Drew continued, looking to impress the Big City cops. "She was really hot. One time we got down to it on her daddy's pool table in the basement. Boy, she had some pair of gazooms, let me tell you. And she never wore a bra!"

Ward stepped drill-sergeant close to the kid and said, "I'd rather fuck the side pocket on that pool table than one of those rich white bitches," in his most octoroon voice, clearly emphasizing his roon over the octo. That shut Trooper Drew up.

"Follow me," he said, looking hurt that he wasn't being accepted by a fellow officer of the law. No pats on the back. No "way to go's." No fraternal winks. Bliss hoped he wouldn't start getting all morose on them. They followed the kid out to the parking lot and got in their cars. The trooper was necessary as a witness, to establish that they were at Spencer's house only for information, not to entrap him, not to gather evidence, just to let the man talk. Now Bliss was afraid Trooper Drew would sequester himself at the kitchen table with milk and Oreos and would be useless to them later. "Wasn't it true, Trooper Wilson, that you were downstairs in the basement at the time of Mr. Van Deusen's alleged 'confession'? That you were lying on the pool table, I believe, caressing the felt with your cheek, moaning softly in some kind of adolescent reverie?" "Yes, sir." "That will be all, Trooper Wilson. And before you step down, you may want to wipe that milk mustache off your top lip."

After driving several miles down twisting roads lined with one mansion after another, Trooper Drew slowed down and put on his blinker. You could only glimpse Van Deusen's house from the street because of the row of high hedges. But once they pulled through the majestic iron gate, however, Bliss could see how huge it was. Three stories, six chimneys, maybe a dozen bedrooms. Bliss expected a moat.

"It's got ten bathrooms," Trooper Drew's voice crackled over the police radio. He seemed to have his bravura back. "Stacey and I took a bath in one of them. It had jets on the side and solid gold faucets. Over and out."

"Never mind the bathrooms, partner," Ward said. "I want to see what's in the garage."

They parked in the circular drive in front of the house. Bliss and Trooper Drew walked up to the door. Ward went around back. Trooper Drew took off his hat and held it deferentially by his chest, like he was talking to a minister. Bliss rang the bell. The door was opened almost immediately by a girl who couldn't be more than sixteen. Sandy brown hair down past her shoulders, which she flicked off to the side. Wide, genuine smile when she recognized the trooper.

"Hi, Drew," she said.

"Hi, Lissy," Drew said back.

"Hey Drew," Lissy said, "I think you need a haircut."

He ran his hand over his bristled scalp and flashed the ol' toothy grin.

"Yeah," Trooper Drew said. "I guess maybe I do."

Bliss scoped trunk and duffel on the floor. Just back from camp. White T-shirt with "Thousand Pines" on the front. Ditto on the shorts. Daughter away all summer. Mean anything? Only that she looked like the girl in the Dumpster. Same age. Same large breasts. Who picked her up from camp? What car did they use?

"How's Stacey?" Drew asked.

"Oh, she's okay, I guess," Lissy said. "She's going with some real loser now. Writes poetry. Wears glasses. He even cooks. Nothing like you, Drew. I don't know what she sees in him." She winked at the trooper, who instantly blushed.

"Hey Lissy," said Trooper Drew, "is your daddy home?"

"Yuh. I think so." She gave a quick who's-the-lug-next-to-you nod in Bliss's direction.

"Oh, yeah. Lissy, this is Sergeant Bliss, from New York. He just wants to ask your daddy a few questions."

Her face grew suddenly hard.

"Questions about what?"

"Your father may know something about a murder that happened about a week ago," Bliss said. "He may have seen something."

"Oh."

"Can we come in?" She seemed worried. But then why not? Mr. Policeman came knocking on the door, wanting to talk with her father. Still . . .

"I guess you can come in. Maybe you should wait in the library. It's just . . ."

"I know where it is, Lissy," said Trooper Drew.

"Oh yeah. Well, it's still in the same place." She forced a laugh, then quickly went to get her father. Not calling him down, like if it was the plumber at the door, or UPS, but going to get him. To tell him something? Tell him what?

Bliss watched her turn and walk up the stairs. The railing was of deep, brown oak. The steps covered with plush Oriental carpeting. A stained-glass window ornamented the first landing, and when Lissy paused for a moment to glance furtively back at them, her face was bathed in gold. Yesterday he was walking through the dingy streets of Brighton Beach, surrounded by crowds of immigrants fresh off the plane, dark eyes wide with wonder and hope. Crowds everywhere, moving like a great dingy sea under the shadow of the train tracks. Today he was encircled by majesty. Bliss wondered if they knew about this, the newly arrived Russians of Brighton Beach. If they knew of these possibilities. That if you followed the Brooklyn-Queens Expressway long enough, it would lead you into heaven, a heaven of trees and circular driveways, dormer windows, rooms for every member of your family, and where your precious daughters would be bathed in golden light.

Trooper Drew led him to a study out of a Dickens novel. Dark wooden shelves up to the ceiling, with the ladders on wheels so you could get to the ones on top. Leather sets of Thackeray, Walter Scott, Trollope, Richardson, Victor Hugo—shit people had bound in fancy calfskin but never read. But Bliss wasn't interested in the books. Unless he saw some titles like *Strangling Made Easy* or *The Whole Body Disposal Catalogue* or *The Guide to Dumpsters in the Tri-State Area.* There was a large oak cabinet against the back wall that looked promising, however. Inside might be Spencer's music collection, which could shed some light on whether he was indeed alias Dumpsterman, jazz aficionado.

"Hey, are you sure you should open that?" said Trooper Drew. "I mean, we're just supposed to be talking to him."

"I'm afraid your memories of the good times you had in this house have dampened your powers of observation, Drew," said Bliss, tilting his head sideways so he could read the names on the albums. "I didn't open anything. This cabinet was very much ajar when we got here. Anyway, you seem to have no problem poking your fingers in the Van Deusens' drawers. Right, Trooper?"

Trooper Drew drew a blank on that and sat in a chair in the corner, sulking. Bliss figured he'd given him one more reason not to go to New York. Bliss knelt down and scoped the records and instantly it was bonus time; the shot *and* the foul; yes, and it counts. Jazz albums to make a serious collector cry. Bliss felt sure they'd found their man. And now he could enjoy the double pleasure of looking at these rarities. Several inches each of Ellington, Armstrong, Basie, Bechet, and Hawkins. And tucked in between some absolute gems, many of which Bliss had never seen before—*Johnny Hodges with Strings, Playing Gershwin.* Ella Fitzgerald's *Let No Man Write My Epitaph.* The original pressing of the Lester Young Trio on Verve, with Nat Cole listed as A. Guye. Original ten-inch Blue Notes, with James P. Johnson on piano. The Hot Lips Page Commodore sessions. Not one but two Frankie Newton collections, the trumpeter whose sad, soft tone was an early influence on Miles.

"Perhaps, Detective, you would like me to play some of them for you."

Bliss froze. The voice was unmistakable. Dumpsterman was there, in the room with him. There was no doubt in his mind. He sensed Trooper Drew jump to his feet, heard him speak.

"Hello, Mr. Van Deusen."

"Hello, Drew. How have you been?"
It was like a radio play going on behind him.
"Just fine, sir."
"And your folks?"
"They're fine too, sir."
"Glad to hear it." Then, what could only have been the sound
of Van Deusen's hand slapping Drew's back. So the trooper's
day wasn't a total loss. Bliss knew he looked ridiculous, kneeling
there, facing the cabinet. That he should have stood up long ago,
stood and turned and faced the man, to see at least what the shell
of the monster looked like. But he couldn't yet. He wasn't ready.
Because the image of the girl came back to him, covered in
garbage, pathetic and . . . wait. He said Detective . . . what
Dumpsterman always called him. And Trooper Drew, at the
front door, introducing him to the daughter as . . . how? . . . as
sergeant.

So this was it. So easy. Now we go for hair samples in the
trunk, blood on the seat cushions. We go for alibis the night of.
Still, Bliss couldn't turn around. His daughters and the girl in
the garbage and Van Deusen's kid all swirled around him like
cartoon birdies. And he saw blood on all of them, leaking
through their eyes instead of tears, their mouths open, screaming silently. And Bliss reached for his gun and pulled it out of its
holster and still not looking at him released the safety and still
not looking at him tossed the gun at Van Deusen's feet or where
he guessed his feet would be. And Bliss hoped he would pick it
up. That good old Spencer would pick up the gun and put it in
his mouth and end it right there on the library rug. Blow his
brains all over the Thackeray and Trollope, stain the stained
glass with blood and flecks of skull. "Do it," he wanted to shout,
but his voice was barely a hoarse whisper. "End it now." He
wanted Spencer to close the mouths of the girls screaming in his
head.

Ward's voice snapped him out of it.
"Here's your piece, partner," he said, handing Bliss his gun.
"I didn't know we were giving out free samples."
Bliss turned now and took in the tall, sporty figure of Mr.

Spencer P. Van Deusen, looking like he just stepped out of a Ralph Lauren ad—khakis, twill shirt, no socks, loafers. But if Ralph knew the secrets locked inside that soul, that lay in the dark heart that beat just under his Polo logo, he would probably be very disappointed in Spencer. Very disappointed indeed.

Behind him his daughter cowered by the entrance to the library, her hand held to her mouth, curled around an imaginary flower. She was whimpering softly. But Spencer didn't hear her or see her. He didn't hear or see anything. His eyes, his whole being, were somewhere far, far away.

Johnny was thinking about Hollywood, how he'd be perfect on a sitcom. The wacky neighbor. That was him. He was born to play the wacky neighbor.

Who is it, honey?

Oh, it's just Fyodor (no). It's just Sergei. (They pronounce it "Sayr-gay," his American neighbors.)

Door opens. (Big applause. The other guy's the lead, but Johnny, *he's* top banana. Now the wacky-neighbor-fun begins. Scheme-time. Another-fine-mess time.)

Comrade Harry, I have big plan vill make us plenty rich. (He uses the heavy accent for this.)

What is it this time, Sergei, you wacky Rusky, you?

My cousin in Chernobyl say he can buy farm very cheap. (Canned chuckles, they know a big payoff's coming.) Grow giant tomatoes. Like bowlink bawl. (Big laugh here. Guffaws and snorts.) And celery, you needink chainsaw to cut down. And . . .

Then he heard the key turn on the lock and the most beautiful woman he'd ever seen walked in. She was at least a foot taller than Johnny, with deep brown skin and a radiant smile. He was frozen in his chair.

"Oh," she said. "Hi. I didn't think anyone was home."

Johnny worked with the accent. He stayed with wacky.

"Yes. I am, how do you say, the cousin of Alexa. From Russia. My name is Sergei."

"Oh. Hi, Alexa's cousin. I'm Shamika."

"*Da.* Yes. How do you say . . . hello."

She reached out her hand and he shook it. Her fingers were longer than his.

"Um . . . look," she said, "I have a superimportant audition so I can't really stay, but I just wanted to drop this off."

"Okay."

"It's some special tea I ordered for Alexa. Umm . . . are you . . . did you just come over? From Russia, I mean. Did you just get here?"

"No. No no no no. Nyet. Noski. I am, how do you say, lying, no no, *living* in Brighton Beach. With my aunt. She is bee-ink not very good cook. She is making liver. Always liver. I am living with liver. Is funny English, no?"

"It's just that Alexa didn't mention . . . I mean she never said anything about a cousin."

"We are family. Is different from bee-ink . . . how do you say . . . friend, no?"

"I guess so. Anyway," she said, "I thought I'd just drop the tea off so she'd have it when she got back from her trip."

"She is . . . how do you say . . . bee-ink on vacation?"

"Something like that. It's actually a yoga seminar. At a spa in California." He held back the white wave of anger that was surging to his face. "She didn't tell you?"

"Oh, *da, da!* Of course she is tell-ink me." He forced a smile. "Eet . . . how do you say . . . eet slipped out from my mind. Ach, here it is on floor. I put back in." He mimed picking up a speck of thought and shoving it back in his ear. She laughed again.

"So you're staying for a few days?"

"Yes. My aunt she is drive-ink me a little . . . how do you say . . . wacky. I can't eat any more this liver. I'm dy-ink with the liver. Also too many bugs. Alexa give me the key while she is gone."

"Well, it's sure tidy here."

"Yes," Johnny said, thinking of the tofu scrambled into the carpet. Thinking of the stains Alexa's blood would make on the linoleum. "Ees very tidy."

"I'll just put the tea on the counter," Shamika said.

Johnny moved toward her, wacky neighbor smile riding on his face, his hand in his back pocket, feeling for the handle of his knife, wondering should he do her because she'd seen him. If he leaves tomorrow, it wouldn't matter. But maybe it's better that no one see him at all. It's *always* better if no one sees you at all. He slipped the knife out and was about to move toward her throat when he thought no, better not. Because a dead Iris/Alexa they wouldn't find for a while. Everyone thinks she's on vacation. But *this* one they'd come looking for right away. Someone gets worried and soon Kojak is knocking on the door because he can't have tall, beautiful ones like this disappearing. Short, ugly ones could be missing for months, dumpy waitresses at all-night diners, toll collectors, whole bridge clubs could vanish and Kojak wouldn't even unwrap his lollipop. But a girl like this, a model . . . well, it wouldn't be American to have her missing. So Kojak would soon be opening the door with the super's passkey and seeing the model dead on the floor, his Greek blood would start boiling because some bastard took something beautiful from this world and, descendant of Plato that he is, Theo would be pissed. None of this would be good for Johnny. So maybe he should . . .

"Well, *ciao*, Sergei. I'm sure I'll see you again sometime. Peace."

And she was gone. Just like that. The door closed, she's down the stairs.

"You see," he said aloud, "without a plan, I can't do shit!"

He kicked over a chair, then quickly caught himself. Don't want to make too much noise. You never know who's listening. Years of living around the KGB taught him that.

So he paced across the room, past pictures of yogis mocking him with cross-legged serenity. He asked himself why, over and over again, *why* does Alexa want her friends to think she's gone to California? What's the point in that? So they won't bother her while she's a prostitute? Maybe. But what does she want? It doesn't seem like business is so bad she needs to become a working girl. It doesn't add up.

Unless Alexa's lying. And *if* she's lying, that means she knew Elena. And if she knew Elena, she must know everything. Everything. Somehow the bitch knows it all. It's the tea. Her and her fucking tea. He grabbed the bag and ripped it open and shook it all over the room, tea flying everywhere. That helped. At least it wasn't so tidy anymore.

Okay, time to plan. Plan. Plan. Plan. What does she want from me? Did Alexa tell the police? No. Doesn't make sense. Kojak would be watching the house. Wouldn't have risked letting the friend up. So she's on her own. But why? He had to think. She'd been gone almost an hour. The Fat Man was probably just finishing watering her garden. She'll be doing the heel work and then she'd be back.

So he had to come up with something fast.

He wouldn't wait. That's the best solution. Like at the surgeon's. She opens the door, he takes the money, then whap! Who cares what she has to say? She walks in, she gives it up, he cuts her heart out, gets the tinkle tip from her purse, and leaves, takes a bus to L.A. No waiting for explanations. The simpler the better.

And he saw the plan and the plan was good.

Johnny started sweeping up the tea. He didn't want to spook her when she first walked in, so he wouldn't have to go chasing her down the stairs. Afterward, he'd spread it over her, like they do at the cemetery, sprinkling on the dirt. Let her steep a while. Maybe it would keep her body from smelling so bad.

Bliss and Ward were being welcomed back into Manhattan by the hoard of nefarious squeegee men who lurked near the entrance of the Willis Avenue Bridge, which crosses from the Bronx into Manhattan. As two of them went to work on his windshield, Bliss thought they were like the sorcerer's apprentices, mysteriously multiplying, appearing out of nowhere, activated years ago during the Reagan era by some magical incantation, and now no one seems to remember the spell to make them go away. Drivers, trapped in the fantasia of their cars, watch as helpless as Mickey while the apprentices move mechanically in their trancelike dance, armed with their squeegees, heedless of any entreaties to cease and desist. Shooting them wouldn't do any good. They'd keep going, like *golem.* Bliss rolled down his window and gave the guy a quarter. The man didn't thank him. His empty eyes searching for new prey as he walked away.

"Someone wants you," Ward said.

It was only then that Bliss realized his beeper had gone off.

"Pull over in front of Bruckner Antiques," Ward said. "I want to see if they have anything special. There's a phone outside you can use." Ward collected the classic images of Negroes—Aunt Jemima cookie jars, Naughtie Nelly boot jacks with their cast iron legs spread wide, postcards of young black boys stuffed inside an alligator's mouth titled "Alligator Bait—Souvenir from Florida."

"Listen, it's no different from the Jews that collect Nazi stuff," Ward told him. "You should get on the bandwagon, partner. I'll pick you up some SS bars and a Gestapo belt buckle for Christmas. A starter set." Ward went into the store while Bliss used the pay phone on the street.

He didn't recognize the number but knew the voice on the other end. Alexa. Not giving her time to explain, he took down her address, jumped back in the car, and tore off toward the bridge into Manhattan. He then had to do an immediate U-turn when he remembered Ward was still in the store. He threw the car door open and leaned on the horn until Ward got in. Then he tore off again, tires squealing.

"The reason I'm in the homicide business," Ward said, "is because the customers are dead, so I don't have to be rushing around places."

"It was Alexa."

"She in trouble?"

Bliss didn't answer right away. He replayed the voice in his mind. It was soft, almost a whisper, like there was a baby sleeping in the room, or someone praying.

"She wants to see me."

"Isn't that special. We should pick up a Whitman sampler on the way."

"She sounded calm."

"Maybe she is."

Bliss put the red flashing light on the dash and hit the siren to cut through traffic on the FDR.

"Does she know where Tolstoy is?" Ward said.

"No."

"Did she say she had the murderer tied up with an extension cord in her closet?"

"No."

"So what's the rush?"

Bliss said nothing.

"Don't you want to see what I bought?" Ward asked him.

"Sorry," he said. "I didn't see you carrying anything."

"Because I wasn't 'carrying' anything. You don't 'carry' a treasure. You 'transport' it. Like they do murderers or sacred chalices."

"So what are you transporting?"

"It's a photo. A publicity shot of Clayton Bates. Heard of him?"

"No."

"He was better known as 'Pegleg' Bates. One of the greatest

tap dancers of all time. And he had a peg leg. Think about it.
What he had to overcome. You lose your leg, partner, you think
you'd set out to be a dancer?"

"Maybe."

"I doubt it. But Pegleg, *he* did. Loses his leg, starts in doing the
shuffle step, the buck and wing. But then, ol' Clayton, he had an
advantage over you. It was *easy* for him to see what he had to overcome. He looks down, sees the better part of a wooden chair staring back at him where his leg should be. He *knows* what's missing
in his life. On the other hand, you think there's something missing
from your life, but you, partner, have no idea what it is. So I'm giving this photo to you, to remind you that you have to decide
what it is that's missing from your life, before you can find it."

"That's very Zen," Bliss said.

But he looked quickly at the picture Ward put down next to
him on the seat. A guy with a peg leg, smiling. He thought of his
wife and kids. It was probably easier to dance with a wooden leg
than with a wooden heart.

"This is for you, partner. A gift. To hang on your wall. To
remind you. To help you."

He dropped Ward off at the precinct and then drove to the
address Alexa had given him. He double-parked and headed
into the building. It was in the elevator on the way up to the
penthouse that the strangeness of the situation caught up to him.
Why was she in a penthouse on Park Avenue? Whose penthouse
was it? And why was she whispering into the phone?

In the last ten floors he managed to work himself up into a
protective frenzy, so that when Alexa calmly opened the door of
the apartment, she found him with his gun drawn and his eyes
bugging out of his head. He felt foolish and more in need of a
vacation than any time in his career.

"My white knight," she said. "My savior."

She was wearing a cream-colored silk gown that was huge on
her. She held several hundred-dollar bills in one hand, a glass of
champagne in the other. "Quiet," she said in a whisper, finger to
her lips. "We don't want to wake him up."

She took Bliss's hand and led him on her tiptoes to a doorway in the back of the apartment. There he saw a gigantic man lying on his stomach on the floor. His back was pink and had long individual white hairs sprouting randomly, making it look like the belly of a pregnant pig.

"Who's this?" he asked.

"His first name's Edward. Or so he says. Johnny called him the Fat Man. Later I'm supposed to put on high heels and walk on his posterior."

"Really?"

"Mmm-hmm. But first I told him I would give him a massage. A real one. He liked the idea. In a few minutes he was asleep. Just like you were." She gently closed the door.

"How did you wind up here?"

"Johnny sent me."

"Who's Johnny?"

"Johnny Tolstoy."

Bliss saw a hardness in her face he'd never seen before. The hardness of someone who, like Bliss, had seen too much ugliness. And the two scars near her eye, which Bliss once saw as little grace marks, now seemed deep grooves enraged with anger.

"Alexa," he said, "I think we'd better have a little talk."

"Fine," she said. "Edward has some champagne in the fridge. I'll go get it."

While she was gone, Bliss dialed the precinct, told them he needed the phone records pulled for the number he was calling from. Maybe Johnny phoned the Fat Man to set something up. It was a long shot, but he had nothing else to go on at the moment. Unless Alexa came up with something good.

She brought the champagne to the living room. They sat on the Fat Man's plush velvet couch, sipping out of glasses with little insignias etched in the bottom, which Bliss didn't recognize but knew were impressive. Above the fireplace was a Monet, and Bliss remembered a party they'd once been to, one of Rachel's Columbia classmates, born rich and married richer, where he had asked if it was a "real Picasso on the wall." "You never say 'real,' Lenny," Rachel informed him. "You say, 'That's a *nice* Picasso.' "

"That's a nice Monet," Bliss said.

"It's a Pissarro," Alexa said.

"Yeah."

She put down her glass and nuzzled against his shoulder. Her robe fell open and he could see her breasts, the skin taut and smooth. Bliss instinctively put his arm around her. She sighed.

"Tell me about Tolstoy," he said.

And she told him, about making some calls to people she knew in Brighton Beach, then tracking down the Bear and being introduced to Johnny in the St. Petersburg.

"So the Bear did know him. That fat fuck."

"Sshhh," Alexa said. "You'll wake up the whale."

"He lied to me."

"But you have no evidence. So what does it matter?"

"We've got a doorman who saw him. We'll put him in a lineup with an apron and a mustache and give him a pizza box to hold. We've also got fibers from Elena's couch. He bring any clothes with him? Anything maroon?"

"Not that I saw."

"Does he know you're Elena's cousin?"

"No. He thinks I'm just another Russian whore."

"Is he our man?" Bliss asked her. "Is Johnny our man?"

"I don't know."

"Did you see a weapon? A sharp knife? Maybe a switchblade? A scalpel?"

"No."

"He leave any mail lying around? Something with his address?"

"Sorry."

"Did he threaten you? Say what would happen if you screwed up? If you didn't give him all the money? Anything like that?"

"No. He's calm. He likes everything organized. He took out an ad in a magazine. The men will call my number and leave a message. Then I call them back."

"Where does Johnny live? Where is he now?"

"I don't know. He didn't say."

"I want to be there when he comes back. I want to talk to him face to face. I'll come stay with you."

"No. He'll never talk about it. He only thinks about what's happening next. He doesn't look back."

"I could bring him in for questioning. Work him over. Me and Ward."

"He's mad. In Russian we say *sumaschedshi*. With someone like that, there's no sense in talking."

"You're sure he's not on to you."

"He wants me to work. He needs money. I'll take care of it."

"What do you mean you'll take care of it?!"

She put her hand behind his neck, tried to pull him toward her, but he jerked away and stood up.

"What kind of phone do you have? Is it new?" Bliss was pacing across the carpet. "Does it have one of those memories?"

"Yes."

"Put my beeper number into the memory where it says 'Police.' Then if he buzzes your door, if he knocks or calls, you just hit the button, I'm there in five minutes."

"He won't do anything. Anyway, I told you I'll take care of it."

"What does that mean?!"

"Shhhhh."

"Don't try to . . ."

She put a finger to his lips. "Be peaceful, Bliss."

"Fuck peaceful. This asshole may have killed three people. Brutally. That we *know* about. You can't take any chances."

"Shhhhhhhh. Please." She tried to pull him down to the couch, but he snatched his arm away.

"What're you going to do, lull him with your herbal tea? His hands'll be around your throat before the water boils. Maybe you get him to the Ouija board and scare him into a confession. Spell out Elena's name. He'll cut a hole in your belly and stuff in the Ouija."

Alexa grabbed his hand. He tried to pull away again but she wouldn't let him. She held on tight. He felt like a spooked horse being comforted by its groom. One of those old black guys you see around the track. Who seem to have the wisdom of the ages in their weathered faces. That was what Alexa was like. In touch with some kind of older knowledge. She eased him down on the cushions and pressed her lips softly against his neck, sucking it just a bit. Slowly she guided his hand toward her breast. She settled it and he felt her nipple hard on his palm, a tiny point that suddenly became the center of his universe, like it was some kind of stigmata and this force surged through him and instantly he was immobilized, all systems down, shut for the night, and it didn't matter anymore. It just didn't seem to matter. He saw the white curtain fluttering, felt the cool penthouse breeze. Sirocco. He leaned against her shoulder and she stroked his cheek. Isn't this what he wanted? That it would all go away? That it wouldn't be his responsibility anymore?

"You'll call me. As soon as he makes any kind of contact with you, you'll call," he whispered.

"Yes."

"You have to."

"I will. I'll tell him the Fat Man wants me back. Johnny needs money. He won't do anything to me if he thinks I can get more."

"Not right away."

"Not at all." She kissed him softly on the lips and held his hand. Left hand. She felt his ring, now playing with it. "You're married."

"Yes."

"You love your wife?"

He felt his mouth go dry.

"Please tell me you do. Because I know you do."

"Yes. I love her."

"I know. I was married, too. But only for very short time. My husband, he was very young and very handsome. He played piano."

"Jazz?"

"Yes. And Classical. And Russian songs. He could play everything. But then he died."

"I'm sorry." Bliss held her hand tighter.

"Yes. I am sorry, too. But he died at his piano. This was good."

She looked into his eyes and he looked back. Her tiny scars mesmerized him. Some secret lay there. She reached behind his neck again and drew his face to hers. She kissed him. He kissed her back. He felt like he was in high school, with a girl who was baby-sitting, making out on the couch. They'd be eating ice cream soon. Watching *Route 66*. He pulled away and smiled at her. She smiled back.

"You kiss well," she said. They went back at it. Then Bliss heard a noise behind him, someone clearing their throat. Shit, the kid's parents are home early. He turned and saw the Fat Man, staring at them, huge ripples of pink blubber layered over each other like some fantastic geological formation.

"Kissing," he said. He screwed up his face in disgust. "Yech!"

A half hour later Johnny heard her put the key in the door. He was sitting on the large pillow on the floor, an herb catalog on his lap, covering the knife. He was playing it cool, *Baretta* style, a patented Robert Blake smirk on his face, the same one Bruce Willis borrowed to make his millions.

But it wasn't her. It was the Bear. *Then* Alexa, cowering behind him. But definitely the Bear in the lead. Johnny felt his sphincter tighten. The Bear saw him. This didn't make sense. This wasn't part of the plan. This wasn't supposed to . . . before he could move he felt the Bear grab his shirt and yank him out of the pillow. Rigid now, pressed up against the wall, his feet dangling, his knife falling on the floor. Then the Bear hit him in the stomach and it felt like someone had a giant fish hook in his belly and was dragging his guts out up through his chest and he had to puke and the Bear must have seen it coming because he tossed him toward the pillow where he landed doubled over and retching.

He could see Alexa picking up the knife.

"Meant for you," the Bear said to her. "You did right thing to call me."

She nodded her head like a pony, clutching the knife to her chest, eyes wild. Panicked.

"Close door," the Bear said. She scurried over.

The Bear kicked him once, twice in the side. Everything, every molecule in his body was raging with pain. He fell over, his head landing with a dull thud, which he heard more than felt. He could see the Bear's feet, walking to the kitchen, getting one of the chairs. He put it down next to him, sat, and rested his foot on Johnny's neck. The shoe smelled of dog shit. Christ, he hated New York.

"You act like dumb Ukrainian fuck-up," the Bear said. "You

do same thing over and over again. Like stupid animal. You going to learn? You going to learn never! I try to be teaching you. I be giving you big chance, but what do you do? You don't wait, like good friend, like trusting friend. You run away. I come to find you, I go down steps to open door to refrigerator myself, so we can laugh at stupid cops together. Have drink. Toast future. I have vodka. I have herring and pumpernickel. I have girl. She love purple. She seeing you in lobby and is telling me she live her whole life waiting to fuck man in purple tuxedo. She is practically wet by time we are getting to basement. But where are you? Nowhere. Nothing in walk-in but borscht and Mexican dishwasher scared like he is seeing ghost. Because you are running away, like stupid peasant, scared of airplane noise."

He pressed down harder on Johnny's neck, mashing his cheek into the floor. Johnny started punching the Bear's leg, slapping at it.

"PLEASE!!" he screamed in Russian, barely able to breath, gasping. "Don't kill me, please. Take my other nipple, but don't kill me."

"I am not killing you. I am just throwing your shoes out window, so you won't run away."

The Bear released the pressure.

"Then, comes again bad habits. So quickly you forget our little deal."

"What deal?"

"You see? You are forgetting already?"

"What DEAL??"

"Where I am getting percentage of what you make. But it is seeming that you are planning maybe to keep all the money again?"

"No, Sascha."

"This not what Iris is telling me. From this one I get telephone. Iris is worrying because she is being afraid what Bear will do if I am finding out that you want to keep all the money. The money she is making from this Fat Man. If you—what does she tell me you say—if you not tell that fat Russian fuck about the money and we be keeping it all."

"She's lying! The bitch is lying!"

"She is lying? *She* is lying? One thousand dollars she is giving me! Because she has faith! This is some fucking expensive lie, Johnny baby. No! The truth is *she* doesn't want to get hurt! But you, Johnny, you I am thinking will never learn. So I come here, over the stinking bridge into filthy, stinking Manhattan, so I can be personally teaching you one last lesson."

The Bear leaned back and laughed, his body shaking, and as it did his foot did a little dance on Johnny's neck. But Johnny felt something change. The Bear wasn't laughing. And blood landed splattering near where Johnny's nose was flattened against the floor. And then the pressure was released from his neck and he looked to see Iris/Alexa with his, Johnny's, knife pressed into the Bear's side, by his kidney, ramming it in deep while her other arm was wrapped around his neck. He could see her muscles bulging. The veins popping. Her eyes on fire. Nothing about this day was making sense.

"October third, nineteen ninety-one," she was shouting in the Bear's ear. "The night before you leave St. Petersburg. Downstairs casino. Band playing. People laughing. Dancing. Then lights out. Then gunshots. Glass explodes. My face cut. Machine guns. Screaming. Matches. Candles. Money set on fire so we can see. What? What do we see?" She pulled out the knife and plunged it in again. The Bear growls in pain. "I see my husband dead! His head on piano! His blood on keys! People wailing. Man standing on table. Shouting. 'The Bear did this!' With his last breath this man was shouting, 'It was the Bear gave us this present, this going-away present!' "

Then she pulled the huge man tighter to her breast, her arm rigid around his neck until his tiny pink tongue popped out and his feet shook and then he was still. She released him and he fell over. Johnny saw her coming toward him. He tried to move but he hurt too much. She knelt down next to him.

"Johnny. Johnny, can you hear me?"

Her voice was soft. Comforting. Like a librarian. Maybe everything was going to be all right. Maybe he just had to get those overdue books returned. Maybe he just had to pay his fine.

Then he felt her opening his hand. Then she was putting the knife in his hand. His knife.

"Hold it," she said. "Please. Hold it tight."

He held it, tried to move it toward her, trying to find something soft, to stick it in something soft, but she darted away and was behind him now. She held his head between her hands and for a moment he was a child back in Russia, and the hands were his mother's, and he was alone with her because he had forced himself awake and crawled out of bed, after his brothers and sisters had fallen asleep and his father was asleep, snoring on the floor where he had rolled off the couch, and finally he was alone with his mother. She cradled his head in her lap, singing to him softly, and combed his hair gently with her fingers. But now the hands were tightening against his temples and he was jolted back to this apartment, to the warm blood around him, and he thrashed with the knife but he couldn't find her. His head throbbed like he was in a vise, her hands were so strong, and then thunk! she banged his head against the floor. And then again. And again. Soft, steady. He saw double. His head was spinning. He heard the sound of his head hitting the floor, the dull thud. But he couldn't stop it. He still had the knife. He tried to find her belly again but had no idea where she was. Then suddenly she was in front of him and she was holding his hand, the hand with the knife. She was kneeling in front of him, staring into his eyes. Inches away he could only barely make her out. Blurry. Like she was behind a screen door. What? What did she want? Now he felt his hand moving, the knife moving toward her, good, yes, she was guiding the knife to her until he felt flesh, a familiar feel, knife in flesh. But why? And then the warm blood dripped on his face. Her blood? She wants to die? But no, because there she was again, in front him, and her mouth was moving, he saw it moving and then he heard her. She was screaming in Russian, screaming into his mouth. A name. Elena! Elena! Through the pain he heard it. That bitch of a name. Over and over she shouted. Then he felt her hand slide to the back of his head and she was ramming him forward and his head was rushing to the floor and he couldn't stop because it wasn't his head and then it hit the floor flush and everything went blood ugly and black.

CHAPTER 31

It had only been a couple of hours since she left. Bliss had stayed with the Fat Man, grilling him about Tolstoy. But Edward refused to say anything without his lawyer present, so Bliss didn't get far.

After leaving the penthouse, he sat for a while in his car, feeling like he was back in college, when the existential moments had hit him hardest. He had reclined the seat and had his feet on the dash and he was searching for words until he found the right one. Purity was what he came up with. There was a purity about her that made him feel weightless when he was with her. That made him speak from his heart. It had been a long time since he said he loved his wife. Equally long since he knew with certainty that he needed to be with Rachel, that they belonged together. Somehow Alexa had brought that out of him. He owed it to her to find Tolstoy, shoot him, and lay him at her feet.

Then the call came and he had the light on the roof and he was charging back through Central Park, thinking how he would play it. He wanted to see this Tolstoy—look into his eyes. Unlike before, with Van Deusen, he was ready this time, to burst in and wrestle the knife out of his hands and press his face into the floor while he embraced the breathless Alexa with his free hand.

It's all right. Bliss is here and everything will be all right. We'll match the knife to Elena's wounds, to the plastic surgeon and the other girl. We'll send him away for life, beyond Siberia. We'll put him in a deep hole and throw starving rats in with him and they'll claw his eyes out and burrow into his belly. Everything will be all right.

But as soon as he saw Ward standing in front of her building, he realized everything was probably not all right. His partner had a grip on a big guy in handcuffs. Bliss jumped out of his car and recognized the Bear's muscle from the restaurant. Not good. Very not good.

229

"You been upstairs yet?" he asked Ward.

"No," Ward said. "But this guy was."

"What'd he say?"

Ward wasn't smiling. Ward wasn't his usual avuncular self.

"Alexa, is she . . . ?"

Ward didn't answer.

Bliss turned and ran up the stairs. But there was no panic in her message. No sense of danger. Two hours ago he was weightless in her arms. He could still feel the hard point of her nipple on his palm, the nerves assembled in that spot like a conga band in Washington Square, keeping a torrid beat, the rhythm of desire. Two flights on a dead run. It must be love. Or something like it he hadn't felt for a long while. Care, maybe. That was it. He'd become a caring person. At his age, it could be dangerous.

He got to the door, opened it, saw the Bear first, on his back, tongue out, eyes popped out like a fly's, blood red blotches on his blue shirt making it almost Hawaiian. Not breathing. Hmmmm, must be dead. That's one. Scrawny guy curled up next to him, out cold, smirking, like he was having a naughty nap. Bliss figured him as *the* Johnny Tolstoy. Blood on his face, but breathing. One in the alive column. Blood splatter Pollock-ed his back. Splatter, not stain. So the blood's not his. Then whose?

He tried to keep his eyes from moving, wanted to stop them from moving, but they wandered. Because that's what eyes do when they see a woman's bare leg. You can tell your eyes all you want that there may be death at the end of the line, but once the eyes see that smooth flesh of the calf, the lure of bare thigh is too much, so they move, on their own, two cells to the left, until they hit thigh, until they meet skirt pulled up, until they see her, Alexa, arm across her throat, eyes wide, unblinking, blood by her neck, soaking her shirt. Her shirt . . . moving. Just enough. No movement means death. Any movement means breath in the vicinity. He sprang to her side. Bliss the gazelle now, the lover from the Song of Songs.

"Alexa," he whispered. He put his ear to her lips.

"Did he see me?" she asked, her voice surprisingly strong.

"Who?"

"The big guy. With the gun. Did he come up here? Did he see me dead?"

"Yeah. I think so."

"He *has* to see me dead."

"He did."

She sat up, pulled her arm away, and the blood went with it.

"They don't like loose ends, these people."

"So you're okay?"

"Yes."

"Your neck's okay. Because the last one . . . that's how he . . . I mean. You're not hurt."

"Just my arm. A small cut, but a lot of blood I guess."

He helped her up. Got her to a chair.

"You're sure he saw me? His name's Malcolm. Dead, I'm not a problem. Dead he doesn't have to come back looking for me."

"My partner said he'd been up here. Tell me what happened."

"He found us."

"Who?"

"The Bear. He came in and Johnny went crazy. He took out his knife, stabbed him in the side. I moved forward, to stop it."

"You shouldn't have."

"But I did. That's when I got cut. Johnny got his knife into the Bear's belly. The Bear fell on him, knocking him over. Johnny's head hit the floor. I guess he blacked out. Then the Bear rolled over and died."

"From the knife."

"How else?"

Bliss looked at the blue tongue poking out of the Bear's mouth like a dog's erection. Textbook post-strangulation tongue protrusion.

So. Problem. So. Someone choked the Bear to death. *Not* just stabbed. Bliss looked at Alexa, saw a calmness in her face that didn't quite jibe with having just watched a death struggle, having just had a killer's knife rip through your arm. People are scared when death knocks close to their heads. "Jesus, one inch either way and I'd have been . . ." People's eyes are exploding.

"My God, you could hear the rattle. His whole body shuddered and then he . . ." He'd been there. People around murder usually cry or turn white or go faint or get enraged. "The fucking creep! He could've killed me!" Spitting on the dead. One stiff he found was soaked with piss. The blood spooks them. Getting touched by blood. He knew. Most people don't like getting splashed with a little milk, never mind warm blood. He'd seen. He knew. But maybe Alexa wasn't like most people. Or maybe it was something else about her. Something that made the connection between them even deeper.

"Turn your head," he told her.

"Why?"

He took a step toward her, getting in her face. "Because when a policeman tells you to do something you fucking do it!"

She did.

"I'll tell you when to look back."

He walked to the Bear and tapped his chin with his toe. The jaw still loose, hadn't frozen up yet. It might work. Bliss cocked his leg and kicked the Bear once very hard, directly on the chin, forcing his teeth to guillotine his tongue. There was an odd popping sound, and the tongue tip flopped to the side and dropped on the floor. Now it looked like he bit it off when his head hit the ground. It reminded Bliss of a piece of chopped meat that fell off the counter when someone was making burgers. He nudged the tongue out of sight under a flap of shirt. She didn't need to see it. Then he went to the front window and told Ward to call it in— ambulance, forensics, coroner, the whole caboodle.

"Okay," he said to Alexa, "you can turn around now."

But Alexa was already in the kitchen, filling up a pot of water.

"You want some tea?" she asked, as if she didn't have a care in the world. And maybe she didn't.

He hated the tie. They told him he had to dress up for the trial, but the tie looked like what they gave you in a restaurant if you forgot to wear one. And the suit made him seem like he worked in the Kremlin. It was the final irony—that he, Johnny Tolstoy, the most alive, the most intellectually free Russian in the world, now looked like nothing more than a common, low-level bureaucrat. With no dream. No vision. Watching the clock, waiting to leave work, waiting to drink. To die.

JAY: *Let me introduce my next guest. Olga Kepelnikov.* [Who is she? Johnny asked himself.] *Now Olga, you own a lingerie shop in Brighton Beach?*

OLGA: *I do.*

JAY: *And do you recognize the man who bought these panties?*

OLGA: *Ven I seen him he vas vith the red hair. He bought brassieres, too.*

JAY: *Thank you, Olga. My next guest is Detective Bliss.* [Another one I've never seen before, Johnny thought.]

BLISS: *He had the knife in his hand.*

JAY: *Holding it?*

BLISS: *Yes.* [This guy was there? Why don't I remember?]

JAY: *And was he conscious at the time?*

BLISS: *No.*

JAY: *Now Johnny and I go way back, Detective. He's been on the show several times. Are you sure it was him?*

BLISS: *Absolutely certain.*

JAY: *Thanks, Detective. Now I'd like to welcome Alexa Gurevich to the show. So, Alexa, things are going well for you?*

ALEXA: *Yes, Jay. Very well. My new movie is coming out soon. It's a thriller. It's about the Bear rushing through the door and Johnny is stabbing him and I'm scared and the Bear is hitting*

Johnny but Johnny stabs him again and again and the Bear knocks him down with his last strength but then the Bear stops moving and Johnny stops moving and it's about to open in theaters everywhere.
JAY: Sounds pretty exciting.
ALEXA: Oh, it is, Jay. It's very exciting. And it's based on a true story, only we changed it just a bit. To make it more believable.

Johnny was going to get bumped. He knew it. He felt it. At the last minute they were going to bump him. Two weeks he'd been sitting around waiting, listening to all the other acts—has-beens and washed-ups and now they'd run out of time. The pet tricks took too long. Jay's monologue got too many laughs.

He imagined the producers talking.

"Cut that Russian comic. Bump him."

"But he's waited his whole life for this, for this one shot."

"Fuck him. Tony Bennett wants to sing *two* songs, not one. Bette wants to do more schtick. We're going to turn down Tony? We're going to cut short Bette the sure bet?"

But no, he was wrong. They *did* want him. He heard right. They were coming to get him in the green room. Knocking on the door of the green room and telling him to get ready, that the jury was in and he'd be going on soon. He fixed his hair, his lapel. Pulled down the cuffs of his shirt so they hung evenly past the sleeves of his jacket. Straightening the tie. He rubbed each shoe against the back of his pants, so they'd be shiny for the long shot. You ready? They asked him. You all set? Need anything? Glass of water? No, he said. He was ready. And they walked down the hall and into the studio and he sat down. They were still in commercial. Everyone was waiting.

Then Jay walked in and the crowd stood up and applauded and Jay banged the gavel and did his opening routine from behind his bench, getting everyone warmed up. Johnny was nervous now and he wished he could go to the bathroom but he couldn't because the stage manager said it was time. He was about to be on. He was about to be on with Jay. With all of America.

And then it happened. They called his name. They called his

name and he stood up and he could feel it, like nothing he had ever felt before. Millions of people watching him. And instinctively, as he knew he would when he finally had the chance, his eyes found the camera. As he had practiced a thousand times in his bedroom he found the camera and he could feel, without even glancing up, that the red light was on and that the lens was now focused only on him.

Bliss was lying facedown on the massage table and Alexa was working on his feet. Sitting on the floor under his head was one of the kids. The girl. She was almost three now, Alexa said. Her friend Shamika the model paid for them to come over. The boy was napping in the crib. The girl, Anya, was playing with a stuffed animal Bliss had brought over.

"That's Babar," he said. "Bah-bar." Little Anya babbled back something in Russian. They didn't have Babar when he was growing up in the Bronx. It was a Rachel thing. "He's king of the elephants. El-eh-phants." More babbling.

"She saying anything in English yet?"

"A little," Alexa said. "You have to keep practicing with her."

"Hey, *bubeleh*," Bliss said to the kid. "You remember what I taught you last month? Go on. Say it. Say 'Aunt Alexa, please buy me a new . . .'"

Alexa gave him a sharp pinch on his calf.

"Teach her something nice," she said.

"Say 'angel,' Anya," Bliss said. "Say 'Aunt Alexa is an angel.'"

She was a beautiful little girl, her brown hair long and curly and flowing to her shoulders. The boy, Alexis, too. Though he was still too young to know for sure. But Anya was definitely a knockout. At first Bliss couldn't look at her, because in her face he saw the dead eyes and then the mutilated body of her mother lying on the floor. But now he saw only the little girl, smiling and happy. Maybe he'd undone one of the curses Ward put on him. Wiped away one of the stains. De-Warded himself a notch. He hoped so.

"Turn over," she said. "On your back."

She was working on his thighs now. Forcing her fingers deep into the muscles until they hurt, then rubbing them softly.

"And with your wife," Alexa said. "Things are good."

236

"Yes."

"You love her?"

"Yes."

"And you say this to her recently?"

"Once, anyway."

"It's a start."

She was gently massaging the inside of his leg, rubbing her hands along the length of his loins.

"But you still think about me," she said.

"Yes," he said.

"Good," she said. "It's not polite to lie. Anyway, I can tell. The sheet looks like a little pup tent."

For the next half hour they were silent. Then Bliss put on his clothes and paid her.

"I'll bring Julia by around seven o'clock. What time should I pick her up?"

"I'm just going to the movies," she said. "I'll be back at 9:30."

"You have Oreos? Can't baby-sit without Oreos."

"I have them."

"Okay. 'Bye, Alexa."

He kissed her on the cheek and headed home to his family.

What is it with you married guys? All of a sudden you decide you want to start having sex again? Take my husband, the cop. Last three years it's been like living with Cardinal O'Connor. Then, out of the blue, he's all over me. Like that insect. What is it? The cicada. For six years you don't hear anything. Then, year seven comes along, they're doing the mambo on every tree trunk. The same thing with my husband. I can't get him off me. Telling me he loves me. Holding my hand. I mean we all want our husbands to be more romantic, more attentive, but we don't ever actually expect them to change. And without any warning? It's starting to get spooky. It's gotten to the point where I'm under the bed looking for pods. Because that's what I think it is. *Invasion of the Body Snatchers.* I don't know.

Anyway, I'm gonna just do a short set tonight. Because I want to get back home. I mean, well, it's hard to be funny when I got this big lug waiting for me, sitting on the bed with this dopey grin that comes over his face when I walk in the room. Anyway, it'll be fall soon. The cicadas will shrivel up and fall off the tree and the birds will eat them. And before you know it, things will probably be back to normal and I'll have plenty of new material. I'll make you laugh again. I promise. But for now, I think I'm going home, to enjoy a little bliss while it lasts.

Thank you very much. You've been a wonderful audience. Thank you and good night.